# All for the Good

*"We know that all things work together for good for those who love God, who are called according to purpose."*

Romans 8:28

*Other Christian romance Fiction*

*by Janet DiFabio*

*Always Faithful - Series*

Always Faithful and True *(Book 1)*

In Good Times and Bad *(Book 2)*

*(Both can be read as a stand-alone novel.)*

All for the Good

Finding Hope at Kringle's Crossing *(Coming soon.)*

# All for the Good

*"We know that all things work together for good for those who love God, who are called according to purpose."*

Romans 8:28

# By Janet DiFabio

**Abiding Spirit Press**

*Where the Spirit leads and grace redeems.*

**Abiding Spirit Press**

*Where the Spirit leads and grace redeems.*

# Epigraph

"We know that all things work together for good for those
who love God, who are called according to purpose."

Romans 8:28

Do you remember life without smartphones, the internet, or social media? I do. I remember passing handwritten notes folded into tiny triangles to friends at school, hoping the teacher wouldn't catch us. Research papers meant hours at the library's card catalog—unless your family had invested in a set of encyclopedias from the grocery store. And typing a final draft on a clunky typewriter with a rotating font ball felt like an accomplishment all its own.

Friday nights were an adventure. My friends and I wandered the mall, met up at the arcade, or cruised around town listening to homemade cassette tapes, praying the player wouldn't eat them. Getting lost meant pulling into a gas station to ask for directions, because GPS didn't exist. And if I wanted to stay out past curfew, I had to hunt down a pay phone to call home.

A quiet night in meant browsing the video store, hoping the newest release was still on the shelf—and remembering to rewind the tape so you wouldn't be charged a dollar. Oh, the good ol' days.

When I drafted this story, I found myself longing for that simpler time—before constant connection, before instant answers, before life sped up. Setting this book in

1990 felt like opening a window to a gentler world, where love had room to grow without digital noise.

As you read, I hope these pages stir your own memories if you lived through those years—or offer a glimpse into a slower, sweeter season if you didn't. Most of all, I hope this story reminds you that even in the simplest moments, God is weaving something beautiful. His plan is always at work, often in ways we don't see until we look back.

Janet

# Acknowledgements

Refreshing this book has been a journey of the heart, and I could not have done it without the love and support of so many dear people.

To my family, thank you for walking beside me through every season of this writing adventure. When *All for the Good* was first published in 2022, Joey was only five, and writing meant squeezing words into the quietest corners of the day. Now he's nine, and with two precious grandchildren under three filling our home with joy, quiet moments to write are rare treasures. Thank you for giving me the space to bring this story back to life.

To my daughter Alyssa, thank you for reading this book from beginning to end and for your honesty, even when it meant telling me the ending needed "more." Your feedback pushed me to dig deeper, and this refreshed version is stronger because of you.

To my critique partner and husband Mike, thank you for sharing your expertise whenever I wandered into unfamiliar topics and for offering honest advice when my ideas needed rethinking. Your personality, humor, and interests quietly inspired the heart of my hero. Without your insight and steady encouragement, this story would not be the same.

To my editor, Beth, thank you for polishing this story for its original publication in 2022. Your early guidance helped me grow as a writer, and your fingerprints still shine through these pages.

To Abiding Spirit Press, thank you for bringing this book to print once again. This imprint was born from a sacred promise and a friendship that changed my life, and its spirit continues to guide every story I write.

To every reader, my prayer is that these stories bring you comfort, joy, and a reminder of God's unwavering love.

Most of all, to God Almighty, thank You for every blessing, every open door, and every moment of grace.

# Chapter 1

Jenna Rossi sat on the edge of Tommy's daybed, quiet and worried as the last night of summer slipped away. No more moonlit walks, no more stolen kisses under the bleachers, no more afternoons wandering the mall together. Tonight was the last time she'd hear him play in person until Thanksgiving.

Tommy stood in front of her, lost in the driving rhythm of his electric guitar, his shoulder-length brown hair swinging with every beat. When he finally caught sight of her tear-stained face, he stopped mid-strum.

"Is my music that bad?" he teased.

Jenna tried to smile. "I'm just going to miss you."

His grin faded, replaced by something softer. He sat beside her. "I'm going to miss you too."

Jenna wished missing him didn't feel so much like losing him. She wiped her cheeks. "I can't believe we have to do this for three more years."

"We made it through freshman year," he said gently. "This one will go fast too." He set his guitar aside. "Before you know it, I'll be back here playing like I never left."

Jenna brushed his hair from his eyes. "Not you. You're talented, Tommy. You'll play your way into the music scene in no time. Then you'll forget about me while you're tanning on some California beach."

He stared at her, stunned. "Are you done ranting?"

"It happens," she muttered.

"Not with me." He took her hands. "And this mountain isn't frozen yet. It's still summer."

She smacked his shoulder. "Very funny."

"Seriously, Jenna." His voice lowered. "I promise I'm coming back to you. I love you."

He pulled her to her feet and wrapped his arms around her, brushing a tender kiss across her lips — just enough to quiet her fears.

"Tom?" His mother's voice echoed up the staircase, sharp enough to break the moment.

Jenna stepped back, her heart thudding. Tommy wiped his mouth on his sleeve and groaned. "What, Mom?"

"It's too quiet up there!"

He rolled his eyes. "She doesn't trust me."

"She's just keeping you respectable," Jenna whispered.

"We're not even doing anything," he muttered, then added, "Besides, she's not nearly as threatening as your dad."

"Thomas James!" his mother called again.

"What, Mom? We're watching a movie!"

"It's getting late. We have an early flight tomorrow."

Tommy sighed. "Okay. Be right down." He kissed Jenna once more. "Translation: it's time for you to go." He backed away and offered his hand. "Come on. I'll walk you downstairs."

They headed toward the living room, where the buttery smell of popcorn drifted through the air. His parents sat in their recliners, bowls in hand, eyes fixed on the TV.

"Have a safe flight tomorrow," Jenna said.

"Thank you, dear," Mrs. Pruitt replied.

"Good night," Mr. Pruitt added.

"Tom, keys are on the hook," his mother said.

"That's okay. I'm walking Jenna home."

"Not tonight. Two black bears tore apart the neighbor's garbage and wandered down the road."

Tommy muttered under his breath but grabbed the keys. "Okay. Fine."

"No back talk, bud!" his father warned.

"Yes, sir." Tommy straightened and followed Jenna out the side door.

Jenna stepped out of the cool house and into a thick, swirling fog. The air was warm and heavy, carrying the scent of rain. She could barely make out the hunter-green Jeep in the driveway. Crickets chirped somewhere in the mist, unfazed by the humidity — or the bears.

Tommy opened the passenger door for her. "I really don't miss living in the middle of nowhere," he muttered.

Jenna's breath caught. "I like it here."

She fastened her seatbelt and stared into the white haze beyond the windshield. River Grove had always been home, a quiet mountain village where neighbors smiled, newcomers were welcomed like family, and the Blue Ridge Mountains wrapped around everything like a comforting blanket. Jenna couldn't see herself living anywhere else.

Tommy slid into the driver's seat, started the Jeep, and eased it through the fog for the short drive to her house. He pulled into the driveway and shut off the headlights.

"Well," he said dryly, "that was a brutal trip. And those bears? Terrifying."

"Tommy," Jenna whispered, "your mom was just being cautious."

"She's overly protective."

"If she were, she wouldn't have let you go to college across the country."

He turned toward her, frustration flickering before softening. "Jenna… why the attitude?"

She looked down, unsure she could keep her voice steady.

"What's wrong?" he asked gently. "Talk to me."

"I thought you liked living here," she said, her voice breaking.

Tommy took her hand, his tone calmer now. "I do. But I need to do this for my future — for our future. If I'm going to make it in music, California is where I need to be for now."

Jenna nodded, her tears quieting. A future. She wanted that with him more than anything, even if the thought of him being gone again made her chest ache.

"And with me gone," he added, "you'll have time to figure out what you want to do."

Time. She wasn't sure she wanted time—she wanted certainty, direction, something from God that didn't feel so blurry.

"You're right," she whispered. "Maybe the community college is where I'll finally understand what God's been trying to tell me."

"That's my girl." He brushed a tear from her cheek. "Promise me — no more crying."

She nodded.

"Hey," he said softly, reaching into his pocket, "I have something for you." He slipped his high school ring onto her finger.

Jenna stared at it, stunned. Her breath caught. She hadn't expected anything—especially not this.

"Will you marry me?" he asked.

For a moment, the fog outside felt like it had slipped into her chest—thick, blinding, impossible to breathe through.

"Oh, Tommy… yes."

His smile trembled with emotion. "I'll get you a real ring when I can."

"This is perfect," she whispered, her fingers tracing his Class of 1989 ring — the birthstone, the Celtic cross, the guitar, and the curve of his engraved signature —

holding onto each detail as if it might steady her against the ache of him leaving again.

"I love you, Jenna."

He leaned in and kissed her — gentle, lingering, full of hope.

## Chapter 2

Bits of breadcrumbs that had settled on the bottom of the toaster burned while Jenna was toasting her morning bagel. Smoke drifted upward, setting off the fire detectors.

"Oh, for Pete's sake!" Frazzled, she flicked on the ceiling fan, then rushed into the dining room and yanked open the slider door. After a few moments, the ear-piercing alarm faded into silence.

"Finally," she muttered, rubbing her ringing ears.

Her father burst into the kitchen, shaking his hands in anger. "I'm awake now, Jenna!" His gruff voice rumbled like thunder, vibrating straight through her.

Jenna nervously licked her lips. "Oh, I—was just trying to keep you on your toes, Daddy."

"What'd you burn?"

"Just crumbs in the toaster."

He let out an exaggerated sigh. "*Amore*, you know it's not that hard to clean the toaster from time to time."

*Amore*—Italian for *love*—did nothing to soften the unforgiving tone in his voice.

"No, sir, it's not." *But you can, too.* She wanted so badly to snap back but knew better than to be disrespectful. "Sorry, Daddy, but I'm running late."

She grabbed her plate and a glass of orange juice, then scooted into the dining room, hoping to escape his criticism. The last thing she wanted was to let his grouchiness stir up her own unstable emotions. She loved her father, but they seldom agreed on anything, so avoiding an argument was wise.

She took a huge bite of her bagel, wanting to finish breakfast quickly, but her phone rang to life in her bedroom. She sprang from her chair and raced down the hallway. As she lunged across her bed, the answering machine had already taken the call.

*Crab apples! I really need a cordless phone.*

She waited a moment, then played back the message.

"Jenna, it's Tommy. I'm about to board the plane. Babe, I'm not looking forward to a six-hour flight. I'll call you later. Love you and miss you."

Jenna sighed. *I miss you, too.*

She moseyed back to her breakfast. She had barely taken a sip of juice and a bite of bagel when her father entered the room carrying a cup of coffee and a cheese Danish.

"What time did you get in last night?" he asked, settling into the head of the table.

"Uh…midnight?" she answered, her voice barely above a whisper. She stared at her plate, not wanting to see his expression.

"What?" Disgust lined his voice.

"Now, Nick," Mom said from the doorway, her calm, steady voice cutting through the tension. "Watch your blood pressure."

Jenna peered up at her mother. *Oh, thank goodness.* The knots in her stomach loosened.

"I gave Jenna permission to stay out later than usual," Mom said, walking toward him.

"For what, Julia? To see that boy?"

"He's leaving today," Mom said, placing her plate on the table. "Now, relax." She walked behind her husband's chair and rubbed his shoulders.

"He went back to college?" Dad asked. "Good, then it's over." Relief softened his dark eyes, and a satisfied smile surfaced.

"Nick!" Mom smacked his shoulder. "What a terrible thing to say!"

"My daughter is too young to date."

Jenna blew out her breath and threw her hands up. "Daddy, I'm eighteen!"

He fell silent. She could see the battle behind his eyes, and when he finally gathered his thoughts, his response was cold and curt.

"Well, you're not old enough to get married."

*Ugh! You're impossible.* He made every excuse as to why she shouldn't be with Tommy. But she was an adult now. She had the right to make her own decisions.

That's it. I'm going to set the record straight.

She twirled the ill-fitted ring on her finger, gathered the broken fragments of her courage, and met his gaze head-on. "Daddy—Tommy and I are engaged."

"What?" her father sputtered, nearly choking on his coffee. "And how do you suppose he's going to support you?"

"He's a musician, Daddy!"

"I hardly call that noise music."

"Now, Nick," Mom interjected. "Not everyone has the same tastes as—"

"Forget it, Mom," Jenna said. "It's not Tommy's job to support us. I'm working, too."

"At a dog shelter?" He threw his hands out, begging her to understand. "*Amore*, life is not easy. Do you think I enjoy working as a mason—carrying back-breaking materials, bending all day, wearing out my knees? You deserve better."

"I didn't say we're getting married tomorrow."

"Jenna," Mom said gently, cupping her hand over hers. "Marriage is a lifelong commitment. It's not like buying a car and trading it in when you get tired of it."

Jenna pulled her hand away. "I know that, Mom. Tommy and I have been together for four years. We love each other."

"Jenna, you have your whole life ahead of you," Mom said. "You're still growing—changing. Why deny yourself the opportunity to explore and discover who you are…who you're going to be?"

"But we know what we want, Mom."

Her father, an expert at controlling a conversation, chimed in. "No! You have no idea what you want. You just graduated high school. You need to go to college like your brother. He became a successful accountant first, then got married."

"Daddy, this isn't about Anthony."

"Listen, *Amore*! You go to college, get a job, save your money, then worry about marriage."

His intensity pounded her until she had to look away. Tears pooled in her eyes as she stared at her ring. *He doesn't get it.*

"So, where's this engagement ring?" he asked.

Jenna's face burned. "Um…" She raised her trembling hand and showed him the ring.

"You call that an engagement ring?"

"It's his class ring…until he can afford the real thing."

"That's a placeholder. When you're ready to get married, you have him come ask me."

Tears escaped Jenna's eyes. She wasn't going to let her relationship fall apart because of her father's old-fashioned ideologies. She waved her hand in dismissal. "I'm late for work."

Jenna slammed the gray car door of her early-eighties clunker and sat for a moment, gripping the steering wheel. Her father's overbearing lecture still churned inside her gut.

*Ooh, Daddy, you're such an ornery cuss, and I hate how you play favorites. In your eyes, Anthony is perfect. Why, Daddy? Why can't you treat me like a responsible adult? What have I ever done to disappoint you? Tommy and I are meant for each other. Stop living in Italy and wake up to the modern world.*

Angry tears spilled as she turned the key in the ignition. The engine coughed to life, but she didn't move. She needed to get a grip before she drove off.

*God, I can't take it anymore. Please help me understand him.*

A sudden calm washed over her — not enough to erase the hurt, but enough to steady her hands so she could drive safely through yet another foggy morning.

She pulled onto the rural road, keeping to the posted speed limit and watching for deer grazing at the tree line. The fog clung low, turning everything into a muted watercolor.

Then a rumbling V8 engine shattered the quiet.

She glanced into her rearview mirror. Faint headlights loomed behind her — a monster-sized Ford Bronco riding her bumper.

*Oh, back off, hotrod.* Her high mileage car handled like a rowboat in the deep seas and couldn't maneuver the sharp turns even on a sunny day. *If you want to crash, then pass me illegally, jerk!*

The arrest-me-red shiny Bronco continued to tail her all the way to a stop sign. When the intersection finally cleared, Jenna pressed the gas — and her car stalled.

"Son of a biscuit! Not again."

Sweat beaded on her forehead. She shoved the shifter into neutral, turned the key, and coaxed the engine back to life. She threw it into drive and floored it while she still had momentum.

"Go, you piece of crap!"

Her car lurched forward, then stalled again in the middle of the intersection.

"No, no, no! Don't do this to me again!"

Honks erupted from every direction. Her heart pounded. Her limbs trembled. She shifted back into neutral, cranked the engine, braked with her left foot, revved with her right, then slammed it into drive. The car sputtered forward.

"Thank you, God."

She petered up the hill, her car barely getting out of its own way, when the hothead Bronco passed her on a solid yellow line, leaving behind a cloud of rancid exhaust.

Jenna choked. *Good riddance.*

Twenty minutes later, Jenna finally made it to work. The sound of her tires crunching through the gravel parking lot alerted the dogs to her arrival.

*Yes, my fur babies, I'm here now to take care of you.*

Even though she was late, she sat in her car for a moment to compose herself. She took a deep breath. *Thank you, Lord, for getting me here in one piece.* She smoothed her windblown caramel-brown hair and gathered it into a high ponytail. Pulling her long hair off her neck rejuvenated her after the stressful drive.

As she stepped out of the car, she heard Max — a black pit bull mix — panting as he dragged a man in a fluorescent yellow raincoat through the fog. As they approached, she recognized the slender man as her boss.

"Good morning, George. I think you're going to have one arm longer than the other by the time you get back."

George chuckled. "Max is eager to be the first to mark his favorite tree." He tugged back on the lead. "Easy, boy. Speaking of being first, it's not like you to be late, Jenna."

"I'm sorry."

"Is everything okay?" he asked.

Jenna shut her car door. "Oh, this old jalopy…every time we have this kind of weather it acts up." She shook her head. "I don't get it."

George shrugged. "Maybe take it to a mechanic."

"My dad test-drove it to work a few times and said it ran fine. Apparently, it only aggravates me."

"Time to buy new."

"I hope not. I haven't saved enough money, and I don't want a loan — especially with college starting on Monday."

"Sometimes we don't have a choice," George said.

"I suppose. It's a shame because the body is solid, and the interior is super clean."

George raised his gray, bushy eyebrows. "But if the heart is no good, then…"

"True, but I don't need this stress right now."

"I understand."

Max grabbed the leash in his mouth and shook it, whipping his big head side to side.

"Easy, boy!" George said, trying to control him.

Max leaped forward toward the towpath.

"Let's talk later about your hours," George said as he sprinted after the energetic dog.

"Okay," Jenna said, heading toward the front entrance. *He's going to be so disappointed when I tell him how few hours I can give him.*

George had depended on her ever since she started volunteering at the shelter at twelve. She was more reliable than some of the employees. She hadn't thought much about it before, but her dedication had helped her land her first job there. Now, six years later, she still worked there and loved every minute of it.

It crushed her to have to cut her hours, but she knew that if she wanted a successful future, college had to become her priority.

♡

Hours later, Jenna returned home. She took a cool, soothing shower to relax after her long workday, then checked her answering machine. No messages.

She sighed. *Tommy, I miss you.*

In the kitchen, her father was doctoring up Italian braciola. The aroma of seasoned meat stirred her empty stomach.

"Hi, Daddy. Can I help?"

"Hi, *Amore*." He picked up the platter of meat and an armful of utensils. "Open the slider door for me, please."

His tone was surprisingly pleasant.

"Okay," she said, hurrying to the door.

As her father stepped onto the back deck, her mother came inside carrying a basket of vegetables from the garden. "Oh, Jenna, you're home."

"Yeah, I just got in. Can I help?"

"Certainly," Mom said, bringing the vegetables to the sink. "You can make the salad."

"Okay."

Jenna grabbed a bowl from the cabinet, set it beside the cutting board, and began slicing a cucumber.

"So, how was your day?" Mom asked.

The question triggered the sour mood lingering inside her. "Well, if I don't include this morning's lecture or my car trouble, I'd say I had an okay day."

Mom turned and put her arm around her. "Your dad and I only want what's best for you."

Annoyed, Jenna stepped back. "Oh? He doesn't seem to care that my car almost killed me entering an intersection this morning."

The slider door opened, and her father walked in. "What happened?"

Jenna let out a breath — half frustration, half disbelief. "Really, Daddy? Did you need to ask? My car is a piece of junk! It kept stalling on me in traffic."

"*Amore*, I test-drove it for two weeks. There's nothing wrong with it."

Jenna clenched her teeth so tightly she thought they might crack. *You're so full of it.*

Mom gently took the knife from her. "I'll finish slicing the cucumbers. Take this tray of condiments and set the table."

Jenna huffed into the dining room with the tray. *He doesn't believe me! He's the most stubborn person I know.*

As she prepared the table, her mind simmered with frustration. She'd had enough of her domineering father for one day. She sat down and rested her forehead in her palm, listening to the conversation in the kitchen.

"Nick, maybe a mechanic should look at it," Mom said.

"Why? And waste money? Julia, there's nothing wrong with it. The car is old. It's going to have some quirks."

Astounded, Jenna jumped from her chair. She stood in the doorway and pointed at him. "Ha! So it *did* act up for you."

Her father flipped his wrist. "So what? It stalls; you restart it. Car runs fine. Heck, it'll outlive me."

Jenna's blood boiled. "Oh, Daddy! You're as stubborn as a mule — and a cheapskate, too."

"That's enough, Jenna!" Mom scolded.

"*Amore*, you don't need a new car!"

"Daddy, you're ridiculous!"

"Jenna, I said that's enough," Mom shouted.

Jenna lowered her head and retreated to the dining room. *I give up.*

Her mother hated their bickering. Whenever she and her father clashed, Mom always played referee, rarely taking sides for fear of adding fuel to the fire.

Jenna rubbed her tired eyes. *I can't wait to move out. Tommy and I will be so happy.*

Moments later, her parents entered the dining room carrying a salad bowl, pasta, and the platter of braciola.

"Time to eat," Mom said, placing the food on the table. "Oops, I forgot the cups."

Her father took a wine glass from the hutch. "I got one right here."

"Good for you, Nick, but Jenna and I don't drink wine."

"Why not? A glass a day is good for you."

Mom rolled her eyes. "No, thanks." She stepped into the kitchen and returned with two glasses of milk, handing one to Jenna.

"Thanks, Mom."

"Jenna, life isn't all that bad. How about a smile? You know we don't serve food at an angry table."

Jenna looked up and forced a grateful smile.

"That's better. Now, let's say grace," Mom said.

After supper, Jenna checked her answering machine again. Still no messages. She dropped her head in disappointment. *Where are you, Tommy? Are you okay?*

He was the second person in her life who had left in just a few weeks. The first was Kellie Wade, her best friend, who had moved to Massachusetts for a four-year college. Since she left, Jenna had lost touch.

*Everybody's gone.*

Distressed, Jenna stepped outside onto the back deck. The night air was warm and heavy with moisture. A faint chant from the neighbor's wind chimes drifted through the darkness, hinting that another storm was on its way.

Whenever she felt down, she found solace under the night sky. She lay back on a lounge chair and gazed up at the stars. The moon's blemished face smiled sadly, as if sharing her melancholy.

Her heart ached. It had only been twenty-four hours since she and Tommy said their goodbyes, but it already felt like forever. She had a longing for him unlike anything she'd ever imagined. She swallowed hard over the lump in her throat.

*Please call me, Tommy… I miss you.*

## Chapter 3

During the closing hymn at Mass the next morning, a wide range of singing voices surrounding Jenna faded as many of the parishioners gushed out of the church like it was a race to reach the parking lot exit. But for Jenna, it was a moment to linger. Jenna knelt in her pew, the faint scent of incense still lingering in the air, and prayed, asking forgiveness for arguing with her father.

*Lord, I know I can be stubborn and short-fused at times, too, so please grant me patience and help me accept my father for who he is.* She also prayed for Tommy. *God, I haven't heard from him yet. I know moving back into the dorm is overwhelming, but I'm worried. Please watch over him. Amen.*

Jenna entered the church fellowship hall in search of her parents. After weaving through clusters of mingling parishioners, she spotted them sitting at a small square table, drinking coffee and eating pastries with another couple.

As she drew closer, she recognized the gentleman with russet hair sitting across from her father. Sal Valente — her father's childhood friend. Beside him sat his wife, Angela, her salt-and-pepper bob framing her warm smile.

*Oh my goodness! They're here!* Her father had mentioned they were moving back from Texas, but she hadn't known when. Tears filled her eyes as joy overflowed her soul. It had been eight years since she'd seen them.

Growing up, Jenna's family had shared countless outdoor adventures with the Valentes — fishing, hiking, camping. They celebrated birthdays and holidays together. They were like her extended family, and she had missed them dearly. A soft ache pressed at her chest; the easy warmth the Valentes shared with their children was everything she wished she felt with her own father.

In her eyes, Mr. and Mrs. Valente were the ideal parents. They showed love openly to their twins, Luke and Liliana — with words, hugs, and smiles. Even amid chaos, they had patience and humor. Unlike her father, who lost his temper easily.

Careful not to slip in her pumps, Jenna hurried to greet them. "Mr. and Mrs. Valente, hi!"

Mr. Valente's eyes lit up. He pushed his wheelchair away from the table and opened his arms. "Bella Jenna, how are you?"

"I'm well, thank you," she said, leaning in for his hug. "It's so good to see you…but what happened?" She pointed to the wheelchair.

Mr. Valente shook his head. "Ah, clumsy me. Six months ago, I injured my back — fell off a two-story roof."

Jenna stared wide-eyed, mouth open.

"No worry." He flicked his wrist. "I heal."

She nodded. "I'll pray for you."

"Thank you, doll."

"Jenna," Mrs. Valente said, reaching out. "It's been a long time."

"Too long, Mrs. Valente."

She gestured to a chair. "Please, join us."

Jenna eagerly pulled up a seat. "So, how's everything? How are Liliana and Luke?"

Mrs. Valente smiled. "The twins are well. Luke is still living with us. Liliana graduated college with a bachelor's in agriculture. She and her fiancé are ranchers in Silver Bit, a rural town outside Dallas."

Jenna lifted her brows. *Liliana is engaged at twenty-two.* She glanced at her mother, then back at Mrs. Valente. "Wow, engaged. That's wonderful news! I'm so happy for her."

"Jenna," her mother said, patting her hand. "Remember, Liliana is older than you."

"I know that, Mother." She turned back to Mrs. Valente. "Did she pick a date yet?"

"No. They want to focus on the business first and hopefully save some money."

Dad cut in. "See, *Amore*, no rush."

Mrs. Valente touched Jenna's shoulder. "Your father's right, honey. You're young. Enjoy life."

"Yes, ma'am." Jenna sighed. *Why does this always have to be about me?* She dropped her chin and toyed with her gold rope chain, Tommy's ring resting close to her heart. Lost in her thoughts, she nearly missed the conversation buzzing around her.

"Did you close on the house?" her father asked.

"Yes," Mr. Valente said. "A two-bedroom chalet on Woodland Way."

"Nice. Woodland Way…that's only a few blocks from us," her father said.

"But we're far from moved in," Mrs. Valente added. She reached for her husband's hand. "If it wasn't for our son..." Her voice cracked. "He's been a tremendous help. A blessing."

Mr. Valente nodded. "Yes, he sacrificed a lot for us since my accident."

Mrs. Valente scanned the hall. "Where's Luke anyway?"

"Angela, he left. He had a lunch date, remember?"

She shook her head. "Oh, right. With all this moving madness, I've lost my mind."

Mr. Valente cupped her hand. "Relax now, love. We're home...for good."

Jenna looked at her watch. "Oh my! I must get to work." She sprang from her chair. "It was so nice seeing you both again."

Hours later, on her way home from work, Jenna stopped at the store to buy some last-minute school supplies. When she arrived home, she dropped her purse and shopping bag on her desk, then plopped across her bed to check her answering machine. It blinked red — a message. Her heart jumped. She pressed play.

"Jenna, it's Tommy. Pick up the phone. It's Sunday, uh, two o'clock. Wait! That would be five, your time.

Anyway, I finally got my phone hooked up. Call me, 858-555-1623."

Jenna desperately searched her desk for a pencil, only to find one with a broken point. *Oh, crap!* She tore open a package of pens from her shopping bag, grabbed a notebook, rewound the message, and scribbled down the number.

She took a deep breath then picked up her neon trimline phone and dialed the given number. The phone rang once, then twice. *Come on, Tommy, answer.* The phone rang a third time, and then a fourth, before someone picked up.

"Hello?" an unfamiliar, wavering voice said. Heavy metal blasted in the background.

Sweat prickled at Jenna's hairline. *Did I call the right number?* "Oh, uh… is Tommy there?"

"One moment, please," the strange voice quivered.

The booming music cut off. Muffled voices followed — one of them unmistakably Tommy. The receiver crackled.

"Dude, you're not my secretary. Take a break. Go for a walk; get lost."

A door slammed.

"Hello?" Tommy said.

"Tommy! Oh my gosh, I miss you."

"Jenna, babe, I miss you, too."

"Who answered your phone?"

Tommy cussed. "Jenna, I can't take it already. My roommate is such a geek. I'll never survive the year with him."

"Really? What happened to Ken?"

"He upgraded to a single dorm."

"Is this roommate really that bad?"

"You have no idea. Harold is a neat freak with OCD. We're total opposites."

"But you're neat, too."

"You don't get it. He divided the room with tape and labeled everything where it belongs."

"No way!"

"Yeah. He even typed his entire life schedule and posted it on the bulletin board — laundry days, bedtime — like I care."

"Oh, my goodness! Can you switch roommates?"

"I have to wait at least a month before I put in a request. That is, if I survive that long."

"Well… if it makes you feel better, I'm miserable here too. My dad is not pleased about our engagement. He thinks we're too young to know what we want."

"What a shocker."

"I'm so done with him running my life."

"Move here so you can be my roommate."

"Yeah, I wish."

"I'm serious, babe. We can get married, then I don't have to live in this dorm."

"I was hoping we were getting married because you love me, not because you hate your roommate."

"I do love you," Tommy said.

There was a longing in his tone that touched a place inside her. "I love you, too."

Suddenly, Tommy grew silent.

"Hold on, babe."

More muffled cussing. Another door slam.

"What just happened?" she asked.

"Gotta go. The geek came back and left again to take a shower. He said our call will disturb his beauty rest."

Jenna rolled her eyes. "Okay. Good night."

The line clicked into silence, leaving her alone with the hum of the dial tone and a hollow ache that felt bigger than the distance between them.

$$\heartsuit$$ *Chapter 4*

The next morning, Jenna circled Lot F twice like a vulture waiting on its prey, until she finally spotted someone pulling out. She slid into the space and let out a deep breath. *From now on, I'm going to have to get here an hour early just to find parking.*

She made the fifteen-minute trek to the Math building, passing at least half a dozen drivers creeping through the rows in search of a spot. She gave each of them a sympathetic head shake.

Inside, she quickly found her classroom — but stepping through the doorway felt like entering a different world. She didn't recognize a single face from high school. Her stomach tightened. *I feel like a fish out of water.*

A clique of girls cackled in the back corner. *Are they laughing at me?* Jenna glanced down at her stone-washed jeans and oversized concert T-shirt, checking herself. She chose the first desk in the first row.

She shifted uneasily, the girls' laughter prickling her nerves. The hum of fluorescent lights buzzed overhead, only sharpening the edge of her anxiety. Doing nothing felt awkward, so she pulled out her schedule and pretended to study it. She listened to their conversation — something about a goofy lifeguard they'd met at the beach. Relief washed over her. *Okay… not about me.*

As she settled in, someone poked her shoulder. Shivers raced up her spine. She looked up — and a familiar smile greeted her.

Adam.

His happy-go-lucky face was always a sight for sore eyes.

"Adam! What're you doing here? What happened to art school in New York?"

"My dad lost his job," he said, taking the seat behind her.

"Oh, wow. I'm so sorry."

He ran a hand through his shaggy jet-black hair. "Nah, don't be. I can always transfer in two years."

"That's true."

Adam's hazel eyes drifted to the ring dangling from her necklace. "Tom's ring?"

She nodded.

"Ooh, getting serious."

Joy rippled through her. She touched the ring. "Tommy and I are engaged."

Adam nodded, but something flickered in his eyes — a pinch of disappointment she wasn't sure she imagined. "Congratulations. I hope he knows what a lucky guy he is."

Jenna smiled, uncertain whether he was sincerely happy or just being polite. A faint heaviness tugged at her chest; she hadn't expected his reaction to matter, yet somehow it did. He'd never hinted at liking her more than a friend, and he'd never been a rival to Tommy.

"Thanks, Adam."

She turned back around as the professor walked in.

Midafternoon, Jenna stopped at the school bookstore to buy her textbooks. The checkout line stretched longer than the return line at the mall the day after Christmas.

She glanced at her wristwatch beneath her stack of books. *If this line doesn't move soon, I'm going to miss my next class.*

"Hey, Jenna!" a vibrant voice called.

She turned — Kellie stood six people back. *Oh, wow! What's she doing here?* She was supposed to have moved in with her grandmother to attend a prestigious college in Massachusetts.

Jenna stepped out of her place in line and moved to stand in front of her. "What're you doing here?"

"Change of plans," Kellie said, trying to hug her without knocking over the books.

"What happened? You should've called me."

Kellie lowered her gaze. "I'm sorry. My grandma passed away, and life got crazy."

A chill hit Jenna's core. "Oh, Kel… I'm so, so sorry."

Kellie wiped a tear, still grieving. "Thanks. Yeah, Grandma was a character. I really looked forward to living with her. I miss her so much."

"If you need anything, please tell me," Jenna said.

"Thanks. Life can sure change in a hurry," Kellie said, her voice catching.

"It sure can."

"Hey, call me," Kellie said. "Let's make plans for Friday. You know… catch up on life."

"Okay. We'll make it happen."

Much later, after a harried day at college, Jenna returned home. She stepped into the kitchen and found her mother preparing stuffed chicken breast with spinach and mozzarella, with a side of green beans.

"Ooh, that looks scrumptious, Mom."

"Thank you. You're home just in time. It's ready."

"Good, I'm starved."

In the dining room, her father served her plate. "How was your first day of school?"

"Exhausting. There was barely any parking, the classes are redundant, and textbooks are *so* expensive."

"Doesn't matter. You need an education."

"Sure, and I'm going to go broke getting one."

"Then you'll have to work more hours."

"Daddy, there are only so many hours in a day. I'm already working weekends. I'm tired."

"You wouldn't be so tired if you didn't spend all hours of the night talking to that boy."

Jenna set down her fork. "That was only last night."

"Then don't make a habit of it."

She pressed her lips together to keep from snapping.

Mom cleared her throat — her gentle way of diffusing tension. "Jenna, I saw Mrs. Bailey yesterday at church. She loved the baby blankets you sewed for the unwed mothers' home."

"And?"

"She was asking if you wouldn't mind sewing lap quilts for the nursing home as Christmas gifts."

Jenna yawned. "I guess so. I'll have to buy more fabric… something suitable for old people."

Mom pressed her lips together to keep from smiling. "Oh, Jenna!"

After dinner, Jenna retreated to her bedroom. She sat at her desk and opened her English Literature textbook. She thumbed through the twenty pages assigned for homework, then closed the book.

*I don't want to read this.*

She pushed her chair in and moved to her sewing table. She picked up the cotton yardage with the Noah's Ark print — bright, vibrant colors she adored. She smoothed her hand over the soft fabric, imagining how lovely it would look in a baby's nursery.

She closed her eyes, recalling the family living class she and Tommy had taken in high school. The course was meant to prepare students for adulthood, marriage, and parenting. She and Tommy had pretended to get married. They carried around a hard-boiled egg as their "baby." Out of the entire class, they were the only couple who didn't crack theirs.

Jenna opened her eyes and smiled at the memory. All she ever dreamed about was marrying the love of her life and raising a family. To her, finding true love mattered more than having a successful career.

She laid the baby fabric out flat when the phone rang. Immediately, she leaped across the bed and grabbed the receiver. "Hello?"

"Hey, wassup?" Tommy asked.

"College stinks. First day and already too much homework… and it's only Monday."

"It'll get easier."

"And my dad is hounding me again."

"What now?"

Jenna twirled the phone cord. "He just doesn't want me to be happy."

"I can cheer you up."

"How? You're there and I'm here."

"I wrote you a song. Wanna hear it?"

Heat rushed into Jenna's cheeks. "I'd love to."

"Okay," he said, strumming his guitar. "It's called *Holding Forever*."

"Aww," Jenna breathed.

As Tommy sang, her heart skipped, then raced. Even miles apart, each word made her feel his nearness — his scent, his warmth, the memory of his touch.

"Tommy, it's perfect."

"Did you really like it?"

"Yes, I loved it. And I love you."

"Love you, too, Jenna."

She held the receiver close, wishing the warmth in his voice could bridge the miles between them.

## ♡ *Chapter 5*

Excited for a much-needed Friday night out, Jenna paced the living room waiting for Kellie to pull up. When she heard the horn honk, she shouted, "See you later, Mom!"

"You're leaving? You be careful."

"We will," Jenna said, racing outside to the maroon four-door idling in the driveway.

"Hey, bestie!" Kellie shouted over the loud music.

Jenna hopped in and fastened her seatbelt. "So, what do you want to do tonight?"

Kellie lowered the radio volume. "Whatever — cruise around, go to the mall, rent a movie… look for guys. Oh, wait! You're engaged now."

Jenna couldn't hold back a smile.

"Look at you! It's settled then. We're going to the mall. We can check out the bridal shop."

"No, that's okay. It's way too soon. Besides, Tommy and I have to get through college first."

Kellie shifted the car into drive. "It's never too soon to plan a dream wedding."

It was a forty-minute drive to Forest Hill Mall. When they pulled into the parking lot, Jenna frowned. It felt just like college — cars with booming stereos cruising the rows for parking while white security trucks with yellow flashing lights patrolled for theft and nuisance activity.

After repeatedly circling the chaotic lot, Kellie finally found a spot way out in Oshkosh.

Jenna unclicked her seatbelt and sighed. At last — freedom. Freedom from a demanding week of college, homework, and parents. "Ready to de-stress?"

"Let's do it!" Kellie said, fluffing her shoulder-length sandy brown hair.

Jenna smoothed her oversized concert tee, suddenly aware of how out of place she felt among the confident peers prowling the mall.

Jenna and Kellie entered the mall through the main entrance near the movie theater. It was a typical Friday night. A group of foul-mouthed heavy-metal teens stood in the red-rope ticket line, spewing obscenities at their rivals until mall security stepped in to break it up.

Kellie flipped her wrist. "Oh, that's so high school."

"So glad we're over that." Jenna laughed. "Hey, but it's free entertainment. No need to buy movie tickets."

"Do we get popcorn with it?" Kellie asked.

Jenna breathed in the buttery aroma. "Yum." She could almost taste the salt and watered-down soda. Tempting as it was, she wasn't much of a movie-theater person. She preferred the coziness of home over uncomfortable chairs and sticky floors.

Jenna nudged Kellie. "If this outing turns out lame, we should rent a movie from the video store down the street."

"Sounds like a plan," Kellie said.

They passed the moderately crowded lounge area with the iconic garden fountain and rubbery shrubs, heading toward the common area.

Mrs. Field's freshly baked chocolate-chip cookies teased Jenna's stomach, reminding her she'd skipped supper. *Why did we enter the mall this way?* If they'd come through an anchor store, the cloud of perfume would've smothered her rumbling stomach.

"Hey, Kel, mind if we stop at the food court?"

"I thought you ate at home."

"No. I'm so sick of spaghetti."

"But your mom's an awesome cook. How can you get sick of her Italian cooking?"

"Uh, let's see…" Jenna tapped her finger on her lips. "Maybe because it gets boring eating the same thing every night."

After eating a cold Italian sub, Jenna and Kellie strolled through the mall past the Time Warp arcade.

"Hey, wait a sec," Jenna said, grabbing Kellie's arm.

"What?"

"Let's see who's hanging here tonight."

Kellie shrugged. "Okay, I guess," she said, following Jenna inside.

Jenna traipsed through the dark, noisy, overly crowded arcade. Memories of Tommy playing *Alien Invasions* made her smile. She pictured him feeding the machine quarter after quarter until his pockets were empty. She never understood how he'd become so addicted to a game he could never win. She shook her head at the silliness and pushed the memory aside.

As she snaked her way to the back of the arcade, she spotted Adam playing pinball. She snuck up behind him and wrapped her arms around his waist.

"Hey, you," she said.

Adam turned. "Hey, Jenna. What're you doing here?"

Jenna shrugged. "Same as you. Escaping the nightmare of Professor Regal's geometry class."

"But I like that class," Adam said.

"Yeah, I guess you would, Mister Artistic."

"Jenna," Kellie said, tugging at her sleeve. "Stop flirting with him. I thought we were wedding-dress shopping?"

Adam gave Jenna a sidelong glance of utter disbelief. "You're still going through with it?"

Jenna playfully smacked his shoulder. "Yes, I am."

"I'm the best man, right?" he asked.

"Yeah, sure, Adam. I'll let Tommy know."

Something in his eyes lingered — not quite jealousy, not quite sadness — but enough to unsettle her.

"C'mon, Jenna," Kellie said, steering her away.

Jenna and Kellie rode the escalator to the third level.

"What's with you and Adam?" Kellie teased.

Jenna's face burned. "Nothing. Why?"

"You're crushing on him, aren't you?"

"No way!" she said, too quickly. "We're just friends."

She turned and focused on the autumn décor embellishing the mall's center hub. Sure, Adam's sensitive nature captivated her, but he wasn't her type — and she wasn't the least bit attracted to him.

Jenna straightened her posture and answered with confidence. "My heart belongs to Tommy, and it always will."

Kellie nodded with a smile. "Okay, okay. I believe you."

On their way to the bridal shop, they passed a jewelry store. Eagerly, Kellie pulled Jenna aside. "C'mon, let's check out the rings."

Jenna stopped at the entrance and glanced inside. A couple stood at the cash register speaking with a sales rep.

"Really, Kellie?"

"Yeah, why not?"

"Because it's Tommy's decision to pick out the ring."

"It doesn't hurt to look. Maybe toss him a few hints."

Jenna rolled her eyes but followed Kellie inside, past extravagant display cases of dazzling neck chains, watches, and earrings. They reached the back of the store where glistening diamonds and elegant wedding bands gleamed under the fluorescent lights.

To Jenna, the perfect ring was anything Tommy picked out. It didn't matter what shape the diamond was or how much bling it had. Honestly, she preferred being surprised. She was an old-fashioned, traditional gal. Thinking about it, she laughed inside. *I am very much like my parents.*

After browsing the many styles and shapes of diamonds, Jenna and Kellie made their final stop at a bridal boutique. They browsed the bridesmaid dresses, admiring all the styles and colors. But without an appointment, Jenna couldn't try on the wedding gowns.

"No biggie," Jenna said, picking up a two-inch-thick bridal catalog. She flipped through the pages in search of her princess gown. "When I find my style, I'm going to make it myself."

The thought warmed her; sewing her own gown felt like stitching her dreams into something real — something she could hold onto while Tommy was so far away.

Pre-wedding bliss burned in Jenna's soul. She couldn't wait to share her browsing experience with Tommy. Before leaving the mall, she stopped at a phone booth to call him. She reached into her change purse for quarters and slipped them into the coin slot.

"Do you have any clue how much this call is going to cost?" Kellie asked.

Jenna waved her hand. "Shush, it's ringing."

She didn't care if it cost twenty dollars. She had to talk to Tommy. But after ten rings, she hung up. "No answer." She glanced at her watch and shrugged. "Who stays in on a Friday night anyway?"

The night grew old. After Jenna arrived home, she took a hot, steamy shower, then nestled into bed under warm flannel sheets. Snuggled against her soft body pillow, she drifted into dreamland.

While in that twilight state, a loud ring jolted her awake.

"Hello?" she answered.

"Babe, wassup?" Tommy asked.

She yawned. "I was sleeping."

"Oh, then I won't bother you."

"No. I'm awake now," she said, rubbing her tired eyes. "Went to the mall with Kellie. We were looking at wedding dresses."

"Cool. Wish I was there to see you."

"No! That's bad luck."

"It is? Well anyway, we should pick a date."

Jenna sat up straight. "Really? When?"

"The sooner, the better, so we can be together."

His velvet tone flowed over her like warm honey.

"Aw, Tommy."

"How 'bout June?" he asked.

"But what happened to graduating college first?"

"Screw college. I miss you," he said.

Tommy's words kindled Jenna's eagerness. She switched on the lamp and grabbed the bridal catalog off her nightstand. She flipped through the pages, rambling about the latest fashions while dog-earing her favorite styles.

"I really want to have our wedding at the River Grove Manor," she said.

"Whatever you want."

"Well, I want you to have a say in it too."

"Like what?" he asked, strumming his guitar.

"Like music. Do you want a band or a DJ?"

"DJ. I want to hear the songs from the original artist."

"Okay. And how about the food?"

"Anything Italian, like you," he said slyly.

"Oh, Tommy, stop!"

"I love you. All I care about is you here with me."

A crackle of energy passed between them.

"I love you, too, Tommy. I can't wait till you come home for Thanksgiving."

"Can't be soon enough."

A loud thump and commotion transmitted through the receiver. Jenna pulled it away from her ear and frowned. *What in tarnation is going on?*

She put the phone back to her ear. "Tommy?"

"Babe, wait a sec."

In the background, she heard Tommy dropping the F-bomb. "Dude, it's Friday night!" A door slammed before Tommy shouted, "It's only freaking eight o'clock!"

"Harold again?" she asked.

"Yeah, unbelievable! I gotta go. Geek says he's got to wake up early tomorrow so he can go to the computer lab. Who does that on a Saturday?"

Jenna shook her head. "I'm sorry. I love you."

"Love you, too."

♡♡ *Chapter 6*

The weeks passed, and October neared its end. Jenna sat in math class with her pencil clenched between her teeth, staring at her test paper. She silently read the first question.

*If a circle has a diameter of eight, what is the circumference?*

She had no idea. She hated geometry. *When am I ever going to use this?* She reread the question, trying to remember the formula. *Let's see... pi equals three point fourteen, I think.*

She peered up at her classmates, all actively working. The sound of their pencils scratching against their test papers broke her concentration. The steady scrape of graphite felt louder than her own thoughts.

*Ugh! I can't think.*

She looked toward the partially open window as a breath of wind brushed her bare arm. The peaceful scenery mesmerized her. Trees splashed with autumn color stretched against the blue sky, their beauty at its peak. It was her favorite time of year, and she was annoyed she wasn't enjoying it. Instead, she was buried under more schoolwork than she'd ever had, plus endless hours at her job just to make ends meet.

She sighed, knowing the frigid winter winds would soon strip the trees of their splendor — and she'd miss it.

A firm hand touched her shoulder, sending chills up her spine. She turned to find Professor Regal standing there.

"Focus, Jenna," he whispered. "You only have thirty minutes left."

She nodded. "Yes, sir." Her daydream shattered, she turned her attention back to her test.

It was lunch break, but Jenna didn't have time to eat. She had to type up a last-minute narrative for English class. She rushed into the computer lab and dropped her books on the counter.

"Hey, Jenna, wait up," Adam called, jogging to catch her. "How'd you do on the test?"

"Horrible. I'll never understand geometry."

"I'd be happy to help you study."

Jenna gave an appreciative smile. "Thanks. I might take you up on it," she said, digging through her bag for her floppy disk.

"Aren't you going to lunch?" he asked.

"No. I have a paper to type."

"Oh. When's it due?"

"In an hour."

Adam glanced at his watch. "Yikes. Aren't you cutting it a little close?"

Jenna shrugged matter-of-factly. "There's not enough time in the day to do it all."

Adam touched her shoulder lightly, offering a warm, encouraging smile. "Good luck."

"Thanks."

Jenna slid the disk into the hard drive and clicked on her English Comp folder — but it was empty.

"Where is it?" she mumbled.

She searched the other course folders, but her narrative was nowhere. *Oh crap! Don't tell me I forgot to save it.*

Quickly, she whipped out her three-ring binder and thumbed through the loose-leaf pages. Relief washed over her when she found the writing prompt:

*How will you create a niche for yourself in this world?*

*Thank goodness for the handwritten copy — and for four years of typing in high school.*

After a grueling day at school, Jenna pulled into her driveway and saw that neither of her parents' vehicles were home. *I'm good with that.*

She unlocked the front door and stepped inside. At once, the delicious aroma of pot roast surrounded her. As she trudged up the steps to the second floor, the only sound was the tick-tock of the grandfather clock. She entered the kitchen and slid her heavy backpack off her shoulders. On the counter, beside the crockpot, she noticed a handwritten note from her mother.

*Jenna—*

*Drove Nonna and Nonno to their doctor's appointment in the valley. Hope to be home by 5, but you and Daddy can eat without me if I'm not.*

*Mom*

Jenna couldn't chill the excitement. She had the whole house to herself. The quiet felt luxurious — no tension, no criticism, just stillness she could finally breathe in. For once, she was home early — but only because Professor Gordon had canceled Psychology class.

She glanced at the microwave clock. Three-thirty. She tapped her fingers on the counter. *First, I'm going to eat lunch. Then I'm going to take a much-needed hot bubble bath before anyone comes home.*

She opened the refrigerator. Lunchmeat or leftover spaghetti and meatballs. *Hmm… what am I in the mood to eat?* Before she could decide, the house line rang.

"Oh, for Pete's sake!" she grumbled. She turned and answered the phone. "Hello?"

"Jenna. It's Daddy."

"Oh, hi," she said, unable to hide her lack of enthusiasm.

"Uh, I need you to do something for me."

Jenna sighed. "What?"

"There's an envelope on my desk with some masonry designs in it. I need you to bring them to Sal's office."

"But, Daddy, I just got home."

"Jenna, this is important. I'm stuck on this job site in Alpine Edge."

"But, Daddy, I don't even know where his office is."

"It's in Deer Creek Plaza, suite 201."

Jenna twirled, wrapping the curly phone cord around her fingers. "Who do I give it to?"

"*Amore*, if Sal isn't there, just leave it with the receptionist at the front desk."

Jenna sighed. "Fine, but you owe me gas money."

"Please, *Amore*. Thank you."

"Yeah, Daddy, bye," she said, struggling to keep her annoyance out of her voice. She slammed the phone onto the wall cradle and muttered, "So much for freedom."

Jenna drove twenty minutes to Deer Creek Plaza. The complex was newly built, several businesses already taking up residence — a florist, a pizza joint, a pharmacy, and a cluster of medical practices.

She coasted through the freshly paved parking lot. The sharp smell of tar sparked her memory of childhood trips down the shore. The Valente family had a summer home on the lagoon in New Jersey, and her family had visited them often for barbecues and celebrations. *So many good times.* She could still feel the burn of the sizzling sun and the salty air on her face. *Yep, good times.*

She set the memory aside and focused on finding Suite 201. *It must be on the backside of the court.* As she pulled around the back, she spotted a white pickup truck labeled *Valente Custom Home Builders.*

She parked beside it and studied the stone-faced building, wondering if it was one of her father's past projects. Regardless, she found Suite 201 by the fancy gold-lettered sign.

Jenna grabbed the envelope from the passenger seat and approached the entrance. When she opened the door, a bell chimed.

"I'll be with you in a moment," a male voice called from the back office.

"No problem," Jenna replied.

She wandered the waiting area, taking in the small space. Stark white paint dulled the walls, but framed sketches of model homes drew her attention. On the back wall, a huge map of River Grove showed a heavily wooded area flagged as the future site of *Melody Lake Estates*.

A nearby table displayed an architectural model of the forthcoming community; another showcased interior design options.

Jenna picked up a brochure and browsed the featured homes. She imagined how fun it would be to choose one. She liked the chalet model, though Tommy preferred ranch style. She smiled, picturing the two of them arguing one day over buying a house.

As she slid the brochure back into the rack, her attention snapped to the cowboy boots thumping against the wooden floor. A young man in a green-checked shirt and well-fitted jeans — drawing attention to all the right places — strutted into the room.

"Howdy," he said, tossing his chestnut hair back with one hand. "Sorry to keep you waiting. How may I help you?"

Jenna smiled. "My father asked me to drop these designs off for Mr. Valente," she said, handing him the envelope.

His brown eyes danced up and down her figure. A long, awkward, *don't I know you?* moment stretched between them.

"Wait a sec," he said, rubbing his well-manicured beard. "Ain'tchya Jenna Rossi?" His slight southern drawl caught her off guard.

"Yeah, and?" she asked, giving him a *who the heck are you?* look.

A stunning smile split across his face. "I guess you wouldn't recognize me." He offered his hand. "I'm Luke — Mr. Valente's son."

She stared wide-eyed for two seconds, then shook his hand. Its warm, rough texture made her heart race. Suddenly, everything clicked.

"Luke! Oh my goodness! How've you been?" she asked, jumping forward to hug him.

He drew her into his powerful arms and lifted her off the floor in a huge bear hug. His masculine scent —

soap, mouthwash, and Drakkar Noir — enveloped her, triggering a new sensation she'd never felt before.

"Golly, look at you!" he said, setting her down. "It's been… how many years?"

"Eight," Jenna replied.

"Whoa! Last time I saw you, you were—"

"Ten."

Luke laughed. "I was gonna say knee-high to a grasshopper." He shook his head. "Wow. I still remember that time at our shore house when all y'all went fishing on the dock, and your brother cast his line and landed the hook in the back of your head."

"Stop!" Jenna covered her ears. "That was awful. If it weren't for your calm mother carefully retracting that hook, I would've been in the ER."

"Sorry, but it's hilarious — looking back now," he said with a devious laugh.

"Yeah, funny," she said, trying not to laugh along.

"Don't know if you heard — our folks are fixin' a camping trip once my dad gets out of his wheelchair."

"I'll pass," Jenna said, waving her hands.

"Oh, c'mon. It'd be fun."

"No way. I prefer indoor plumbing."

"We've got that. An RV. Sleeps eight."

"Oh. In that case… maybe."

Luke pointed toward the door. "Hey, I'm closing for the day. Wanna grab a bite to eat? Catch up on old times."

"Oh, uh… I can't. My parents have supper waiting," she said, toying with her neck chain — Tommy's ring warm against her skin.

Luke lifted his chin in acknowledgment. "So… when's the wedding?"

He stood firm, arms crossed over his broad chest.

Goosebumps tickled her arms. "What? How'd you know about that?"

"Your folks mentioned it."

"Oh." Jenna dropped her gaze, not wanting to discuss it. She looked back up. "What about you? Seeing anyone?"

"Nope."

"What about that lunch date you had after church?"

"That was strictly business."

"Uh-huh. I see."

"So… about this fiancé," Luke said boldly. "Does he treat you right?"

A small, firm voice inside Jenna insisted she set the record straight. "Tommy's a good guy."

"Do I know him?"

"Probably not," Jenna said, opening the suite door. "I gotta get going."

"Yeah, sure," he muttered.

She hurried to her car and fumbled with the key in the lock.

"Hey, Jenna!" Luke called from the doorway.

She looked up.

"Congrats on your engagement!"

Jenna closed the door to her gas guzzler. What the heck was that all about? During her twenty-minute drive back home, her mind wavered over her conversation with Luke. *Does he treat you right?* What was that supposed to mean? Luke didn't even know Tommy. His question disturbed her. It clung to her thoughts like burrs, irritating and impossible to shake.

When she pulled into her driveway, neither of her parents were home yet. As she entered the house, conflicting thoughts continued to stir her emotions. *What's not to like about Tommy? He's respectful, loyal, and caring. Okay, so he has long hair, wears leather, and listens to heavy metal music. So what? He doesn't drink, smoke, or do drugs.*

She wondered if Luke's query stemmed from her parents' dislike for Tommy. But Jenna didn't care. She loved Tommy and that was all that mattered.

She pushed the negative thoughts aside and entered the kitchen. Her stomach growled, reminding her that she hadn't eaten all day. She lifted the lid on the crockpot and made a face. Suddenly, the pot roast no longer seemed appealing. *Oh, forget it. I lost my appetite.*

She left the kitchen and moseyed down the hall to her bedroom and closed the door. She was too exhausted to think. She changed into her nightshirt, settled into bed, and turned out the light.

Drifting into the wisps of sleep, her phone rang.

"Hello?" she yawned.

"Hey, I have awesome news," Tommy said.

"What?"

"Me and my buddies—Kevin, Jeff, and Scott formed a band. We got this gig, playing at this bar Friday nights."

"Oh, wow! That's awesome, Tommy."

"I'm so close to my dream. It's so unreal."

"I'm so happy for you."

"For us, Jenna. Oh, I miss you."

"I miss..." Jenna's voice trailed off mid-sentence when she heard a knock at her bedroom door. "Wait a sec," she told Tommy, then shouted at the door, "What?"

Her door opened. "You're in bed already?" Dad asked.

"Yeah, I'm tired."

"You didn't eat supper."

"I'm not hungry," she said as her stomach rumbled.

"Did you drop off that envelope like I asked?"

"Yes, sir."

"Was Sal there?"

"No."

"Who'd you give the envelope to?"

"Luke."

A satisfied smile softened her father's harsh features. "Oh! So, you saw Luke?"

"Yeah, Daddy." *Can I get back to my phone call now?*

"Nice young man, isn't he?"

Jenna rolled her eyes. "I guess so. Um, Daddy, I'm really tired, and I have a test tomorrow."

"Okay, *Amore*. Good night," he said, closing the door.

Jenna put the phone back up to her ear.

"Sorry about that Tommy."

"What was that all about?" he asked.

"Oh, my dad's work stuff."

"Who's Luke?"

"My dad's friend—he works with him."

"Uh-huh. And should I be jealous?"

"Oh, puh-leeze! He's practically family."

"How old is he?"

"Um, twenty-two."

"Do you think he's hot?"

A knot tightened in her stomach; she hated when Tommy slipped into insecurity.

"Tommy, stop!" I love you and only you."

"Okay. I trust you," he said.

Jenna and Tommy's phone conversation dragged on late into the night until their words faded.

## Chapter 7

Jenna ran her tongue over her lips in a nervous gesture as she waited for Professor Regal to hand back her graded geometry test that she had taken earlier in the week. *I hope I passed.*

"Most of you did phenomenal," Professor Regal said as he walked up and down the aisles, placing the papers face down on the desks. "If you have any questions, I will be available after class."

"Yes!" Adam whispered loudly, rejoicing over his perfect score.

When Professor Regal placed Jenna's paper in front of her, nerves danced in her stomach. *Please tell me I passed.* She took a deep breath, braced herself, and flipped it over.

A big, fire-engine-red F filled the top of the page. *What?*

She spun in her chair toward Adam. On the edge of an emotional breakdown, her voice cracked. "I failed."

"I'm sorry," he said, gently taking her paper. He scanned the problems she'd missed and handed it back. "I'll help you, so you don't fail the course."

Jenna nodded. "Thank you."

But the day didn't get any better.

Professor Henderson handed back her English paper — the one she'd typed last minute on Monday about creating one's own niche in the world. She received a D. Jenna read the teacher's comment:

Having a family is nice, but what are you passionate about? How will you earn a living?

A bitter taste of disappointment rose to choke her. The comment felt like a slap — as if her dreams weren't good enough for the world she was supposed to fit into.

*You've got to be kidding me! What's wrong with having a husband and family if that's my niche?*

She believed in the simple things. A career and a big paycheck weren't going to satisfy her soul.

She stewed in her thoughts. *Should I talk to her? Or just let it go?* It was a subjective topic — arguing wouldn't change her grade. *Oh, screw it. I give up.*

By the end of the school day, Jenna was ready to give up. She stepped outside the humanities building, and the smell of approaching rain flooded her senses. She looked up at the dreary sky as a dark smudge of clouds scudded overhead.

*Go figure. The only day I'm late for school and parked somewhere in Oshkosh.*

She schlepped across the parking lot, her overstuffed backpack dragging at her shoulders. The first drops of rain dotted the pavement.

*Oh, great. If I don't get drenched now, I'll be soaked later walking the dogs at the shelter.*

At her car, she fumbled through her backpack for her keys. Of course they were buried at the bottom beneath all her heavy textbooks.

Just as she unlocked the door, the sky let loose. She tossed her pack inside and hopped in, slamming the door behind her. For a moment she sat there, watching rippling sheets of water roll down the windshield. The storm drummed against the roof, matching the heaviness pressing inside her chest. After ten minutes, the torrential downpour tapered to a slow, steady drizzle.

Jenna turned the key in the ignition and pleaded silently.

*Please start.*

The engine listened and turned over.

She gasped. "Wow. Something went right today."

She backed out of her spot and shifted into drive—only for the car to stall.

"Oh, c'mon, you piece of junk! Don't do this to me. I *must* get to work sometime today."

She cranked the engine again and revved it hard to get the RPMs up. When she shifted into drive, the car lurched forward.

"Thank you!"

When Jenna clocked in at the shelter, the dogs announced her arrival. Their constant barking declared it was feeding time. *I'm coming, my fur babies.* She opened the kennel door and twitched her nose at the strong dose of bleach permeating the air. George was disinfecting the last pen.

*Oh boy. I'm late.*

George shut off the hose and looked up. "Tough day?"

Jenna nodded. "What gave it away?"

"You're late again."

She glanced down at her high-top sneakers. "I'm sorry. My sociology class ran overtime."

"No worries. The Boy Scouts volunteered today—walked and fed all the dogs."

"I really am sorry."

"Forget it—this time." George smiled. "Linda's here today, out walking Ruby." He pointed to the pen across from him. "Only one left to walk is Ranger."

Jenna turned and saw Ranger, a sweet coonhound/lab mix, sitting patiently at the door. "Aww, poor old guy." She opened the pen, greeted him with affection, and clipped on his retractable leash. "C'mon, boy. Let's go."

Dusk was settling in, so she grabbed a flashlight on her way out. She walked Ranger down to the towpath, following the wet pavement along the canal. Cold rainwater dripped intermittently from the colorful autumn foliage overhead. It wasn't ideal weather, but the outing was good for both her and Ranger.

Jenna used the quiet to withdraw into her thoughts. *What am I doing with my life? Apparently what I want is wrong. According to Professor Henderson, I should be focusing on a career. But nothing is going right. I'm failing.* Her eyes pooled with tears. *I just want to be with Tommy.* Thinking about him made her mind come alive again. *I love him so much.*

Suddenly Ranger tugged hard on the lead, yanking her out of her thoughts. He veered off the towpath down a worn, muddy trail.

"Oh, Ranger! Where're you going?"

They trekked through brown leaves and frost-bitten brush toward the main road near the shelter. Ranger pulled her full speed to a pebbled creek, where he stopped short and barked continuously.

Breathless, Jenna asked, "What is it, boy?"

Then she saw it — an injured red brindle greyhound lying lifeless at the creek bank.

"Oh, good Lord!" She rushed to the dog's side and assessed its condition. The dog was conscious, but its breathing was shallow, its eyes glazed. "Oh my gosh… you poor thing." She spotted the tag on its collar and shined her flashlight on it. "Carmella. 343 Mountain View Road…"

She looked up at the dark storm clouds swallowing the last traces of daylight. She stood. "I'll get you out of here somehow."

Rain began dappling the creek. A crack of thunder boomed overhead. Jenna grabbed Ranger's leash and bolted, sprinting back toward the towpath. When she reached it, she spotted Linda walking Ruby back to the shelter.

"Linda! Wait up!" she shouted.

Linda turned at the urgency in Jenna's voice.

"What's wrong?"

"Quick! Get George. There's a dog at the creek in critical condition."

Hours later, Jenna sat in the vet's emergency room, waiting for what felt like an eternity. She dropped her head into her lap and prayed that Carmella would recover. Focused on her plea with God, she flinched when a troubled voice called her name. She jerked upright, her heart thudding from the sudden break in silence. A middle-aged woman stood before her.

"You must be Jenna."

"Yes, I am."

The woman grabbed Jenna's hands and cupped them in her own. "You saved my fur-baby's life."

"It wasn't me," Jenna said softly. "It was Ranger."

"But you cared enough to bring her here—unlike the person who hit her with their car and left her to die."

Jenna's jaw dropped. "Oh my gosh… really?"

The woman wiped a tear from her eye. "Ten days ago, Carmella escaped from our fenced-in yard. We've been searching everywhere for her. And thanks to you and Ranger, she's going to be okay."

Jenna's tension evaporated like a puddle on a scorching summer day. "Oh, thank God."

The woman nodded. "Is Ranger available for adoption?"

"Oh, yes. Speak with George."

"I definitely will. Thank you," the woman said.

Dog-tired, Jenna arrived home. The instant she closed the front door, her father came out of his office, voice first.

"Where've you been?" he shouted.

"At work."

"At ten o'clock at night?"

"We had—"

"How do you expect to earn a degree with these failing grades?" he demanded, holding up her progress report.

"Ugh!" Jenna groaned, stomping her feet. *I should've never signed that waiver.*

Dad's voice escalated. "*Amore*, we have a right to know. You're living under our roof!"

Jenna dropped her head in shame. "I'm trying, Daddy, but these classes are hard."

"It's not enough! When I came to this country, I had to learn the English language. I had it much tougher than you."

As her father lectured, Jenna fell into a pit of apathy. His words blurred. Her thoughts drifted to the future — to the altar where Tommy waited for her.

"Jenna," Mom called, descending the stairs. "Have you given any more thought about a career?"

Jenna gave a pathetic shrug. "I don't know."

"How about a vet?" Mom asked. "You like working with animals."

"No," Jenna said.

"Why not?" Dad grumbled.

"Because I can't stomach that stuff. I hate science."

"How about a secretary?" Dad suggested. "You dress up, work in a nice office—"

"No way. I'm not making anyone's coffee."

"Jenna," Mom said calmly, "just put some effort into those grades. Eventually, something will interest you."

"And no more talking to that boy all night," Dad added.

"But Daddy, I'm—"

"How're you going to pay this?" he asked, waving the phone bill.

"Don't worry. I've got it covered," she shouted.

"You can't be wasting hundreds of dollars on a phone bill. School is your top priority."

"I—"

"*Amore*, no more, or I'm yanking your line!"

"Fine!" Jenna yelled.

"And from now on, be home by nine!"

"Daddy, if you'd just listen… I had an emergency. I found an injured dog hit by a car."

His features softened. "Next time, you find a phone booth and call home."

"Yes, sir."

Jenna pulled her backpack over her shoulder and bolted up the stairs. She stormed down the hall to her bedroom, slammed the door, leaned against it, then slid down to the floor. *Oh, God… can anything go right in my life? My car is a piece of crap, Mom and Dad hate Tommy, and my future has no direction. I am a failure.*

Overwhelmed, her energy drained out of her. *I can't do it anymore, God.* Salty tears rolled down her cheeks; her mouth puckered in a cry of frustration and anger. Her chest tightened, each breath catching like she'd forgotten how to breathe.

She reached up and clutched the glass picture frame on her nightstand. Gingerly, she touched the junior/senior prom photo of her and Tommy posing inside the gazebo. She remembered how neither of them knew how to dance, how their friends pulled them onto the floor during their favorite love song. The moment had been amazing and so romantic. Like that night, she wished he could take her in his arms and make everything all right.

Time slipped away as the memory played in her mind. Disengaged from reality, she jumped when her phone rang. She crawled across the floor and answered it.

"Hello?" she sniffled, trying to steady her voice.

"Hey… what's wrong?" Tommy asked.

"Nothing."

"Don't lie. I hear it in your voice."

"Just a rough day."

"What happened? Talk to me," Tommy pleaded.

Jenna's voice broke into deep sobs. "I'm flunking school and my parents are furious," she cried, then rambled about her junky car and her woes at work.

"Look at the bright side," he said gently. "You saved the lives of two dogs."

When her sobbing finally subsided, Jenna whispered, "I guess if you look at it that way."

"See? Now that's my girl."

"You always know how to cheer me up." She wiped her tears. "Gosh… Thanksgiving can't be here soon enough. I can't wait until you come home."

Silence stretched.

"Tommy?"

"Yeah… um, about Thanksgiving… I'm not coming home."

"What? You're kidding. Why not?"

"I got this gig, and—"

"Oh, Tommy…" Sourness stirred in her stomach. "I—" Her voice trailed off as tears resurfaced. The hope she'd been clinging to all day slipped through her fingers.

"Jenna, listen. My parents are flying out here to see me perform. They invited you along."

"What? Really?"

"Yeah. They have a timeshare."

Jenna couldn't cool her enthusiasm. "Oh, Tommy! That is so awesome. I can't wait!"

Hours later, after they said their good nights, she lay in bed filled with energy and anticipation. Thinking about Tommy and their future together gave her a fresh sense of purpose. There were no shadows of sadness left in her heart.

# Chapter 8

Daddy loosened the collar on his Sunday dress shirt. "No, *Amore*—you're not going to California to see that boy!"

"But Daddy—"

"What did we just talk about the other night? Huh? Jenna, your grades come first."

Quivering with anger, she slapped her arms to her sides. "Fine! I'm moving out!"

She turned on her heel and stomped off in a huff. She slammed her bedroom door and plopped onto her bed. *Why God? Why can't I go?* As she lay there, sobbing, she heard her parents bickering through the hollow walls.

"Nick, it's only for four days," her mother said.

"No, Julia! She's got to hit the books. If she's going to have any kind of future, she needs a good education."

"Please, Nick. Let her go, or we'll lose her."

"No, Julia! Not until she improves her grades."

Jenna buried her face in her pillow not wanting to hear anymore arguing. Deep sobs shook through her. In moments like these, she wished the ground would just swallow her up. *God, I'm sorry. All I want is peace and happiness in my life.*

The shouting died as if someone had lifted the needle from a record. The sound of heeled shoes tapping against the hardwood floor grew louder, then stopped. There was a knock at her door.

"What?" Jenna answered rudely. "I'm getting ready to go to work now."

The bedroom door opened, and her mother stood in the doorway. "I'm sorry, Jenna, but your father only wants what's best for you."

"Is that so? Maybe he doesn't know what that is."

Mom entered and sat on the edge of the bed.

"He does, and so do I. We both feel a college degree is the key to success."

"I don't care about riches. I just want a simple life," Jenna said, crossing her arms. "Maybe it's time I make my own decisions."

"And what? Fly to California?" Mom asked.

"Yeah. It's only for Thanksgiving," Jenna said, her voice hoarse, strained with pain. "It's difficult being apart from Tommy."

"I'm sure it is, but attending an outstanding university is a lifetime chance for him," Mom said, placing her hand on her shoulder.

"I guess," Jenna mumbled, staring down at the floor. Disappointment settled over her like fog on a riverbank. She needed to be with Tommy. "If I pick up my grades by Thanksgiving, then can I go, please?"

Mom shook her head. "You'll have to ask your father." She shifted her position and eyed Jenna's sewing table. "I see you've been busy." She stood up and smoothed her hand over a white satin and lace bridal purse that Jenna had made. "This is beautiful." She then picked up a dazzling rhinestone studded ring bearer pillow. "Wow, you made this too?"

Jenna nodded.

"Very nice," Mom said, impressed.

Jenna's mood lifted. "Tommy and I haven't settled on a date yet, but I wanted to start prepping."

"You have plenty of time," Mom said, walking toward the door. She stopped and turned. "It's okay to dream about the future, but first, you need to live in the present. And right now, the present is your schooling."

Jenna rolled her eyes at her mother's remark. She picked up her bridal handbag and shook her head dismissively. *They just don't take me and Tommy seriously.*

She set her bridal creations aside then dove across her bed to call him. After six rings, he picked up.

"Hello," he yawned.

"I can't go," she said, her voice breaking.

Tommy's voice perked up. "What? Why?" But before she could answer, he erupted into cuss words. "It's your dad again, isn't it?"

Jenna drew in a bolstering breath. "No, it's my fault. I must do better in school."

There was a mocking note in his voice. "Your dad just won father-of-the-year award."

"No, Tommy! It's me! I—"

"I can't stand your dad."

"I'm sorry," she said, dropping her head to her pillow. She pinched the bridge of her nose. "Listen, I gotta leave for work. Can we talk later?"

"Yeah," he said.

"Thanks."

Jenna hung up the phone. The heat of Tommy's anger and dislike for her father seeped into her blood. *Daddy isn't going to ruin my chances for happiness.* Her father had pushed her too far, and she had the right to some of that anger too. Seriously annoyed, she quickly changed out of her Sunday clothes into a pair of jeans and a sweatshirt, then left the house without saying goodbye.

Anger and frustration festered in Jenna's gut all through work. While walking along the towpath with Boomer, a boxer-mix, her father's words reverberated in her head.

*No, Amore, you're not going to California to see that boy!*

"Whatever!" Jenna blurted aloud.

A prickling awareness crept over her. She glanced up at a park bench where a lean, powerful runner was stretching his legs. He shot her a narrowed look — unmistakably a what's-your-problem expression.

Jenna gave a tiny wave and a forced smile. "I'm good."

As she continued toward the shelter, she shook her head. *That guy must think I'm nuts talking to myself.* But she didn't care. Her father's obvious hatred for Tommy gnawed at her, along with his lame excuse for not letting her go to California.

*Daddy is ridiculous to think he can stop me. It's my life.*

A sudden flicker of clarity cut through her anger. *Yes, it IS your life... but your father wants you to be prepared.* Common sense finally settled in. *If I want a future with Tommy, I'm going to have to work on my grades.*

She sighed. I need to tell George I have to cut my work hours so I can focus on my studies.

# Chapter 9

After several weeks of serious swotting, Jenna grew tired of the musty smell of aging books, loud whispering, and creepy old men reading the newspaper. But she knew she had to push herself if she wanted a future with Tommy.

She grabbed a scrap piece of paper and a stubby pencil, thumbed through the card catalog, and wrote down call numbers. *Mr. Dewey Decimal better have these titles available.*

She climbed the stairs to the psychology section and scanned the shelf. She pulled out three books on parenting styles then went back downstairs to the study area.

She chose a quiet cubicle in the back corner where no windows would distract her. She set down her heavy stack of books. The thud echoed through the quiet building. She looked up to find the librarian staring at her, finger pressed to her lips.

Jenna's face burned. She mouthed, "Sorry."

She sat and flipped through the chapters, careful not to rustle the pages too loudly.

She reread her assignment: Compare and contrast authoritarian and permissive parenting styles. She held her pencil to her lips. *That's easy. Daddy's authoritarian.*

Engrossed in her rough draft, she jolted when someone tapped her shoulder. She looked up to see Kellie standing there.

"Finally, you're here!"

"Sorry I'm late," Kellie said in a loud whisper. "I got out of work late."

"Oh. Well, you're not missing much."

"Ooh-la-la, but you are," Kellie said, setting her backpack down. She kept standing, eyes locked on the front desk. "Look what the cat dragged in."

"What?" Jenna asked, standing up.

She caught the backside view of a beautifully proportioned male body dressed in greasy denim overalls that hugged him in all the right places. His muscles rippled under a blue plaid shirt, and strands of chestnut hair strayed from beneath his backward ball cap. Something about him tugged at a distant memory. *Why does he look so familiar?*

She studied him more closely. When he turned, she saw his strong profile and well-manicured beard sculpting his square jaw.

Jenna's pulse accelerated. "Oh my gosh!" Heat flooded her cheeks as she dropped back into her chair, burying her face in her hands.

"Isn't he gorgeous?" Kellie whispered, starry-eyed.

"No," Jenna mumbled. "That's Luke."

"You know him?" Kellie squeaked.

"Yes. Now shush! He's a close family friend."

"Girl, where've you been hiding him?"

"Ladies!" the librarian snapped. "Might I remind you there are patrons studying?"

"We're sorry," Kellie said, quickly sitting down. She popped back up for another peek. "Oh fudge, he's gone."

"Good," Jenna said.

That evening, Jenna sat in bed with her cushy body pillow propped behind her. She held the phone to her ear, listening to the acoustic strum of Tommy's guitar as he sang her favorite song. His deep, rich voice soothed her tender emotions.

"I love that song," she said softly. "But I wish I could listen to you play live with your bandmates."

"You tried, babe. Can't help that your father is a stubborn old coot."

"I know… but I can't flunk either," she said, the weight of her new determination pressing against the ache of missing him.

"I guess," Tommy replied, his voice dipping into a glum tone.

"Just think — Christmas will be here in no time, and we'll be together then," Jenna said, clinging to optimism.

"But I need you now," he murmured. "I miss you."

His words warmed her, yet a small knot tightened in her stomach — wanting him didn't make the distance any easier.

"I miss you, too.

## ♡ *Chapter 10*

nother week passed, and it was Thanksgiving Day. The comforting aroma of turkey roasting in the oven permeated the air, mixing with the woodsy smell of seasoned oak crackling in the fireplace.

After Jenna finished helping her mother with meal prep, she entered the festive dining room where acorn string lights draped over the doorways, and pinecone candle holders, pumpkins, and fall foliage tastefully adorned the rustic banquet table. Thanksgiving was her favorite holiday, but the harsh wintry weather made it feel more like Christmas.

She stood by the slider door to the back deck and watched the fine snowflakes fall gracefully from the sky. It was hard to believe that four inches of snow had fallen already making the roads too treacherous for travel. Fortunately, for her, she wasn't going anywhere. However, her grandparents, and her brother Anthony and his wife Holly, couldn't make the two-hour trip from the city to River Grove to share in the holiday feast. Jenna sighed in disappointment. Since she wasn't spending Thanksgiving in California, she was looking forward to celebrating it with her family.

When the grandfather clock chimed noon, a terrifying thought washed over her. The Valentes would be there shortly, and living only a few blocks away, the weather wouldn't deter them. Though she loved being in their company, she cringed at the reality of dining with Luke. She had no room for his nonsense in her busy schedule.

Jenna returned to her bedroom and changed out of her sweatpants into a designer pair of high-waisted tapered jeans. Instead of a frumpy T-shirt, she topped it with an off-the-shoulder black sweater. She paused, staring at her reflection. *Why am I suddenly trying so hard?* She knew the answer— she just didn't want to face it.

She added a cotton headband to her styled hair and brightened her complexion with a little makeup. Feeling a bit more confident, she smiled at her reflection. *Okay, now I'm ready.* Even if she wasn't ready for Luke.

Jenna sat at her desk and opened her math textbook. She had two full pages of geometry to finish over the holiday weekend, and since finals were right around the corner, she needed to get a grip on the concepts if she wanted to pass the course.

She read the first math question out loud. "What is the area of the triangle below?" She studied the diagram. She knew there was a formula for figuring out a triangle's area but didn't remember it. She pulled out her spiral notebook and flipped through the pages for a sample problem. "Where is it?"

The phone rang.

"Ooh, that's got to be Tommy," she said, springing out of her chair to answer the phone. "Hello?"

"Hey, I'm finally free from the dungeon and Harold."

"Lucky you. Wish I was free of my dad and away from all this snow."

"Babe, you should see this place—ocean views outside my bedroom window."

"Nice. Wish I was there."

"Me too," Tommy said, clearly bummed.

Jenna dropped her focus on her paper. "Hey, do you know the formula for calculating the area of a triangle?"

"What? You're doing schoolwork?"

"Yeah, I have to get it done."

Tommy sighed. "What does it matter now?" Resentment tainted his angry words. "Your dad won."

"But I still have to try, or I'll fail the course."

Tommy sighed. "I'll let you go then."

"No, wait! I have all weekend to figure it out."

"I have to go anyway," he said. "My mom wants to walk the beach before we go out to dinner."

Jenna groaned, "Fine."

"I'll call you later."

"Sure. Have fun." *Without me.*

She hung up and felt an incredible void. She should be there too. If only she had focused on her studies from the beginning, she'd be with Tommy right now.

She imagined holding his hand and walking barefoot along the beach, listening to waves crash on the shore. But no — she was hibernating on a cold, snowy mountain. *This really stinks!*

Jenna sprawled out on the floor with her textbook. Math was not her subject. Even after weeks of tutoring with Adam, she still struggled. She thought about him — probably having the time of his life in Florida. *Oh well. It's up to me to figure this out.*

She skimmed the index for the page number on area, then flipped back to the chapter. While she reviewed the example, there was a knock at her door.

"Yeah?" she answered without looking up.

The doorknob jiggled, and the door swooshed open.

"Howdy," Luke said.

The sound of his charismatic voice froze her brain. Her heart took over, pounding like a hammer on a nail head. She kept her eyes glued to her textbook, pretending to be busy.

"Hey."

"Whatcha working on?"

"Geometry."

"Need some help?"

Determined to resist the pull of his warm Southern drawl, she kept her eyes down. "Nope. I got this."

"Then why're you not in California?"

That hit a nerve. She shot him a *mind your own business* glare — but his charm touched something deep inside her, and frustration seeped in. She dropped her head into her textbook. "I have to pass this class, and I have no idea what I'm doing."

"Okay, okay. Don't pitch a hissy fit," Luke said, stepping inside. The tantalizing fragrance of his cologne drifted in with him — warm, masculine, familiar. It traveled along her nerve endings, sparking her memory of their first encounter.

"Let me see the problem," he said.

She lifted her head and handed the textbook and worksheet to him. "It's question number one."

Luke sighed then lowered himself onto the floor beside her. His nearness made her body tingle. She tried to look at him dispassionately, but excitement kept blooming inside her, uninvited and impossible to ignore.

*Shake it off, girl. You love Tommy.*

Luke pointed at the page. "This is the formula. Now look at the triangle and plug the numbers in."

"Okay," Jenna said, taking the pencil.

"Now do the math."

Seconds later, she asked, "Is the answer 20?"

"Yes, that's correct."

She smiled. "It makes sense now. Thank you."

Luke looked at her, pleased and impressed. "Good. But now look at the next one. It's tricky."

He wrote out the equation on scrap paper. His left arm bumped hers again — a warm, accidental brush that made her breath catch.

She looked at him with a warm mixture of curiosity and wonder. "How do you remember all this?"

"I use it every day in construction. Roof pitch, flooring material, countertops—"

"Alright already!" she shrieked. "I get it."

"Thank God," he said.

Her phone rang.

"Ooh, I have to take this," she said, grabbing it. "Hello?"

"Hey, bestie," Kellie said. "What's doing?"

"Homework."

Luke stood up. "Catch ya later," he said, leaving the room.

"Who's that?" Kellie asked.

Jenna smiled with shameless delight. "Luke."

"You mean the hunk from the library?"

Jenna laughed.

"Really? C'mon, set me up."

"No way!"

"Why not? He's so fine. Did you tell him you saw him in the library?"

"No way! That was so embarrassing."

There was a soft knock at the door, and Mom poked her head in. "Time to eat, Jenna."

Jenna covered the phone's mouthpiece. "Okay, Mom. Be right there." She uncovered it. "Kel, I have to go."

Kellie's voice held a sulky tone. "Fine."

Early evening, after enjoying the delicious feast, Jenna handed Luke his black leather trench coat from the hall closet. The coat felt cool and smooth in her hands, and for a split second she wondered why her pulse jumped just from touching something that belonged to him. She pulled on her own long-hooded wrap coat, the soft fabric brushing her neck like a comforting hug.

She poked her head into the living room where both her parents and the Valentes were watching a football game, waiting for turkey comatose to set in. The glow from the fireplace flickered across their faces, and the room smelled of cinnamon, oak, and leftover gravy — the kind of cozy warmth she usually loved.

"We're going for a walk," Jenna said.

Preoccupied with the game, Dad gestured for her to go without looking away from the TV.

Mom waved them off. "But don't get lost, you two. We have plenty of dessert."

"Ugh, I'm stuffed," Jenna said, patting her stomach.

"Sure'nuff, Mrs. Rossi," Luke said, following Jenna downstairs. "There's always room for your pumpkin pie."

His voice carried that easy, teasing warmth she was starting to recognize — and feel — far too quickly. As they stepped into the chilly stairwell, Jenna caught the faint scent of his cologne again, something woodsy and clean that mingled with the cold air and made her heartbeat thump a little harder than she wanted it to.

She tugged her coat tighter around herself. *Okay… deep breath. It's just a walk. Nothing more.*

But her heart wasn't listening.

Luke held the front door open, and Jenna stepped out onto the covered porch. The cold evening air kissed her cheeks, and the whiff of chimney smoke cleared her stuffy nose. She peered up at the frosty moon as it tried to reveal itself through the heavy webbed clouds. The new fallen snow lay silently around her — fluffy heaps burying cars, carpeting the streets, and weighing heavily on the arms of the evergreens. The world looked hushed, enchanted, like River Grove had been dipped in powdered sugar.

As Luke pulled the door closed, his breath formed a plume. "Sweet gingerbread! It's as cold as a cast-iron commode out here."

Jenna laughed, the sound puffing into the air like a tiny cloud. "You're not used to it, cowboy."

"No, but I do miss it," he said, blowing into his hands.

"You do?"

"Sure thing. Texas was hot as hades. I much prefer the four seasons and what River Grove has to offer."

"I do too," Jenna said, her voice softening. "But right now, I could be soaking up the sun and digging my feet in the sand with my love."

Luke looked at her intently — a quick, unreadable flicker — then strode off the porch into the deep snow.

"What?" Jenna asked. She trudged forward, stepping into his footprints to catch up. "What's wrong with that?"

"Nothing." He continued toward the recently plowed road. "Ain't no hill for a stepper," he said.

"What?" She stopped, baffled. "Where do you come up with this stuff?"

He turned, snow crunching under his boots. "No problem can't be solved if you set your mind to accomplishing your goals."

Jenna blinked as she pondered his words. *He's right. A little effort goes a long way.* She nodded. "Okay, I get it."

They walked on silently, admiring the picturesque scenery. Many houses were already decorated for Christmas. White lights and colored lights brightened the darkness, illuminating yards full of blow-mold Santa Clauses, leaping reindeer, and snowmen. Wreaths trimmed foil-wrapped front doors, and strings of garland shimmered on porch railings.

"What happened to cornstalks, pumpkins, and fall mums? Man, Christmas starts earlier every year," Luke said.

"I'm okay with that," Jenna said. "Besides, the weather kind of dictated it."

♡

They followed the road until it curved sharply into the darkness. Just before the bend stood the community center and playground, well-lit by lampposts.

Luke pointed. "Oh, I remember this place! My dad used to take me and my sister sleigh riding when we were knee-high to a grasshopper."

"Fun times," Jenna said.

Luke brushed snow off the wooden fence and leaned into it, resting his foot on the lower rail. "Golly, River Grove brings back some fond memories."

"I'm sure."

"I see they still have the ice rink."

"Yep, and they still go all out in December with the tree lighting ceremony, caroling, and hot chocolate."

"My sis skated here all the time." His voice dipped. "This will be our first Christmas apart."

Jenna placed her hand on his forearm. His coat felt cold beneath her palm, but his arm was warm and solid underneath. "I'm sorry." She remembered how close he and Liliana were — like two peas in a pod. "So how is Liliana doing?"

"She's great! She and her fiancé raise horses."

"Cool. So, do you stay in touch often?"

"Yeah, I reckon we talk every other day or so. We've always looked out for each other, so it's hard not being there, ya' know?"

"Oh, I know. But aren't twins supposed to have some telepathy connection?"

Luke shot her a half-cocked grin. "Yeah, something you and your fiancé don't have."

"Ha, ha, funny," Jenna said, scooping up some snow. She formed a ball and threw it at him, hitting him on the shoulder. "Take that!"

A grin twisted Luke's lips — not playful this time, but mischievous. "Bless your heart," he said.

Jenna smiled innocently and batted her eyelashes, but that didn't stop him from packing a snowball.

"Try and catch me first!" she said, vaulting over the rail fence. She humped through the heavy snow toward the playground.

"I'm fixin' ta knock you clear into California, girl!"

There was nothing like a good old-fashioned snowball fight but playing with Luke was like fighting fire with someone holding a flamethrower. He pitched one ball after another, pegging her not once but twice in the back.

Jenna ducked underneath a catwalk bridge to avoid being hit again. She shaped another snowball, but as soon as she peeked out, an icy cold snowball grazed her face, stinging her cheek.

"Okay, okay, I surrender!" she shouted, both hands raised.

Luke plodded through the deep snow toward her. "I guess you forgot I was one heck of a pitcher in high school."

Jenna cautiously stepped out from underneath the play area. "Yeah, yeah. Done with me now?" she asked.

Luke laughed.

"Quit it," she said, smacking him on the shoulder. "Not funny. You got me in the face."

"I'm sorry."

He pulled off his glove and brushed the icy flakes off her cheek with his tender hand. His fingers were warm and gentle, the touch sending a tiny spark down her spine.

"You should be," she said, pouting. "Now let's get out of here. I need some hot cider and a warm fireplace."

"Hmm, sounds good to me," he said, wrapping his arm around her as they headed toward the glow of home.

Jenna's heart fluttered — just once — before she forced it still. *Stop it. You love Tommy.* But the warmth of

Luke's arm lingered anyway, unsettling her in ways she didn't want to name.

# Chapter 11

Jenna spent the next week at the library with Adam and Kellie, cramming for finals. They sat in the research area on the second floor, hoping it was far enough away from the noisy children's corner, the photocopying center, and the cranky librarian who guarded the stacks like a hawk.

After an hour of English Literature, Kellie had had enough and went home. Adam drilled Jenna with endless math problems.

"Make sense yet?" he asked.

Jenna nodded and slumped back in her chair. "I think so." She exhaled hard. "All I want is to pass the exam tomorrow so I can move on with my life."

Adam patted her shoulder. "Girl, you got this!"

She reached up and touched his forearm. "Thanks."

"No problem." Adam checked his watch. "How 'bout we blow this joint and get ourselves a pizza?"

"Okay, but it's my treat," Jenna said, closing her textbook.

As she packed up her belongings, a familiar scent of cologne drifted through the aisle — warm, woodsy, unmistakable. Her senses sharpened. When a gentle hand touched her shoulder, her body tingled from the contact.

She turned to find Luke standing behind her.

"Studying hard? Or hardly studying?" he asked.

She frowned, trying to steady her heartbeat. "I studied hard. And I'm going to ace my final tomorrow, thank you."

"Ain't no hill for a stepper," he said with a wink, then walked off.

"Wait, Luke! What're you doing here?"

He pivoted on the heel of his boot, held up a thick auto repair manual on Pontiacs, then strode out the main entrance.

"Who the heck was that?" Adam asked.

"Kellie's crush — good thing she left."

"What?"

Jenna giggled. "Nothing. He's just a family friend."

"Oh."

"But I swear my dad sends him to spy on me."

"Really?"

"I wouldn't put it past him."

"Shoot! I'm glad it's not like that with my folks."

Jenna twisted her mouth. "'Cause you're a guy."

At Alfonzo's Pizza, Jenna and Adam grabbed a table by the front window and watched the cold pouring rain wash away the remnants of that freak Thanksgiving snowstorm. The neon OPEN sign flickered against the wet pavement, casting a red glow across their table.

"This weather is nutty," Jenna said, pulling off her coat and draping it over the chair. The damp chill clung to her skin.

"Uh-huh. Glad I was in Florida when it snowed," Adam said, shaking rain from his sleeves.

"Tommy's parents escaped it, too. But no, I had to stay behind," she said, her tone sour enough to curdle the cheese on their pizza.

Adam winced sympathetically. "Sorry, but I think it was worth it."

"Huh?" Jenna asked, lifting her soda.

"Your grades. Your future," Adam said.

Jenna groaned. "Now you sound like my parents." She took a sip. "Tommy is my future, and I miss him."

"Don't you two talk every night?"

"Not lately. We're too busy."

"How's the wedding plans going?"

"Good… until my mother intervened."

"Oh?"

"She has me sewing these lap quilts for the nursing home for Christmas. Between that and studying, my wedding plans fell by the wayside."

"It'll happen," Adam said, giving her a reassuring smile.

Jenna rolled her eyes. "You really do sound like my mother."

Later that night, Jenna called Tommy, but the answering machine picked up. "You know the drill, leave a message."

After the tone, Jenna said softly, "Hey, Tommy. Where are you? I miss you. Call me… no matter how late it is."

"Hello?" a pip-squeak voice answered.

Jenna jerked the phone away from her ear and stared at it. *You're not Tommy.* She brought it back. "Who's this?"

"Harold. Who am I speaking with?"

"Jenna. Do you know where Tommy is?"

"Nope. Hasn't been here much lately."

A cold prickle crept up her spine. "Oh? Well, tell him to call me."

"I can't, Jenna. You see, the problem is, he comes in too late. And if he calls you, it'll wake me up."

Jenna let out an exasperated sigh. "Never mind. Bye."

She hung up and sat on the edge of her bed, still clutching the phone. *This nerd is unbelievable.* She pressed her lips together. *No wonder Tommy's never there.*

A tiny knot formed in her stomach — one she didn't want to acknowledge.

The next morning in Math class, Jenna sat at her desk, her leg bouncing uncontrollably while Professor Regal stood at the podium barking out instructions like a drill sergeant. His voice ricocheted off the cinderblock walls, sharp and commanding, but Jenna barely heard him.

Her mind spiraled. *What if I fail this exam? Will I still pass the course? If only I had one more day to study...* Insecurity swelled inside her, tightening her chest until she could hardly breathe.

A supportive hand touched her shoulder. Warm. Steady. Grounding.

"Don't worry," Adam whispered. "You got this."

Jenna turned and mouthed, "Thanks." His confidence in her felt like a lifeline.

Professor Regal passed out the exam booklets, the pages snapping like warning shots. After he gave the signal to begin, Jenna scanned the test questions.

Her pulse slowed. Her shoulders relaxed.

A smile tugged at her lips. *I know I got this.*

Evening rolled in. Jenna sat at her sewing table, finishing the binding on the last lap quilt she was gifting to the nursing home. She wished she could have sewn more than just three, but the simple cross-block pattern was time-consuming in the little time she had. Otherwise, she would have loved to create a more intricate design.

Mom poked her head inside the room. "You were quiet tonight at supper. Everything okay?"

"Yeah, just tired."

Mom entered and admired the folded-up lap quilts on the desk. "What a beautiful job, Jenna! And I like your color choices."

"Thanks." Jenna stood up and held one of the finished quilts in front of her. "This is it. Wish I could've done more."

"Mrs. Bailey will be pleased. I'll take them to her tomorrow," Mom said. She turned toward the bedroom door and stopped. "How did you do on your exams?"

"Okay, I guess," Jenna answered.

"You studied hard. I'm sure you did well," Mom said, leaving the room. "Good night."

"Night, Mom."

Jenna cleaned up the scraps of material and stored away her scissors and pins. With the holidays coming, it would be a while before she'd have time for more sewing projects. Besides, she didn't have the extra cash to buy the white satin fabric and embellishments she needed to sew her own wedding gown.

She picked up the pattern she had bought weeks ago and studied the sketch on the envelope in awe. She loved the gown's modest style — a sweetheart neckline with cap sleeves, fitted bodice, and floor-length train. It was suitable for a summer wedding and not too complicated to create.

She set the pattern aside, recalling what Kellie once told her. *You're nuts to sew your own wedding gown!*

Jenna smiled, knowing she'd proudly show Kellie her ability to create her dream gown — and one day, stand at the altar and exchange vows with her love.

Speaking of love, Jenna sat down on her bed and called Tommy. The phone rang one ring after another.

"C'mon, Tommy, pick up," she mumbled.

She looked at the clock. It was only six-thirty there. *Maybe he's eating dinner.* With that thought, she was about to hang up, but then she heard a click.

"Hello?" she said into the phone.

Silence. Another click. Then a dial tone.

"What the?" she grumbled.

Someone had picked up and hung up. She shook her head in disgust and slammed the handset into the cradle.

"Ugh… Harold."

A simmering knot of anger formed — one she didn't want to acknowledge.

The next morning, Jenna joined the crowd of students hovering around Professor Regal's classroom door. She stood beside Adam, bouncing on her tippy-toes, hoping to get a glimpse of yesterday's exam grades posted on the wall.

"Nervous?" Adam asked.

"Just a little."

Jenna's stomach churned. *What if I fail? Will I still pass the course? What if all that studying wasn't enough?* She tallied numbers in her head, trying to calculate the exact grade she needed to survive the semester. *C'mon, people.*

*Move out of the way!* She tugged at a hangnail, waiting in anticipation like a little kid at Christmas.

Finally, the crowd parted.

Jenna stepped forward. She took a deep breath and steadied herself. *Please tell me I passed.* She ran her index finger down the encrypted list until she found her ID number.

Next to it was a letter B.

Her breath caught. Tears of relief pooled in her eyes. She turned to Adam, her voice trembling. "I passed… I can't believe I passed."

Adam smiled, warm and proud. "I knew you could do it."

Later that afternoon, Jenna waited for Kellie in the parking lot at the *Ready, Set, Style Hair Salon*. She had been going there for cuts and perms most of her childhood and was always happy with the results. Roy and Ruthe had run the place for over forty years — warm, dependable, professional. But last week she learned they'd retired and handed the business over to their granddaughter, Tina.

Jenna had graduated high school with Tina, and had never been fond of her. She remembered the stories: Tina prancing around the cosmetology classroom like a know-it-all princess, complaining about the elderly women who came in for discounted services, bragging about accepting tips she wasn't supposed to take. Two-faced. Gossip. Backstabber. Jenna had avoided her then, and she hoped Tina had changed now that she was running her grandparents' salon.

While she waited for Kellie, Jenna slid a cassette into her car stereo. As she sang along to her favorite hair band, joy bubbled inside her. She'd passed geometry — passed *all* her courses — and the relief felt bottomless. Her parents would be proud. Maybe now her father would stop harping on her about Tommy or hinting that he wasn't good enough for her.

Once Kellie arrived, they entered the busy salon. The foul, rotten-egg smell of a perm saturated the air, and the roar of hairdryers drowned out the music overhead. A woman with a push broom greeted them and directed them to the waiting area.

Kellie picked up a hairstyle book and flipped through the current cuts. Jenna grabbed a bridal magazine and scoped out the latest makeup trends and updos. They pointed out styles to each other, laughing quietly — until Tina stepped out from the supply area, mouth first.

Her high-pitched voice pierced through Jenna like nails on a chalkboard. The burgundy bombshell was just as obnoxious as she'd been in high school. One look at Jenna and Kellie, and it was senior year all over again.

"Hello ladies," Tina said, flipping her long spiral 'do away from her perfectly oval face. She scooted behind the receptionist desk and opened the appointment book. "Are you two on the schedule?"

"Yes. I'm with Michelle," Jenna said. "And Kellie has an appointment with Patty."

"Okay, just checking," Tina said, closing the book. "Cuz we're really busy today."

She strutted away, smiling at a few clients as she moved through the salon, then spun around and strolled back toward the waiting area.

Tina lingered over Jenna's shoulder. "Wedding planning?"

"Uh-huh," Jenna replied, keeping her tone neutral.

Tina's eyebrows shot up. "Are you still with Tom?"

Jenna gave her a bland half-smile. "Yeah. It's called a long-distance relationship."

"Oh, well I figured since you're looking at bridal gowns you were with someone who was committed only to you and not to some fantasy music career."

Kellie stared blankly, mouth gaping open.

Jenna lashed back. "Excuse me! What is that supposed to mean?"

"Nothing," Tina said with a shrug. "If you don't mind sharing your man with millions of groupies."

Jenna's voice tightened with anger. "I trust Tommy! Besides, he's not that kind of guy."

Tina pasted on a smile of nonchalance. "Okay." She pointed toward the chairs. "Michelle is ready for you now."

Their gazes battled for a moment before Jenna turned toward Michelle's station. Had she not been desperate for a haircut, she would've walked out of the salon.

Jenna and Kellie stood in the parking lot outside the hair salon, talking and shivering. Dark storm clouds from Tina's ominous forecast regarding Tommy lingered overhead, heavy and brooding, leaving Jenna with a knot of doubts about their future. The cold bit through her coat, but the chill inside her chest was worse.

"From now on, I'm done with this salon," Jenna said, rubbing her arms.

"But I thought you like how Michelle does your hair."

"I do, but I'm through doing business with Tina, especially if she's going to get all up in my business with Tommy."

"Oh, please!" Kellie said, tossing her wrist. "She's just trying to get under your skin. You know she had a crush on him all through high school."

"She has a boyfriend," Jenna said. "He took guitar lessons at the same place Tommy did."

Kellie bounced on her toes, trying to stay warm. "I'm telling you, she's jealous. Always has been. Besides, she has her bad-girl reputation to uphold."

"I suppose." Jenna huffed into her hands, her breath fogging in the air. "I'm freezing. I'll call you later."

At home, Jenna stood in front of her full-length mirror and admired her fresh new look. Her hair was soft, shiny, and full of body. Michelle's magic never failed. She wished Tommy were there to see her bouncy layers now; she knew she wouldn't be able to get her hair that smooth and alive again until her next haircut.

She sat down at her desk, her mind still dwelling on Tina's crude remark. Was there truth to it? *Should I call Tommy on it or wait until he comes home for Christmas?* She pulled out her pocket calendar and flipped to December. Winter break would start in only four days, and Tommy still hadn't given her his flight information. Since he'd been so difficult to reach lately, she considered calling his parents. Maybe they'd invite her along to pick him up at the airport. What a nice homecoming surprise that would be.

Jenna bounced onto her bed and reached for her phone. But instead of calling Tommy's parents, she found herself dialing his number. The line rang four times before someone picked up.

"Hello?" Harold answered.

"Oh, hey. Is Tommy there?"

"No, nor is he ever here. He packed up all his clothes and his guitar and left."

"What?" Jenna's pulse skipped. "So… he got a dorm transfer?"

"No. He still stops by to pick up his books before heading to class, but I have no clue where he's been sleeping."

A haze of confusion muddled Jenna's thoughts. "Okay. Can you leave a sticky note on his books for me?"

"I guess."

"Tell him to call me ASAP."

"Okay," Harold said.

A heavy door boomed in the background.

"Who you talking to?" Tommy's angry voice rumbled.

"It's Jenna," Harold piped.

"Give me the phone," Tommy said. "Now, take a walk."

"And then what?" Harold asked.

"Keep walking."

The phone crackled as it exchanged hands. Moments later, sneakers squeaked against the vinyl floor, followed by another door slamming.

"Jenna, wassup?" Tommy asked.

"Tommy! Where've you been? I left messages—"

"I know. These freaking exams… I'm so over it—"

"I was worried. You should have called me."

"I'm sorry," he said.

Insecurity crept in, tightening Jenna's chest. "I thought maybe you had other interests."

"What? Why would you think that?"

"Rumors from Tacky Tina."

"Who?"

"Tina from high school. She insinuated you were having too good of a time with groupies to stay committed to me."

Tommy spewed a few cuss words. "Jenna, I love you. Do you hear that? I love you."

"Well, I don't know. You haven't returned my calls, and Tina's implication made me think twice."

"Tell Tina to stick a sock in it."

"And Harold says you moved out of the dorm."

Agitation settled in his voice. "Ugh! I can't stand that dweeb! I'm staying off campus with my bandmates."

"Oh. Well thanks for telling me," Jenna said.

"I'm sorry. I thought I told you. Life got busy."

"Apparently too busy for me."

"Stop, Jenna! I miss you."

"Well... when're you coming home?"

Tommy hesitated. "About that... I'm not."

"What?" Jenna shrieked.

"We're doing gigs Thursdays to Sundays through winter break. This is my chance. I can't give it up."

Jenna sighed. "This is what I'm saying. You don't have time for me anymore."

Tommy's tone softened. "So come here for Christmas, and I'll make the time."

His plea filled her with a longing that had lain dormant for months. "I'd have to convince my parents... then try to get a last-minute plane ticket."

"Please. I couldn't ask for a better gift."

Jenna's heart wanted to go more than ever, but she'd have to jump through hoops to get there. "I don't know, Tommy. Are your parents coming?"

"No. They're visiting my brother in New York."

"Oh," Jenna uttered, toying with his ring.

"Please! I need you. I miss you," he begged.

Jenna licked her lips. "I have to talk to my parents."

# Chapter 12

Jenna followed her nose to the comforting aroma of freshly baked Christmas cookies in the kitchen. Yum, she could almost taste the sweet frosting on her lips.

Cookie sheets clacked against the rack as Mom removed another batch from the oven. She turned toward the center island and began kneading a new ball of dough. Peering up at Jenna, she said, "Be careful not to slip."

Jenna looked down and noticed the layer of flour dusting the floor. *What a mess.* She lifted her gaze to the counter where decorative plates of homemade cookies sat wrapped in cellophane — chocolate chip, gingerbread, jam-filled. It looked like a bakery exploded.

"I think you outdid yourself, Mom."

"Not really. I made just enough for the church cookie exchange, the annual tree lighting ceremony, and us."

"Just… enough?"

"Wanna help? You used to love decorating them."

Jenna shook her head. "No thanks. I, uh…" Her throat tightened. "Umm, is it okay, Mom, if I go to California to spend Christmas with Tommy?"

Mom set down her rolling pin. "What? And miss Christmas with the family?"

"Well… Tommy's not coming home again. He got this gig and—"

Mom shook her head. "Anthony and Holly are coming, and so are Nonna and Nonno."

"But I passed all my courses." Jenna stomped her foot, her voice cracking. "And I worked so hard, too!"

Mom dropped her head. "Then go ask your father."

Jenna let out a heavy sigh. "That's like talking to a brick wall."

She poked her head into the living room where her father slouched in a chair, eyes glued to the boob tube, watching some fuzzy old black-and-white western. She perched herself on the armchair adjacent to him and looked at the tree. Twinkling white lights chased one another up and down the branches, mesmerizing her — giving her an excuse to avoid the conversation she didn't want to start.

Jenna rubbed her weary eyes. *How do I bring up Tommy and California without starting WWIII?* She glanced at her father, his harsh features carved with pride, engrossed in the classic shootout about to happen.

"Hey, uh, Daddy?"

"Shush! This is the best part." He sat up straighter, jaw clenched.

"Can we talk?" she asked.

"*Amore*, not now." He waved her away. "Can't you see I'm watching a movie?"

"Like you haven't seen this before," she muttered. She stood and stalked out of the room, practically running over her mother in the doorway.

"Jenna?" Mom called.

"Forget it, Mom!"

Jenna continued down the hallway toward her bedroom when her father called her back.

"*Amore*, what do you want?" he bellowed.

"Oh, for crying out loud!" Jenna shouted, turning around. She marched back into the living room and plopped into the chair. "I thought you were too busy watching TV."

"Commercial break," he answered.

Jenna ran her hand through her hair. "You said if I passed all my courses, I could go to California. So… can I?"

Silence hung heavily in the air.

"Well, can I?" she asked again.

Dad cleared his throat. "Your brother and sister-in-law are coming for Christmas. We missed them at Thanksgiving."

*Maybe it'll snow again and they won't make it this time either.* Jenna fidgeted under his piercing stare. "I know, but Tommy has to work and can't come home."

His cleft chin hardened with stubbornness.

"C'mon, Daddy! I did my part."

"How 'bout his parents. Are they going?"

Jenna dropped her head. "No."

"Dorms are closed. Where's he staying?"

"Off-campus with friends."

"Well, you're not staying there!"

"No, Daddy. I have money. I'll get a hotel room."

He shook his head. "Save your money. Stay home."

"C'mon! I budgeted for this. I can pay for my hotel room and buy my plane ticket, too."

Her father sighed. "*Amore,* you've never flown before."

"Yeah, so? There's a first time for everything."

He shook his finger at her. "No! You're not ready. You don't need to see that boy."

She stood up and shouted, "You're impossible!" then stomped out of the room.

Jenna slammed her bedroom door so hard that her blue and silver embellished Christmas wreath fell to the floor. Rage crawled up her neck like hot lava. *You don't need to see that boy.* Her father's words pricked her like stiff needles from a fresh-cut pine tree. *You never keep your promises.* Bitter tears stung her eyes. It was excuse after excuse as to why she couldn't go.

*You've never flown before.* Dad had said.

*Yeah, and there's a first time for everything,* she had fired back.

A first time for everything? Jenna smacked her forehead. *What was I thinking?* No wonder Daddy said no. *He doesn't trust me.*

Jenna stared at the phone. Now she'd have to call Tommy and tell him she couldn't make it for Christmas. Tears formed in her eyes. *He's going to be so ticked off.* She sniffled. *Tommy, please don't give up on me.*

There was a soft knock at the door before it opened. Mom stood in the doorway. "I'm sorry, Jenna."

"You guys really know how to ruin my life!"

Mom sighed. "Do you honestly believe that is our motive, to ruin your life?"

Jenna threw her hands out wide. "You don't get it, Mom! You have no idea what it's like to live apart from someone you love."

"You two will have your whole lives to be together."

Jenna sighed. "The future is too far away. What if he meets someone else?"

Mom's green eyes widened at the absurdity of Jenna's words. "Now hold on just a minute! If he loves you like you say he does, he'll wait for you."

Jenna dropped her head. She had fallen prey to insecurity, vulnerable as an orphaned fawn beneath a circling eagle. She knew Tommy would meet countless attractive ladies in the music industry, and that likelihood weakened her self-confidence. Determined to keep jealousy at bay, she reached deep for her willpower and held Tommy's ring to her heart. Thinking about what Tina had said, she needed to see him — to claim him as her man.

Armed with ammunition, she stood up and grabbed a stack of graded test papers off her desk. "Look, Mom," she said, handing them to her. "Look at all these A's! I worked my tail off and I can't believe you guys went against your word."

"AFTER Christmas," Mom said.

"What?" Jenna asked.

"Dad and I acknowledge your hard work. You proved yourself accountable. You can fly out the day after Christmas and stay until New Year's Day."

"Really, Mom? Oh, thank you!"

Complete euphoria coursed through her. Although it would only be a week with Tommy, she'd take it, especially having her parents' approval.

# Chapter 13

Christmas was a big deal in Jenna's family. From the day after Thanksgiving, the cheerful activities began. Care packages were shipped to servicemen and women overseas, meals were served to the needy at the church hall, and carols were sung at the nursing home — just a few of the many seasonal traditions that stitched River Grove together like a patchwork quilt of kindness.

On Christmas Eve, Jenna shared dinner with her grandparents and extended family, followed by a candlelight midnight Mass. The glow of the candles, the scent of pine and incense, and the soft echo of *Silent Night* drifting through the sanctuary wrapped her in a peace she hadn't felt in weeks.

Late Christmas morning, Jenna, her parents, Anthony, and Holly gathered in the living room around the festively decorated seven-foot Douglas fir. The twinkling lights cast dancing shadows on the walls, moving in time with the carols playing softly in the background.

As her family took turns opening gifts, Jenna's eyes landed on a handmade angel ornament she had crafted in kindergarten — bowtie-shaped pasta painted white, dusted with silver and gold glitter, and glued together with all the determination of a five-year-old. The sight of it tugged at her heart.

*Oh, I remember making this.*

She touched the shiny textured ornament and allowed her mind to wander back in time.

She had been so excited to give that angel to her mother. She remembered wanting to hurry home after the children's Mass so she could set out milk and cookies for Santa and change into her new reindeer-print footsy pajamas. Anxious to move the night along, she had climbed into bed and told her mother she was too tired to listen to *The Night Before Christmas.*

*Patience, my love. Tomorrow will come,* Mom had said, opening the book. After reading the story, she kissed Jenna's forehead and whispered, *Sweet dreams, my precious angel.*

Jenna smiled at the fond memory. Even back then, Mom knew her secrets. Not much had changed.

"Earth to Jenna!" Anthony bellowed.

His hearty voice startled her, hurling her back to earth barely fast enough to catch the gift he tossed at her. She stared down at the box, perfectly wrapped in silver foil and tied with shiny gold ribbons and a bow. She smiled inside, knowing her brother was incapable of wrapping anything so neatly. Holly's handiwork, no doubt.

Jenna peered up at Anthony. An undefinable emotion sparkled in his brown eyes. He seemed overly cheerful — even for Christmas. "Thanks, bro."

Anthony raised his pointer finger. "Wait, sis, don't open it just yet," he said, trying to look all serious.

She slanted him a wary look. *Why?*

His eyes shifted from her to Mom and Dad. He handed them each an identical box, then put his arm around Holly.

"Okay. Now, everyone, open it," he said.

Jenna pulled off the bow, careful not to tear the pretty paper. She hated destroying wrapping paper.

"Get real, Jen… open it!" Anthony said.

She looked up at him. His wide smile and white teeth beamed back at her. *What could be in this box that has him so excited? A gag gift? Something special I can take to California?*

"Rip it open, sis! We're not saving the paper."

Jenna smirked. "I'm going to take even longer now."

Holly laughed — but Jenna knew it was only to cover her annoyance in front of Mom and Dad. Holly was always too serious, with little tolerance for goofing around. Not wanting to cause a scene, Jenna smiled politely at her, then focused on opening the gift.

She lifted the lid off the box and peeled back the perfectly folded tissue paper. She held up the black shirt with gold lettering and read it aloud. "Future Auntie." Her jaw dropped. *Already? They just got married.*

Jenna looked at Mom and Dad as they held up their shirts. Dad looked as thunderstruck as she felt.

"What's this?" Dad asked, staring blankly at the shirt.

Mom read hers. "Only the best parents are promoted to grandparents." She threw her hand to her heart. "Oh, my goodness!"

Anthony reached for Holly's hand, tucking it comfortably between his. "Yep, we're expecting!" he announced proudly.

Mom beamed with delight. She stood up and hugged the two of them. "Congrats!"

Dad sat there in a daze with his mouth open. When the fog cleared, he asked, "When?"

"June thirtieth," Holly said, her face glowing with bliss.

"Congratulations," Dad said. Then he pointed to Anthony and launched into a sermon. "Now, son, you take care of her. You save money now, so she can stay home when the baby comes."

Holly chimed in. "We'll try, Dad, but I worked really hard in corporate to get where I am today. I'm not sure I'm ready yet to let my position go."

Dad's expression pinched. He cleared his throat and stood up. "I need to bring in more firewood."

The kitchen timer went off, and Mom excused herself to check on the turkey.

Holly turned to Anthony and traced the hard angle of his face. "I'll see if your mother needs help."

"Okay," Anthony said, helping her to her feet.

"Ooh, it's hot in here," Holly said, pulling off her linen blazer and revealing her tiny baby bump. "Why in the world does your father want to put more wood on the fire?"

"Because he likes a good argument," Jenna mumbled. She could almost see the fireworks now — her father complaining that his first grandchild must go to daycare because Holly wants to keep working.

Anthony replied, "Dad likes the house hot. I'll see if he needs some help." He held Holly's stomach. "I love you, beautiful."

"I love you, too," she said, kissing him.

Jenna felt the intensity of their affection, only causing her to miss Tommy even more. Her heart jolted and her pulse pounded thinking about him. *Only one more day.*

Holly followed Anthony to the doorway but stopped and turned to speak with Jenna. "Heard you're going to California."

"Uh-huh," Jenna answered as she organized the open boxes under the tree. "Leaving tomorrow."

"First time flying?" Holly asked.

"Uh-huh."

"You nervous?"

"Nope. Just excited to see Tommy."

"Don't take this the wrong way, but I'm shocked your father is letting you go at all."

"Why? I *am* eighteen."

Holly sighed. "I mean the way he is."

"Oh, like how he expects you to stay home with your baby?" Jenna shot back.

Holly rolled her eyes. "Touché."

"Daddy is stuck in his ways. Can't change him."

"I respect that," Holly said, "but I need him to respect my decision to keep my career. It *is* the nineties."

Jenna laughed. "Good luck with that."

"Thanks." Holly pointed toward the kitchen. "Well, I should probably see if your mom needs help."

"Okay," Jenna nodded. "By the way, congratulations."

"Thank you," Holly said.

Jenna watched Holly click-clack out of the room in her spiked heels and red fitted power suit. *She has everything I dream about — love, a home, a baby. She doesn't even see how blessed she is.* Sure, Holly was successful, but to Jenna, the love of a family meant more than the passion of a career.

Jenna grimaced. *Geez, I'm sounding more like my father every day.* She smacked her forehead to knock the absurdity out of her head. *Enough is enough.* She leaned forward and gathered up the shredded wrapping paper scattered across the floor.

## Chapter 14

It was a bitter cold December twenty-six. Another Christmas had come and gone. Joyous moods had faded, radio stations had stopped playing holiday music, and trees had already been tossed to the curb. Typically, for Jenna, it was the most depressing day of the year — but not this year. This year, she woke up at dawn, bright-eyed and bushy-tailed for her flight from Stonebridge International Airport to Sandy Ridge, California.

The airport was the closest civilian airport, a grueling two-hour drive south of River Grove. The early morning commute started out well, traffic moving steadily along the interstate. But as they neared the jaunty city, the maniacal traffic whirled around them. Vehicles headed into the city elbowed their way toward the exit ramp, while vehicles leaving the city were expelled onto the highway like a slingshot.

Arriving in the wee hours of the morning, the airport looked like an endless sea of twinkling lights. Jenna's heart raced when her father pulled into short-term parking. *We made it!* She stared out the window at the massive airport. The main entrance was a constant revolving door of travelers and rolling luggage. *I hope I don't get lost.*

When she opened the car door, she winced at the frigid blast of arctic air that slapped her in the face. She stepped out and zipped up her puffy down coat. She certainly wasn't going to miss the brutal weather. *Warm, sunny California, here I come!* She shut the door, and the thump echoed through the parking garage, making her arrival feel real. *This is it.* In about eight hours, she'd be wrapped in Tommy's arms.

Inside the airport, the noise and animation were overwhelming. Huge TV monitors overhead flickered flight information while faceless voices over the PA system announced arrivals, departures, and delays.

As Jenna traipsed through the airport, she passed a constant stream of changing faces. Some stood in line at the ticket counter, others waited at baggage claim, while more passengers shuffled toward security. It seemed like total chaos. Babies fussed, young children whined, and some travelers just looked plain confused.

After passing through the metal detector, Jenna and her parents sat at the viewing window and watched planes take off while waiting for her boarding call.

When the attendant announced her flight, Jenna sprang from her chair as if propelled by some intense force. She turned and handed her coat to her mother.

"Here, I don't need this!"

Mom's eyebrows shot up in disbelief.

Jenna threw her hands out wide. "What? I'm not going skiing on the beach. Just bring it back when you pick me up."

Mom sighed. "Okay." She stood and hugged her. "Have fun, but not too much fun."

"I will, Mom. Don't worry."

Jenna turned to her father. His pained expression made her feel as though it were their final goodbye. *Oh, dear Jesus… does he think my plane is going to crash?* The chilling thought slipped through her mind like a probing knife.

"You be careful," he said.

Jenna took a deep breath against her apprehension. "Daddy, I'll be okay."

"You sure you have enough money?"

She patted her shoulder bag — ID, credit card, cash. "Yeah, Daddy."

Mom nudged him. "Nick, let her go before she misses her flight. Jenna, we'll be waving as your plane leaves the runway."

Dad hugged her once more. "Don't forget to call."

"Okay, but let me go now," Jenna said, pulling away. She grabbed her carry-on and headed toward her gate.

"*Amore!*" her father called out.

Jenna stopped and turned at the pleading voice.

"I love you," he said.

The intensity in his eyes shook her resolve. *He never says that.* For a moment, she wavered. *Maybe I shouldn't go.* Holding back her tears, she nodded and waved goodbye. "See you in a week."

Jenna boarded the plane, found her seat, and settled in. She looked out the window toward the airport viewing gallery, but it was too dark to see her parents. She squeezed her eyes shut and felt herself retreating inward. A goodbye had never felt so emotional.

She closed the shade when the flowery scent of perfume drifted toward her. A retired couple had taken the two empty seats beside her. The woman smiled softly and introduced herself and her husband, then pulled out a crochet hook and a pink ball of yarn.

"I hope to finish these booties for my new granddaughter before we land," she said, looping the yarn with practiced ease.

"Aww, they're adorable," Jenna said, admiring the craft. She'd always wanted to learn crochet, especially now that she was going to be an aunt, but never knew anyone who could teach her.

"Young lady," the old gentleman spoke. "Where are you headed on a long flight all by yourself?"

"Oh. I'm visiting my fiancé. He's in college," Jenna said.

"He should be visiting you, my dear," he said.

His wife nudged him. "Oh, Arthur, don't be an old stick in the mud."

"Ada, I'm not! I'm—"

"May I have your attention," the airline attendant announced over the loudspeaker. She introduced herself, then reviewed the safety procedures.

Shortly afterward, the lights dimmed, and Jenna felt the thrum of the engines and the vibration of the plane. She watched out the oval window as the scenery slid past. Finally, she was on the highway in the sky, about to soar amongst the fluffy clouds.

As they reached altitude, she fixed her eyes on the wing's flashing red lights. In some strange way, she found it relaxing — even hypnotizing. She should nap, but she was wide awake, too excited to sleep.

She was so close to being reunited with Tommy.

## Chapter 15

Jenna exited the terminal gate with her carry-on luggage. Excitement boosted her impatience as she meandered through the mingling crowds, scanning faces, searching for Tommy.

She spotted him standing near a vending machine, wearing his favorite snug jeans that fit him all too well, topped with an open bomber jacket. His shoulder-length, baby-fine hair was neatly groomed, feathered away from his face.

The moment their eyes met, happy tears streamed down her cheeks. "Tommy!" she called.

His gorgeous face broke into a huge smile. "Hey, babe," he said, greeting her with open arms.

Jenna hugged him, but the strong odor of Aqua Velva aftershave mixed with cigarette smoke irritated her nose. Caught off guard, she pulled away. "Have you been smoking?"

Tommy frowned at her accusation. "No, no, of course not! You know I have asthma. It's the guys — you know, living with them, everything reeks."

Jenna shrugged, not totally convinced he was telling the truth. A sudden chill slipped between them, like she was hugging a stranger. Certainly not how she had envisioned their reunion. Strange… after years apart, hugging Luke hadn't felt like this. That embrace had been warm, familiar grounding. This one felt… off.

Tommy caressed her cheek. "I'm so glad you're here." He held her chin in his hand and tilted her face to his. He drifted closer and whispered, "I missed you."

At the first touch of his lips, those lost, forgotten feelings stirred awake, causing Jenna's heart to tumble in her chest.

"Oh, I missed you, too," she said.

"Then let's get out of here!"

The Spanish-style hotel where Jenna reserved her room was situated downtown Sandy Ridge, two blocks from the waterfront and only four blocks from Tommy's apartment.

After Jenna received her room key, she and Tommy rode the elevator to the third floor. She found her room and unlocked the door.

"This seems like a decent place," she said, placing her luggage on the rack. "First, let me call my mom and then we can do whatever you want."

"Okay," Tommy said, roaming the spacious room.

Jenna sat at the tiny table and picked up the room phone. She dialed collect and waited for the operator to connect the call. *C'mon, Mom…pick up. You must know my plane landed by now.*

"Hello, Jenna?" Mom answered.

"Mom, hi! I made it. I'm at the hotel."

"Okay. Is Tom with you?"

"Yes, we're about to get something to eat."

"Okay. Be careful, and remember, behave."

Jenna rolled her eyes, knowing exactly what her mother meant. "Yes, Mom, I will," she said as Tommy began rubbing her shoulders.

"Call me later."

"Okay, Mom." Jenna squirmed at Tommy's insistent touch. "I'll call you only if it's not too late."

"All right. Ba-bye," Mom said.

"Bye." Jenna hung up the phone.

Tommy leaned in and sprinkled kisses along her neckline, tickling her skin with every touch. "I missed you," he whispered.

"Oh, Tommy!" she said, pushing him away.

"What?" he answered defensively. He stood there with his mouth open, astounded by her sudden resistance.

"I missed you, too, but…we should get going."

"Not yet," he said, reaching for her hand. "Come here. I need a hug."

Giving in to longing, she stepped forward into his warm embrace. A yearning for love flooded her body. "I'm so happy we're finally together."

"Me, too," he said.

Tommy drew her face to his and kissed her deeply. He lifted her slightly off the floor in a spontaneous burst of emotion, holding her close.

"Oh, Tommy! What are you doing?" She clung to him, her limbs trembling. "Put me down."

Tommy carried her to the bed and gently laid her down, kissing her with urgency. "I love you so much," he uttered between kisses.

His words soothed the longing in her heart.

"I love you, too," she said, returning his kiss with reckless relief. "I can't wait until we're married," she breathed.

Tommy's expression shifted. "Let's not wait," he murmured. His hands wandered to the neckline of her blouse. With each button he flicked loose, she felt him become more aroused. "Let's make love now," he said.

"What?" Her breath caught.

"I want you," he said as he slipped his fingers underneath her bra strap.

Jenna's nerves twisted and her stomach flipped. Her heart wanted closeness — but her convictions rose stronger. She was supposed to avoid temptation.

She halted his hands. "Tommy, we can't," she whispered through heavy breaths. She eased away from him. "Remember, we vowed to save ourselves for marriage."

Tommy looked away. "But babe, we're finally alone. Don't you want to know we're… right together?"

Jenna swallowed. "Don't you think we already know that?"

Tommy blew out his breath and backed away. "Yeah, I guess." He stood up and adjusted his jeans. "We should go."

"Tommy, please don't be mad at me."

"I'm not. It's cool," he said, walking toward the door. "C'mon, let's blow this joint."

Jenna bit down on her lower lip. "Tommy, wait!"

He stopped and held the door for her.

She grabbed her purse and followed him into the dim corridor. He walked with long strides, and she struggled to keep up. *Why is he acting this way? Did I upset him?*

Jenna caught up and stepped in front of him. "Stop for a second, Tommy." She pressed her hand to his chest. "Talk to me. What's wrong?"

"Nothing," he replied, pushing her hand away and taking another step forward.

"Wait!" She pointed at him. "You're upset because I said no. Aren't you?"

Tommy stopped and sighed. "I'm not mad at you."

"Then what?" Jenna asked.

He combed his fingers through his long hair. "Look… we've been apart for four months. We're finally alone, and I just wanted to be close to you. Really close. And you pulled away."

"I didn't pull away. I love you. But you promised we'd wait."

Tommy dropped his head. "You're right. I'm sorry." He wrapped his arms around her. "I wanted to show you how much I love you and how much I missed you."

Jenna gave a half-hearted shrug. "I missed you, too, but I'm not ready yet."

Tommy's eyes dimmed. "Okay, then."

"So… you're not disappointed?"

"Well… I'm not going to pressure you."

"You still love me?"

"Of course," Tommy replied easily.

Jenna traced her finger along his jaw. "Thank you for understanding."

"Yeah," he mumbled, urging her along.

Jenna and Tommy walked four blocks to the off-campus housing complex where he and his friends were living. As they strolled along the palm-tree and cactus-lined streets, Tommy pointed out the University and mentioned that the center of town was also within walking distance. When they reached the main entrance to the apartments, Jenna stopped in awe.

The upscale, two-story Tuscan-style building featured an outdoor sparkling pool and a calming spa surrounded by lush tropical landscaping.

"Whoa, Tommy! Look at this place."

"I know, right? It's been a treat staying here over winter break. I dread moving back in with that dweeb when classes start up again."

"But you'll only have to deal with him until May."

Tommy gave her a sideways glance. "Only?"

"Yeah, it'll go by fast."

"Right. That's like saying living with your dad until we get married will go by fast, too."

Jenna shrugged. "I guess you're right."

Tommy opened the arched wrought-iron gate and led Jenna down a paver-stone sidewalk. They stopped midway at a ground-level unit. "Here we are," he said, pulling his key from his pocket.

"This is beautiful," Jenna said.

Tommy unlocked the door. When he pushed it open, the heavy stench of cigarette smoke hit her like a wall.

"Oh, crud, Tommy! What did you guys do to this place?"

The ritzy apartment was a pigsty. Stale empty beer cans and full ashtrays littered the kitchen floor. Open pizza boxes with partially eaten slices sat on the counter. A half-dozen unlabeled VCR tapes were strewn across the living room floor, along with a lacy black bra hanging off the arm of the leather couch.

Tommy's ears turned beet red. "Dudes!" he shouted.

A bedroom door opened. A rumpled red-headed guy in gray sweatpants stood in the doorway.

He yawned. "Oh, you're back."

"Yeah… apparently a tick too soon. Kevin, I thought you said you were going to clean up this dump hole."

"Sorry, man. I hit the pillow and crashed."

"Where's Jeff and Scott?" Tommy asked.

Kevin shrugged. "No clue." His blue eyes landed on Jenna. "Oh, hey, you must be Jenna."

Jenna nodded, too stunned to say anything.

Another door opened abruptly, and Jenna shuddered. A handsome blond with a super-gelled shoulder-length mane and double pierced hoop earrings stepped out of the bathroom wearing nothing except a towel draped over his shoulders.

Tommy shielded Jenna's eyes. "C'mon, Scott. Have some respect for my girl."

Scott laughed. "Sheesh, Tom. Respect begins with you," he said, strutting to the second bedroom. Before closing the door, he shouted, "If you were wondering, Jeff went to the bar to set up."

Tommy shook his head and draped his arm around Jenna. "C'mon, let's get something to eat."

With no hesitation, Jenna opened the front door and stepped out, wishing she could erase what she had just seen.

"Sorry about all that," Tommy said.

"No big deal. I grew up with an older brother."

"I don't only mean Scott. I mean the mess."

Jenna pointed at the door. "Yeah, what's that about?"

"Last night's leftover Christmas bash."

Jenna clapped her hands together. "All righty then. I have a feeling California is going to open my eyes to a whole new world."

# Chapter 16

Jenna walked hand in hand with Tommy to the center of town where everything came to life. Cars zipped up and down Main Street, and mobs of people carrying shopping bags schlepped their returns to the stores. The clean and friendly little beach town looked like the North Pole without the snow. Huge Christmas displays lit up every storefront, lights trimmed the palm trees, and joyful music drifted out from speakers above the shop doors.

Although the town sparkled with holiday spirit, the seventy-degree weather felt strange. Having lived on a mountain her whole life, Jenna was accustomed to frigid temperatures and white Christmases.

"Wow! Look at this place, Tommy!"

"Sweet, isn't it?"

"I love it!"

"Beats freezing your nuts off in Pennsylvania."

"Uh, Tommy. I don't have that problem."

"You know what I mean."

"Yeah, sure," Jenna said, nudging him lightly.

They continued onto the next block.

"Oh wait!" Tommy said suddenly.

He stopped abruptly at the crosswalk, forcing foot traffic to weave around him.

"What's the matter?" Jenna asked.

"I just remembered something."

"What?"

"Your gift."

He pulled her aside, away from the crowd, stopping right in front of a local jewelry store. Warmth flowed through Jenna's body.

*Ooh… he picked out a ring.*

Tommy reached inside his jacket pocket and pulled out a wrapped box. "This is for you."

Jenna's heart fluttered wildly. *This is it. He's going to propose.* She looked around, scanning their surroundings. *But why here? In the middle of noise, chaos, and exhaust fumes?*

"Open it," he said, practically bouncing.

Jenna's pulse skittered as she peeled off the red paper. She took a deep breath and opened the clamshell box.

Her enthusiasm deflated like a hot-air balloon. It wasn't a ring. It was just a locket.

"It's beautiful, Tommy," she said, trying to sound pleased. She lifted the locket and opened it. "But… who are these people?"

"Oh, that's the stock picture it came with. I didn't have a recent photo of us."

"Oh." *Well, you could've used our junior/senior prom picture.* She forced an appreciative grin to hide her disappointment. "We'll just have to change that before I leave." She leaned in and kissed him. "Thank you."

"Glad you like it," Tommy said, rubbing his hands together. "Now, let's get some food."

In agreement, Jenna's stomach rumbled. "So, where're we going to eat?"

"The Riff Tide."

"Huh?"

"It's the bar we play at."

"Oh," she sighed.

"What's wrong?"

"Nothing." *A romantic place would've been nice.*

"We're playing a set tonight." He wrapped his arm around her. "You're going to love this place!"

His enthusiasm unraveled the knot in her stomach. Although she had hoped he'd take her somewhere quiet and special, she reminded herself she'd be happy anywhere as long as she was with him.

The Riff Tide was another block over in a brawling, noisy, daredevil section of Sandy Ridge. Flashy sports cars with blasting stereos cruised up and down the strip. Rowdy teens hung out of car windows shouting at people loitering on street corners. Police cruisers patrolled the area with steady vigilance.

Jenna gripped Tommy's hand tighter. "You come here every night?"

"Yeah, why?" he asked.

"This isn't like River Grove at all."

"Nope. It's much more exciting."

Jenna let out a deep sigh. The thought of him constantly visiting this dicey side of town wove an unsettling path through her consciousness. She wasn't thrilled with the idea of him frequenting the area.

Tommy led her to the parking lot entrance behind the bar. He unlocked the door and held it open.

"You have your own key, too?" she asked.

"Yep. This way we can get set up early and rehearse."

"Oh."

The smoky atmosphere was oddly quiet. Chairs were flipped upside down on the round tables that circled the room. The bar was empty, and the stage sat in darkness.

"Where is everyone?" Jenna asked.

"Oh, they don't open for another two hours."

"Then why are we here?"

Tommy took her hand and led her to the stage.

"Check this out!" He picked up his guitar. "Imagine performing here in front of a huge, rowdy crowd — rockin' this place out."

"I can't. I'd be a nervous wreck."

"Nah. The energy is insane. When you're playing, it's like you're in a zone — totally engrossed in your music. Then when it's over, you're like… in euphoria."

Jenna watched the enthusiasm light up his face. The excitement in his voice warmed her heart. *This is what he was born to do.*

She placed her hand on his shoulder. "I'm so happy you found your niche."

"Cool, right!" he said, hopping off the stage.

"Hey!" a throaty voice bellowed from backstage. "The rock star is back!"

Jenna turned to see a six-foot-three guy wearing a sleeveless black T-shirt that showed off bulging biceps, black leather chaps over faded denim, and combat boots. He looked confident, striking, and dangerous.

"You must be Jenna," he said boldly, offering a charming smile.

Jenna returned the smile. *Who the heck are you?*

"Oh, hey," Tommy said, giving him a fist bump. He turned to Jenna. "Meet Jeff, my bassist."

"Hi," Jenna said.

Jeff lit a cigarette. "Dude, did you see the crowd lined up out there? It's gonna be a wild night!"

Tommy nodded and turned to Jenna. "We should eat now." He took her hand and led her to a table near the stage, lowering two chairs. He offered her a seat, then pointed to the bar. "I'll see if Hank can fire up the grill. Want anything to drink?"

"Sure. How 'bout a Coke?"

"Comin' right up," he said, walking away.

While Tommy disappeared behind the bar, Jenna headed to the ladies' room. She pulled the door open and turned the corner.

Two high-maintenance gals — a sun-bleached blonde with big spiral hair and a blazing redhead with a teased pixie cut — stood in front of the mirrors, gabbing loudly about some wild party they'd gone to the night before.

Avoiding eye contact, Jenna slipped into an empty stall. She hung her purse on the hook and glanced down at her clothes. Her tapered black jeans, red blouse, and black blazer suddenly felt too polished, too conservative, too *River Grove* for this crude bar scene.

She shook her head, dissatisfied with her appearance.

She tried to mind her own business, but their giggling and bragging about getting wasted made her feel increasingly self-conscious. *Hurry up and leave.*

The chatter softened while aerosol cans hissed and perfume bottles spritzed. Seconds later, stilettos clicked across the tile, and the door closed with a thud.

*Oh, thank goodness. They're gone.*

Jenna opened the stall door and gasped. A hazy cloud of Aqua Net hairspray and Gucci Rush perfume drenched the room.

She stood at the sink. While she washed her hands, she studied herself in the mirror, wishing she looked as good as she had when Michelle cut and styled her hair. She reached into her purse for makeup and a brush. She freshened up her look and repositioned her headband.

She sighed. *I just can't compete.*

On her way out of the restroom, she noticed a sign that read: ONE OCCUPANT PER STALL.

She stepped back. *Whoa. I am definitely not in River Grove anymore.*

Jenna returned to the table. She spotted Tommy across the room perched on a bar stool, both hands and mouth moving animatedly, but she couldn't see who he was talking to. She ran her hand through her hair. *I thought he was bringing us sodas.*

Tommy let out an enormous belly laugh. *What was so funny?* She peered up at him and saw a slender hand reach from behind the bar and touch his forearm. The cackling grew louder.

*What the—?*

Jealousy clawed at Jenna's skin like acid rain. She grabbed her purse and pushed in her chair. *Stay calm,* she told herself as her heart tripped over its next beat. *Don't make a scene. Don't berate him.*

She approached the bar and recognized the bimbo flirting with Tommy — the platinum blonde she'd crossed paths with moments ago. *Who is she, and why is she hanging all over him?* They were too giddy, too upbeat to be just friends. And that tight dress with the plunging neckline wasn't helping Tommy's testosterone levels either.

Jenna swooped in like a hawk claiming its prey. She walked up behind him, wrapped her arms around his waist, and rested her head on his shoulder. "Hope I'm not interrupting."

Tommy jolted. "Oh, hey! Hank's grilling our burgers and fries right now."

Jenna glared at the blonde standing in front of them. "Funny, you don't look like a Hank."

The blonde sucked in a shallow breath and gave a gentle shake of her head. "No, I'm Sheri."

Tommy coughed to cover a laugh. "Sheri's a waitress."

Jenna smiled blandly. "Uh-huh." *Like I'm supposed to believe there's nothing more to that story.*

Tommy must have sensed her insecurity because he hooked his arm around her and tightened his hold. He made eye contact with Sheri and said, "This is Jenna, my girlfriend from Pennsylvania."

A vain smile curved Sheri's bottom lip. "So, this is the country girl you mentioned."

"Yep, that's me," Jenna said, forcing a polite smile. *And you must be the floozy he didn't tell me about.*

Tommy turned to Jenna and brushed the tangled hair out of her face, tucking it beneath her headband. "We should get back to our table before they open the doors."

"Fine by me," Jenna answered without delay.

Not more than a few minutes after Tommy and Jenna settled in at their table, Sheri's friend with the teased pixie cut served their meals. She placed the plate in front of Tommy and licked her luscious red lips. "Good luck tonight," she said in a sensuous voice.

A sudden luminous smile lit Tommy's face. "Thanks, Lexi," he said.

Insecurity closed like a fist around Jenna's heart. *I'm going to lose him to all his groupies… just like Tina said.*

"Oh! Lexi," Tommy added, clasping her wrist before she could leave. "Before I forget — meet my girlfriend, Jenna."

Hearing him refer to her as his girlfriend eased her uncertainties. She smiled easily. "Hi," Jenna said.

Lexi gave her a once-over, then flashed a polite smile. "Nice to meet you."

As the clock ticked closer to showtime, red and green recessive ceiling lights penetrated the dark room, house music began playing overhead, and the smell of week-old cooking grease drifted in from the kitchen.

Jeff whistled to Tommy from the stage. "Hey, super stud! Time to warm up those vocal cords."

Tommy nodded. "Be there in a second."

He cupped his hand over Jenna's. "I gotta go."

"Okay," she said, nodding.

He leaned in and kissed her — long, eager, and far more intense than she expected.

"Tommy," she whispered, "they're waiting for you."

He responded with a pleased hum, then eased away. Before walking off, he stole one more lingering kiss, leaving her no doubt about how much he'd missed her.

She watched him until he disappeared behind the stage, then noticed Sheri gawking from behind the bar. When their eyes met, Sheri lifted her chin and gave a quick shake of her head — a gesture meant to look confident, but it only revealed insecurity beneath the surface.

Jenna looked away. Deep inside, she felt like a total loser sitting at the table all by herself. With no one to talk to, she scanned the incoming crowd, pretending she was looking for someone so she wouldn't seem like a friendless stray.

This place certainly had its fair share of lookers. Up at the bar, solo drinkers, cougars with caked-on makeup, and women dressed to attract attention had already begun their wheeling and dealing. Jenna tightened her grip on her purse. She had to be careful not to draw the eye of a drunk looking for company.

She sighed. *What am I doing in a place like this? Would Luke have brought me here?*

## Chapter 17

Another hour had passed. Suddenly, the lights dimmed, and the audience fell silent apart from an occasional clack from a cue ball and the clank of a beer bottle. The stage illuminated, and Tommy and his bandmates appeared. They all looked pumped, excited, and even a little nervous. All eyes focused on them.

Tommy approached the microphone. "Good evening, and thank you for coming out to celebrate the holiday season with us…"

He introduced himself and the band, then launched into their first song. Their energy radiated through the crowd, who left their seats for the dance floor. Hands shot into the air as people jumped up and down, getting into the music. Surprisingly, many knew the lyrics. The evening was off to a rocking start.

Tommy played a couple of cover songs, then spoke to the audience again. "You know the saying — save the best for last," he said, plucking his guitar. "This next song is one of my own that I wrote for my girlfriend, who happens to be sitting right there," he said, pointing to Jenna.

Jenna felt the blood drain from her face when all eyes turned toward her. *Oh, no, no, no…*

Tommy continued. "She flew here all the way from Pennsylvania just to be here with me tonight. So, I'd like to dedicate this next song to my girl, Jenna."

He motioned for her to come up on stage.

Jenna shook her head violently. *No way.* But the spark of desire in his eyes lured her out of her chair. Slow, clumsy, and stiff, she climbed the stairs. Somehow, her pounding heart and shaking knees carried her to his side.

Tommy hugged her, then strummed the intro. The familiarity of the tune tugged at her heartstrings, and tears clouded her eyes. It was their song — *Holding Forever* — the one he sang every night before they ended their calls.

Mesmerized by his dreamy eyes looking straight into hers, she forgot about the hundreds of eyes watching her. For a moment, the world fell away. The moment belonged to them.

Their song was the last of Tommy's set for the night. While the next band performed, Jenna and Tommy rambled to the pool tables to play a friendly game of eight ball.

Jenna grabbed a cue stick and found a corner to stand in while Tommy set the rack. As she waited, she observed the bar crowd chugging their beers and telling their stories. Their talking had gotten louder and unruly and the bull crap was undoubtedly flowing freely now. With any luck, they'd be too pie-eyed to notice how awful she was at playing pool.

"Ready to break?" Tommy asked.

"Sure," Jenna said.

She leaned forward and placed her hand on the table in a closed bridge. She focused her aim and took her shot. But she tapped the cue ball too low, causing it to pop into the air and off the table. *Oops!*

Heat rushed into her cheeks. She glanced around. Thankfully, the drunks' blathering continued nonstop, and no one had noticed her blunder.

Tommy laughed. "Scratch!"

"I told you I stink at this," she said, resting her hands on her hips.

"I'll show you how it's done," he said, sauntering to the table. He took his shot and pocketed three balls. "I call stripe."

As Tommy continued with his turn, the sweet smell of perfume wafted through the air. Another Goldilocks dressed in black suede and lace, leaving nothing for the imagination, strolled by. Tommy's wandering eyes left the game and studied the feminine sway of her hips as she made her way to the bar.

Jenna poked his backside with the pool stick. "Hey, focus on the game!"

"I am," he said, taking his shot.

The cue ball smacked a striped ball inadvertently, slamming the eight ball into the side pocket.

"Ha, I won!" Jenna said.

"That's because I let you."

"Yeah, right," Jenna mumbled.

While Tommy racked up a new game, Jeff, Scott, and Kevin joined them.

"We'll play you," Jeff said, clutching a mug of beer.

"I'll sit this one out," Jenna said, stepping back.

"You sure?" Tommy asked.

She yawned, "Uh-huh."

Jenna took a seat in the corner and tried her darndest to stay awake while the boys played another two games. Weary, she could barely focus — until the game paused suddenly and Goldilocks returned with a full tray of drinks, flirty eyes, and a do-me smile.

Adrenaline rushed through Jenna's body. Fully alert, she caught Tommy and Goldilocks exchanging meaningful glances, and every female cell in her body went on red-flag alert.

*Am I missing something here? I may have been born at night, but it wasn't last night.*

Her mind leaped back to Tina's harsh comment: *I figured since you're looking at bridal gowns you were with someone who was committed to you and not some fantasy music career.*

Jenna reminded herself: *Tommy's not like that. Besides, I trust him.*

She wasn't going to let jealousy rip away her outer calm. Instead, she brushed her insecurities off as being overtired.

Jenna hopped off the bar stool and approached Tommy with a hug from behind. "I'll be right back."

Tommy nodded vacantly, totally consumed with pocketing the eight ball.

She shrugged. "Whatever," she mumbled, then snaked her way around the dance floor, trying hard to avoid the mobs of sweaty, dancing strangers.

At the far end of the bar, she requested a Coke.

While she waited, someone nudged her arm. She turned to find a yuppie flashing an amiable smile.

"Did anyone ever tell you that you have the cutest dimples?" he asked with a silvery voice.

Jenna brushed aside his compliment and eagerly awaited her drink.

His breath warmed her cheek as he murmured, "Can I buy you a drink, beautiful?"

"No, thank you."

He studied her from head to toe. "You're not from around here, are you?"

Jenna shook her head. "Is it that obvious?"

He nodded. "Where you from?"

"Pennsylvania."

"Pennsylvania? You look like you should be from Beverly Hills. You here alone?"

"No." *But it sure feels like it.* Jenna pointed toward the billiard area. "I'm hanging with the band that just performed."

"Cool. I've seen them. They're good if you like heavy metal."

Jenna tossed him a baffled look. "If you don't like heavy metal, then why're you here?"

He pointed his chin at the bartender. "Russ — he's a good friend of mine." He extended his hand. "Where's my manners? I'm Liam."

Jenna accepted his handshake. "I'm Jenna."

Liam pointed to the exit sign. "My BMW is parked right outside in preferred parking. Want to ditch this place? I'll show you everything California has to offer."

Jenna cracked a tiny laugh. "I don't even know you."

"C'mon. I'm a nice guy." He waved his glass. "Hey, Russ! Tell this lovely lady I'm a nice guy."

The bartender kept mixing drinks. He peered up and smiled. "I'll vouch for him. He's a good guy… and a cop."

Jenna shook her head. "I gotta go. My fiancé is probably wondering where I went."

"Fiancé? You didn't mention you were engaged."

"You didn't ask," Jenna said, grabbing her glass.

"It's no secret. I'm off duty," Liam said.

Jenna shrugged and strode off.

She weaved her way back to the game area where Tommy and his bandmates were now playing darts.

"Here she is!" Kevin shouted.

Tommy tossed his dart, then turned to Jenna. "You disappeared."

*I'm surprised you even noticed.* "Did you miss me?"

"Of course," he said, wrapping his arm around her.

"I was at the bar."

"Oh? You okay?" he asked, sitting beside her.

Boom. Crash. Boom. Drums crashed through Jenna's head. The music was so loud it overrode her heartbeat and echoed through her nerve endings.

"No, I'm not. My head is pounding," she said.

Tommy turned to Sheri, who strolled by with a tray of drinks. "Do you have, uh, like a glass of sparkling mineral water or something for Jenna's headache?"

Sheri placed a bottle in front of Jenna. "Here's a beer. It'll relax you."

"No thank you," Jenna said, pushing the bottle away.

"Let loose, honey. Don't be a wallflower," Sheri said.

"She doesn't need that," Tommy said.

Alcohol was never Jenna's thing — never mind she was underage. She liked being in control and didn't want to depend on it to socialize or have fun. And she certainly didn't want to come home smelling like a brewery or hugging the toilet.

Jenna yawned. "I think I'm just overtired."

"Here, sweetheart," Scott said, handing her his drink. "Try this. It'll fix everything that ails you."

Jenna put her hand up. "No thanks."

"You sure?" he asked, tossing a shot of whiskey down his throat.

"Lay off, Scott," Tommy said. He stood and helped Jenna out of her chair. "I'll walk you back to your hotel."

"Thanks," she said.

"Dudes," Tommy shouted. "I'll catch you guys later."

Jenna and Tommy walked in silence, mentioning nothing about their evening. When they reached her hotel room, she swiped her key and invited him inside.

"Sorry I ruined your evening," she said.

Tommy's voice went high. "Why would you say that?"

"It's early, and I took you away from your friends."

Tommy waved his hand. "Nah, I understand. It's been a long day for you."

Jenna nodded. "It has been."

"So, what do you think of the guys? Cool, right?" he asked.

"Yeah, sure. I guess."

"Don't sound so convincing."

"Well, I just met them, and I don't know them."

"They're cool, and we play great together."

Jenna nodded. "I can see that. But to be honest… I don't think much of Sheri."

Tommy looked away. "She's sweet."

"Ah-huh. More like *sweet on you.*"

"C'mon, Jenna. Get real."

Jenna shrieked, "Oh my gosh! I can't believe you don't see that. She was all over you tonight. How would you feel if another guy hit on me and I went with it?"

"She likes my music. Nothing more," he said.

Jenna threw her hands up. "Fine."

Tommy sighed. "Don't do this."

"Do what?"

"I don't want to fight."

"We're not. We're having a healthy argument."

Tommy softened. He caressed her cheek. "Look… how 'bout you get a good night's sleep, and I'll take you to the beach tomorrow."

Jenna smiled, pleased with his offer. "Okay."

Tommy clutched both her hands in his and brushed a gentle kiss across her forehead. "Good night."

Exhausted, Jenna changed into her nightshirt and climbed into bed. She lay there like a limp rag doll after a child's day at play and stared up at the textured ceiling. It was too quiet — even too quiet to sleep. Her mind drifted far from dreamland while worries and insecurities swarmed her like pesky gnats on a humid day.

*Why do I feel like Tommy and I aren't connecting? Was there something going on between him and Sheri?* The questions hammered at her, and the more she tried to ignore them, the more they persisted. She was trapped by her own destructive emotions and needed to break away before they ruined everything. *Let it go, Jenna. It's all good. Tomorrow will prove it.*

She closed her eyes but couldn't smother her sour thoughts. "Ugh!" she groaned, kicking off her covers. She had to talk to Kellie. She glanced at the clock. Midnight in River Grove. *She might still be awake.*

Jenna turned on the table lamp and reached for the phone. She dialed Kellie's number collect and waited for the operator to make the connection.

"You're going to pay for these charges," Kellie said.

"I know. I will."

"I'm kidding. I was waiting for your call. How's it going?"

"I don't know, Kellie."

"Uh-oh. What's wrong?"

"I feel like… our long-distance relationship is coming between us — Tommy and me."

"Why do you say that?" Kellie asked.

"Tonight, instead of giving me an engagement ring, he gave me a locket that didn't even have our picture in it. And instead of taking me to a romantic restaurant, he took me to the bar where he plays. Oh, and then there were all these flirting floozies—"

"Girl, stop it! The only thing coming between you and him is jealousy. I've seen the way he looks at you. Tom loves you."

"Yeah, but that was high school. We've been apart for a year and a half, aside from semester breaks. It's really affecting our relationship."

"Only if you let it," Kellie said.

"But do you remember what tacky Tina said about sharing him with groupies? I don't want to do that."

"Yikes, girl! Do you hear yourself? Don't let Tina mess with your head."

"I'm not, but there's Sheri. I see how she looks at him and how he reacts to her attention. Tommy and I no longer have that bond."

"Oh, stop," Kellie said.

"Maybe… maybe I should give him what he wants. Maybe that would make him happy."

"Jenna, not if you're not ready. Don't lower your values. It's better he be mad at you than you give in to sin."

Jenna gnawed on a hangnail. "But I don't want to lose him to some floozy."

Kellie sighed. "Jenna, listen to your heart and follow your head. I know you, girl. Don't question your decision to live by God's standards just to please him. If he loves you, he'll wait."

Jenna expelled a long, tired breath. "I suppose."

"Listen, get some sleep and you'll feel differently in the morning."

"You're right, Kellie. Good night."

## Chapter 18

The next morning, Jenna woke to bright sunlight pouring through a gap in the heavy drapes. *Thank you, Lord, for a restful night's sleep.* She sat up and stretched, letting the quiet of the room settle around her.

But as she shifted beneath the sheets, a familiar longing tugged at her heart — not physical, but emotional. She wanted closeness with Tommy, wanted to feel secure again, wanted their relationship to feel like it used to. And simply telling him she loved him no longer felt like enough.

*Lord, forgive me for letting my emotions run ahead of my judgment. Today I'll be spending the day with Tommy at the beach. Please help us keep our hearts steady and our choices honoring to You. Amen.*

She slid out from beneath the cool sheets and tottered to the bathroom. The cold tile made her cringe, and she hurried to turn on the shower. She grabbed her cucumber-melon body wash and stepped into the warm spray, letting the steam loosen the tension in her shoulders.

Today would be better. *It had to be.*

It was a gorgeous December day to go to the beach. The warm sun shined its joyful face, bringing the morning temperatures into the high sixties. Jenna looked up at the sky; it was a magnificent blue with big, fluffy clouds drifting lazily overhead. A warm breeze swirled around her, blowing salty sea mist across her cheeks.

Jenna hadn't been to the beach since she was a little girl. Her family used to spend weekends at the Valentes' shore home in Fishermen's Point. The Jersey shore was the childhood place she remembered most fondly — the thrilling boardwalk games and rides, building giant sandcastles, evening barbecues at the Valentes' house. But thinking about it now, she realized it wasn't the activities that made it magical. It was being surrounded by close friends and family.

Listening with both an open heart and ear, Jenna heard seagulls squawking overhead as they searched for their next meal. As she and Tommy reached the entrance to the pier, she noticed fishermen's lines hanging off the edge, each one hoping to catch dinner.

Memories poured in as they walked along the pier. She recalled one of the most tranquil moments down the shore — sitting on the dock with Luke, legs dangling over the edge, waiting patiently for a tug on the line. Even as a little girl, fishing had been a peaceful escape… well, except for the time she got a hook stuck in her head. No vacation was ever perfect.

Her memories were swept away when she spotted a couple surfer dudes paddling out to catch the waves. She wondered what it felt like to ride nature's power. *I'd love to try just once.*

Tommy noticed her watching them. "Yeah, those guys are out there from daybreak to dusk, roaming the shore, waiting for the next big wave."

"Have you ever thought about learning to surf?"

"Nope," he said.

"I'd like to give it a try."

"No thanks. I'll pass."

Jenna shrieked, "Where's your sense of adventure?" *I bet Luke would give it a whirl.*

"Touring around the world with my guitar," Tommy said.

"Oh, right." She dipped her hand into her canvas tote and pulled out a disposable camera. "Let's get our picture taken."

"For what?"

"The locket, silly. C'mon!"

He followed her toward a lonely old fisherman who had just cast his line back into the water. Jenna asked if he'd take their picture, and the man nodded kindly.

Afterward, she and Tommy walked barefoot in the warm, wet sand along the shoreline. Every now and then, they stopped to pick up sea glass or to feel the cold, foamy seawater swirl around their feet.

"Oh, guess what," she said, touching Tommy's forearm.

"What's that?" he asked, eyes fixed on the waves.

"Anthony and Holly are expecting. I'm going to be an aunt! Isn't that cool?"

Mesmerized by the ocean, Tommy didn't respond.

"Hel-lo? Did you hear me?"

"Huh? Oh, yeah. Cool," he said, totally disengaged.

Jenna shook her head, then picked up a washed-up stick and drew two overlapping hearts in the sand. Inside the outline, she printed their names and the date they became a couple.

She nudged Tommy's arm. "Look."

Tommy glanced at her sand art. "Cute and creative — just like you," he said, wrapping his arm around her.

She smiled at him, but before she could say anything, a strong wave rolled in from a nearby boat and washed her love letter away.

"Oh no!" he said, half-laughing. He reached for her hand. "C'mon, let's go."

They moved inland to sit a spell. Jenna dropped her sandals and plopped down on a sunset-orange beach blanket. She leaned back on her elbows and lifted her face toward the warmth of the sun. A cool breeze blew her layered wisps away from her face.

She admired the peaceful view. Bright beams of sunlight shimmered across the Pacific Ocean like glass gems. She was in awe of the sea's majestic blues and greens and how they blended with the light blue sky. The water seemed endless, and she wondered what lay beyond it — all the infinite opportunities stretching across the horizon.

She touched Tommy's forearm. "Do you ever think about the future?"

He shrugged. "Yeah, I guess."

"What do you see?"

"Umm…" Tommy flipped his long hair. "Fame. I see myself playing in huge venues and touring all over the world."

"Okay… and what about you and me?"

"Yeah, of course." He nodded with assurance. "Why? What do you see?"

Jenna closed her eyes and smiled. "I see us." She grasped both of his hands. "Oh, Tommy, I can easily leave the mountain for year-round climate like this just to be with you."

"What?" Tommy asked, his eyes searching hers. "But you said—"

"Never mind what I said. I'd be happy anywhere as long as we're together."

Tommy rubbed the back of his neck.

"Now what's that look?" she asked.

"You sure? I mean, you love River Grove."

"Absolutely," Jenna said, bobbing her head. "Sure, I love River Grove, but I love YOU more."

She leaned into him and kissed him softly — gentle, lingering, full of affection. Tommy reacted, returning her kiss with enthusiasm that made her heart race.

"Let's go back to the hotel," she breathed.

Tommy's eyes clung to hers, searching for her expression. "What? But yesterday you—"

She silenced him with another tender kiss, then drew a ragged breath, "I'm ready now."

Tommy beamed with approval. "Let's go then."

Jenna's heart thumped anxiously as her trembling hand fumbled inside her bag in search of her room key. *It's in here somewhere.* Meanwhile, the phone inside her room started ringing. A flicker of apprehension coursed through her.

Jenna let out a heavy sigh. "It's probably Kellie."

"Relax," Tommy murmured. He kissed her neck and shoulders, eager and impatient as a summer storm.

Jenna finally pulled the room key from her bag, but Tommy's closeness made it hard to swipe the door fob. When she managed to unlock the door, the ringing stopped.

"Oh, well," Jenna uttered.

"If it's important, they'll call back," Tommy said.

He pushed the door open and led her inside. He framed her face with his hands and kissed her. The warmth of it excited her yet alarmed her at the same time.

"Tommy…" she breathed, pulling her hand back. She wanted to give him more, but her conscience tugged hard.

I…"

"Shh, don't talk," he said, kissing her even more eagerly.

He glanced down at her white eyelet romper and began unbuttoning its neckline. His gentle touch made her heart race. She peered up at him. His dreamy eyes held a promise of satisfaction, easing her insecurities.

"Let me show you what you mean to me," he said, taking her unsteady hand and guiding it toward the button on his board shorts.

"Tommy," she gasped, redirecting her hand away from his south pole. She wanted to give him more but was feeling repentant. "I..."

He looked at her urgently. "I won't disappoint you."

The phone rang again, startling her.

"Let it ring," he said, trying to draw her close again.

But the phone continued to tremble with persistence, totally killing the moment. Jenna's desire plummeted, and she squirmed out of his embrace.

"I'm sorry; I have to answer it."

Tommy sighed, clearly annoyed.

She picked up the phone. "Hello?" she said, sitting down on the edge of the bed.

"Jenna, where've you been?" Mom shrieked.

Jenna rubbed her eyes. "Hi, Mom."

"I've been trying to call you all morning."

"Why? I was at the beach!"

"Your father is in the hospital."

"What?" Jenna asked, leaping to her feet.

"He had a heart attack."

"What? When?"

"This morning, at work," Mom said.

"Ohmygod, ohmygod, ohmygod!" Jenna ran her hand through her windblown hair. "Okay, okay," she said, spinning in circles. "I've got to get to the airport…Mom, I'll call you with my flight info."

"Okay. Leave a message on the machine. Anthony will pick you up."

"Okay, Mom."

Jenna hung up.

Tommy drew in a shaky breath. "Now what?"

"I have to get home!" Jenna said, rushing past him while refastening her clothes.

He followed her into the bathroom. "Why? What's going on?"

"My dad had a heart attack," she said, stuffing her toiletries into her suitcase.

Tommy's eyes grew alert. "Bad?"

"I don't know," Jenna said, slamming her luggage shut. "Come home with me."

"I can't. I'm playing tonight."

Frustrated, Jenna slapped her hands to her sides. "But this is an emergency. Can't you cancel?"

Tommy stiffened. "No! We're a single band playing tonight. I can't lose this gig."

Jenna shook her head. "So be it. I've got to go."

"But you just got here. You can't leave me!"

"I have to."

Tommy heaved a ragged sigh, then reached for her hand. "Please… don't go."

Jenna touched his face one final time. "I'm sorry, but he's… my father." She rose to her tiptoes and pressed her lips to his cheek. "Goodbye, Tommy."

# Chapter 19

Jenna paid the cab driver. "Thanks," she said, then leaped out of the taxi with her luggage in tow. The combination of exhaust fumes and noisy buses battered her senses, adding to the chaos already tangled in her thoughts. *I was here just yesterday.* Bitter regret tugged at her conscience. *I shouldn't have come in the first place.*

She pushed through the revolving door and stopped inside the main entrance, unsure where to go. Holiday travelers swarmed around her — some jolly, some not so jolly. She turned right and headed toward the ticket counter.

*Oh, no, no, no!* The endless zigzag line stretched farther than she could see. *I'm never going to get home.*

She set her luggage down at the end of the rope line and waited for what felt like an eternity.

Finally, the attendant waved her over. "How may I help you?" the harried woman asked.

"I need an emergency flight home," Jenna said, presenting her return ticket.

The craggy attendant stared at her like she was nuttier than a fruitcake, then dropped her gaze to the monitor and clicked away at the keyboard.

"Is it possible?" Jenna asked.

The attendant shook her head. "The next flight to Stonebridge International Airport leaves in twenty-five minutes."

Jenna sighed. "Oh, thank God!"

"But it's full," the attendant added.

"Really?" Jenna's shoulders slumped. "I have to get home."

"Sorry, miss," the attendant said, handing back the ticket, "but this is still valid for New Year's Day."

Jenna clenched her jaw. "I can't wait five days. Can't you bump someone?"

The attendant gave her a warning glare as turbulent as a violent storm.

"Please!" Jenna pleaded. "My dad had a heart attack. I must get back home to him today!"

The attendant's eyes softened.

"Let me check another airline."

Jenna exhaled shakily. "Thank you."

The attendant typed again. "Blue Highway has a flight departing at three. I can put you on standby."

Jenna nodded. "I'll take it. Thank you."

The two-hour wait for departure gave Jenna enough time to call home and change out of her beach romper and sandals into something more suitable for travel.

Afterward, she settled into a chair near a flocked cashmere Christmas tree with her portable CD player and listened to holiday music from her favorite artists. At once, vivid memories of Christmas trickled into her consciousness, sending her back to that morning. The heat of the fireplace had warmed the cozy living room where she and her family gathered around the twinkling tree to open gifts and listen to carols. She recalled how happy her father had been that day — how his mood had transformed from stern and harsh to cheerful and loving.

Jenna lowered her eyes. Christmas was only two days ago. *What happened since then?* Her thoughts plunged into a whirl of emotions as she remembered her father's farewell at the airport. *Amore, I love you,* he had said.

It suddenly dawned on her what his words meant. *Oh, God! I'm never going to see him alive again.* Guilt gripped her heart. *And it's all my fault.*

Jenna yanked her headphones off just in time to catch the tail end of an overhead announcement.

"…Flight 428 is delayed."

*What?* Jenna snatched her boarding pass from her handbag and checked the flight number. *428 — that's me. No, no, no! I've got to get home!*

She leaped from her chair and scanned the noisy, rambunctious airport for someone who might confirm what she thought she'd heard, but everyone around her seemed too wrapped up in their own business to be bothered.

*Oh, what's the use?* She sat back down and massaged the pain pounding at her temples. She closed her eyes and prayed for her father's health.

Two hours had passed when the boarding announcement was finally made for her flight. Jenna quickly grabbed her things and rushed to the gate.

Inside the plane, she found her seat near the wing. She shoved her luggage into the overhead compartment while eavesdropping on a middle-aged couple already seated in her row. They were gabbing about the weather in Pennsylvania and the possibility of more heavy snow.

"Lenny," the woman said, "we were delayed in anticipation of landing safely during the lull of the storm."

*Snow? You've got to be kidding me.* Jenna sat down and sighed. *I'm never going to get home to Daddy.*

She rested her head against the seat and closed her eyes.

Halfway into her flight, Jenna's stomach churned. The smell of hotdogs and sauerkraut clashed with the stinky tuna fish sandwiches and her seatmate's faded perfume. It was a good thing she didn't get a window seat — the aisle was safer in case she had to run to the bathroom to vomit.

*God, I want to go home. Please, God, get me home.*

Unable to tolerate any food, Jenna dozed off until the pilot announced a flight diversion.

"May I have your attention?" he said. "Due to blizzard conditions, we are unable to safely land at Stonebridge International Airport. Instead, we will be landing at Bedford City Airport until the storm subsides."

*What?* Jenna clamped her lips shut to keep her sobs from breaking loose. *No… this can't be happening.*

As soon as the plane landed in Bedford City, Jenna gathered her personal belongings and rushed through the gate to the ticket counter. "Excuse me! When will Flight 428 depart again?"

"We're sorry, miss, but all planes are grounded due to the impending storm."

Jenna threw her hands out in frustration. "What storm? There's barely a coating."

"A nor'easter. There's a winter storm warning south of here — that's why you were diverted." The attendant handed her a voucher. "We're offering passengers a free hotel room until the storm passes."

Jenna sighed. "But I have to get home to my ill father before—"

"I'm sorry, miss. We can only wait out the storm."

Jenna swallowed hard. "Thanks."

She stepped away from the counter and joined the other discontented passengers in the pay-phone area. When a booth opened, she called home. The phone rang off the hook. She glanced at her watch. *No wonder Mom isn't picking up. It's two a.m.*

The answering machine clicked on.

"Mom! It's me," Jenna said. "How's Daddy doing? This stupid snowstorm grounded our plane at Bedford City. They gave us a voucher for a hotel room, but I'm sticking it out here at the airport. I want to be the first one at the departure gate in the morning. Let Anthony know. Hopefully he didn't drive to Stonebridge to get me. I'll call you in the morning. Bye."

She hung up and ran an anxious hand through her hair. *This is ridiculous. Stupid snowstorm!* She checked her watch again. It was only eleven o'clock in California. She stared at her calling card and considered calling Tommy. *Why not? He's probably worried sick about me.* She dialed his number, but it rang endlessly.

Jenna slammed down the phone. *Whatever.*

She jerked her thoughts away from Tommy and focused on the task at hand. *I've got to get out of here tonight.* She tapped her chin. *Bedford City is only three hours north of River Grove. I can rent a car.* She shook her head. *No, I can't. I'm not old enough. Guess I'll be sleeping on the airport floor.*

Jenna grabbed her stuff and exited the phone booth. *Where did everybody go?* The place looked more like a ghost town than an airport. With most flights grounded, there was no reason for anyone to stay.

She tugged her luggage behind her. The rolling wheels and tapping of her ankle boots echoed across the vacant terminal. The abnormal silence and lack of people was eerily troubling. *Maybe it wouldn't be a bad idea to take advantage of the hotel voucher rather than sticking around here all night.*

She waited for the ping of the elevator when she heard a familiar voice above her call her name.

"Jenna!"

She looked up to the second level and saw a man dressed head-to-toe in heavy winter gear dashing down the escalator toward her.

"Jenna!" he called again.

She blinked in bewilderment. *Who is that dressed like an Eskimo?* She stared as he stalked across the airport in long strides. *Is that Luke?* When she realized it was, it took strong willpower to keep her jaw from dropping.

"Howdy," Luke said.

His sudden appearance rattled her nerves.

"What're you—where's Anthony? How's my father?"

"Whoa there!" he said, holding up a hand. "One question at a time."

"Sorry."

"Anthony and your mom are at the hospital. Last I heard, the doc was running tests on your father, so we'll have to wait and see."

Jenna dropped her gaze. "Oh."

"Hey," Luke said, lifting her chin. "Have a little faith."

"Faith?" Jenna asked. "You have no idea the hell it's been trying to get home — flight delays, diversions — how'd you even find me here?"

"My pager," Luke said, patting his side.

"What?"

"The airport sent me alerts on your flight status."

"Oh. I didn't know that was possible."

Luke pointed toward the exit. Tiny slivers of ice pelted the glass door. "Uh, we should get going."

"Okay," Jenna said, grabbing her luggage. But as she stepped forward, Luke cut her a sharp glare that stung her cheeks.

"What?" she asked. "Why are you staring at me like I'm batshit crazy?"

"Where's your coat?"

"I don't have one."

Luke shook his head. "Bless your heart."

"Stop it!" she yelled, smacking his puffy shoulder. "It was like seventy degrees in California!"

"Well, let me clue you in. It's eight degrees here in Pennsylvania, and it's snowing."

"Well, I didn't know!" she argued.

He pointed to her luggage. "Don't you have something warmer to wear?"

"No, not really."

Without another word, Luke removed his coat and handed it to her. "Here. Wear mine."

"No. I'll be fine."

"Take it. I dressed in layers."

"Fine," Jenna said, accepting it.

She pulled his coat on over her floral baby-doll dress. The subtle smell of cedar and cologne clouded her worries and brought her a renewed sense of strength.

Jenna followed Luke to the exit. When she stepped out into the dark cold, a gust of icy wind lashed the hem of her dress and stung her bare legs. Luke wasn't exaggerating. The weather was brutal, and she was suddenly, fiercely grateful for his warm coat.

The winter sky hung low, spitting dime-size snowflakes into her face as they traipsed through the sloppy, wet parking lot. Slush seeped into her ankle boots.

"Ugh! If I wanted wet feet, I would've kept my sandals on. Where did you park—Timbuktu?" she shouted.

"Don't get all het up about it. I'm parked over yonder," he said, pointing at the white Ford Ranger.

Jenna spotted the company pickup backed into a corner spot under a fluorescent lamppost. It was no longer shiny pearl white but charcoal gray from road salt and cinders. It was so filthy she could barely make out the gold lettering on the side: *Valente Custom Home Builders.*

The logo triggered a memory. The last time she'd seen the truck was when her father asked her to drop off a manila envelope at Mr. Valente's office. She remembered how annoyed she'd been that day, having to go out of her way for him.

*Oh, what I would do for a second chance.*

She lowered her head as tears trekked down her cheeks. Lost in a mental fog, she quivered when a firm hand touched her shoulder.

"It'll be a lot warmer inside the truck," Luke said.

Still dazed, she peered up at him. "Oh. Right."

Luke arched a quizzical brow. "Everything okay?"

"Yeah. I'm fine."

He helped her climb into the truck and closed the door. Instantly, the new-vehicle scent surrounded her. She settled onto the split-bench seat, grateful it was soft cloth instead of cold vinyl. She fastened her seatbelt and looked around the shadowy interior. For a work truck, it was remarkably clean and comfortable.

She gazed out the window while Luke brushed snow off the windshield. Flashing yellow lights from plow trucks idling nearby caught her eye. Not much snow had fallen yet, but she had a bad inkling the drive to the hospital would be hazardous.

Luke opened the driver door, and a blast of arctic air blew in with him. He noticed Jenna sitting with her arms tightly crossed, shivering.

"Don't tell me you're still cold," he said, rubbing his hands together.

"I wasn't until you came in," she grumbled.

Luke blinked in surprise. "I reckon I feel a draft too," he shot back.

He adjusted the temperature controls, flipping the dial from defroster to heat, but the fan still blew frigid air, chilling her even more.

"Really, Luke?" she asked, shivering.

"What? I can't help it the engine cooled off already."

"Then turn the fan down until there's heat!"

"I didn't tell you to wear summer clothes."

"Whatever! Can you please just drive now?"

"Hey, don't rile the wagon master."

Jenna rolled her eyes. "How far is the hospital from here anyway?"

"On a good day, about two hours."

"Well, how long did it take you to get here?"

"Three hours."

Jenna shook her head in disgust. "This is awful."

Luke patted her shoulder. "Listen, come hell or high water, I'll get you there."

"What experience do you have driving in the snow?"

"Don't worry. I've got plenty of arrows in my quiver."

"How? There's no snow in Texas."

"Would you like to drive then?" he asked.

"I would if I knew how to drive stick."

"I'd teach you, but now's not the time," he said.

Suddenly, his pager beeped and buzzed. He twisted in his seat to unclip it from his belt.

"Who is it?" she asked.

"Not sure."

He reached under his seat and pulled out a leather phone bag. He plugged the phone into the cigarette lighter and dialed the unknown number.

"Hello, someone paged me with this number," Luke said, running a hand through his crunchy hair. "Yes, I can hold."

As he waited, Jenna bit her lower lip in anticipation.

"Yeah, I found her," he said, glancing up at Jenna.

As Luke listened, Jenna watched the seriousness settle over his face. His brow furrowed, his expression somber — as if something of grave importance was being relayed.

"Okay. We're about to leave the airport now," he said, glancing at the dashboard clock. "Six, at the earliest."

Jenna narrowed her focus. "What's going on?"

Luke lifted his index finger to hush her. "Yeah, sure," he said into the receiver, then handed the phone to her. "It's your momma."

"Thanks." Jenna grasped the phone. "Mom—"

"Jenna, I'm so glad Luke found you."

"How's Daddy doing?"

"He's being prepped for surgery."

"What? Why?" Jenna shrieked.

"He has a blockage," Mom said.

"He's going to be okay, right?"

"He's in the best of care, Jenna."

Jenna heard the uncertainty in her mother's voice and replied softly, "No doubt, Mom."

"We'll know more in a few hours."

"Okay. We're on our way."

"Tell Luke to be careful driving. This storm is bad."

"Okay, Mom. Bye."

Jenna ended the call and handed the phone back to Luke without a word.

He placed a supporting hand over hers. "Everything's going to be okay."

Tears thickened her voice. "Yeah. Sure."

Jenna sat in silence, watching the wipers shove wet, fat flakes off the glass. Heavy, blinding snow fell, turning the highway into a frozen mess. She noticed the only tires treading the snow were their own.

*Of course — because no one else is stupid enough to be out in this.*

She fidgeted in her seat, clinging to a sliver of hope that they wouldn't crash. The blowing snow was piling up faster than debt on Black Friday.

*This is bad.*

Occasionally, Jenna glanced at Luke, who hadn't said a word since the airport. His left hand held steady on the steering wheel, his right rested on the shifter, and his eyes stayed locked on the white road ahead. His calm composure kept her edgy and alert.

*How can he stay so calm?*

"You okay over there?" he asked.

"No. No, I'm not. Your music is too loud," she yelled.

"What?" he asked, turning the volume up more.

"This hillbilly music sucks!"

"What? This is 'Lovin' You' by Austin Ryder."

"Who cares? You're driving way too fast!"

"I'm doing thirty miles per hour."

Jenna threw her hands out. "You can't even see the road! You're going to run us into a ditch!"

Luke purposely slammed on the brakes.

Jenna grabbed the 'oh-shit' handle above the door. "What're you trying to do, kill us?"

"No! I'm proving to you that I've got this," he said, navigating the skid with practiced ease. "Don't get your granny panties in a wad."

"Who do you think you are, a racecar driver?"

With a badass grin, Luke nodded.

Jenna crossed her arms. "Just slow down, and don't talk to me, okay?"

Completely ignoring her request, Luke asked bluntly, "So, where's your boyfriend?"

"Excuse me? You have some gall! For your information, T-o-m-m-y had to work."

"So? I work, too."

"Some people don't have the privilege to call out."

"These circumstances are different," Luke said.

"If he didn't do the gig, he'd lose it all."

"Fame and fortune ain't everything."

"Well, it is to Tommy. He's incredibly talented."

"If he is, he'll have other opportunities."

"Listen here, Luke!" she snapped. "Not everyone has the luxury of working for 'Daddy.'"

"Don't even go there," Luke shouted. "I don't get stuff handed to me on a silver platter. I worked damn hard to get where I am. And I made a lot of sacrifices in my life doing it."

Jenna dropped her head. She knew he'd taken on a load of responsibilities after his father's accident, but she hadn't realized how deep the wound went. "I'm sorry."

"Don't be. All I'm saying is we have choices to make."

Jenna squeezed her eyes shut, willing herself not to cry. "I know that, Luke. That's why I'm here and not in California right now."

"My point exactly. You made the right choice to come home. But your fiancé should be here, too."

"Well, he couldn't be — and that's okay, because we understand each other."

"Hey. I'm looking out for your best interest."

"Oh? And are you insinuating Tommy isn't?"

Luke sighed. "Just remember who you are. And trust the guidance of your family. Guard your heart. Know what I mean?"

Jenna clucked her tongue at his infuriating speech.

"You know what, Luke? I'm through talking to you."

She shifted in her seat and stared out the passenger window at the blinding snow. Luke's words were wreaking havoc on her nerves.

*Why is he all up in my business? What does he know?*

She had enough anxiety worrying about her father. She didn't need Luke filling her head with doubts about Tommy.

# Chapter 20

Bleary-eyed, Jenna stared at the digital numbers above the elevator door as they counted down to one. When the metal doors opened, the bright overhead lights stunned her tired eyes. It had been a long night driving.

She followed Luke into the vacant elevator and pressed the button for the third floor, but before the doors closed, an oversized teddy bear tied to a bundle of bouncing baby-boy balloons floated in with two sets of jubilant grandparents and a wheelchair.

To avoid her toes being crushed, she stumbled backward into Luke; her body pressed tightly against his. Placed in an awkward predicament, she lifted her chin and uttered, "Sorry."

Luke placed his hand on her arm. "No worries. My coat adds plenty of padding between us."

Jenna gave a short laugh. "Yeah."

Although she agreed, it wasn't the response she expected — or necessarily the one she wanted to hear.

She grabbed the wooden handrail when the elevator lurched to a stop. A chime signaled their floor, and they politely made their way out.

The cardiac wing was right around the corner. Jenna scanned the waiting room. A woman with a headscarf and a teen with a baseball cap pulled low stood at the glass partition waiting for news. Another couple sat on a vinyl couch watching a comedy on TV, trying hard to suppress their chuckles.

Jenna wondered where her mother and Anthony were. She turned to Luke. "Maybe they're downstairs having breakfast?"

"Want me to check?" he asked.

She shook her head. "Maybe they're in with my dad." She pointed toward the front desk. "I think I'll check with the receptionist first."

"Okay," he said.

Before heading in, Jenna peered out the window at the aftermath of nature's violent pillow fight. Although the storm had passed, intermittent gusts kicked up swirls of powdery snow, congesting the early morning sky.

She tapped the glass. "Hey, it finally stopped snowing."

"Go figure," he said.

Jenna removed Luke's coat and slowly handed it back to him. "Thanks for everything," she said appreciatively.

"No problem."

"Hey, uh…" She pointed toward the waiting room. "I know it's been a long night, and I'm sure you're whipped, so…"

"Nah, I'm fine." Luke wrapped his arm around her and walked her inside. "I don't mind staying. Besides, we're like family."

Luke picked a quiet corner and plopped into a chair. He crossed his feet at the ankles and closed his eyes.

Jenna sank into a chair across from him. Her body sighed in relief. *I'm finally here, Daddy.* She pressed her palm to her mouth and stifled a yawn. Exhaustion swept over her, and she dozed off.

Jenna squirmed to get comfortable in the cramped chair, but the familiar scent of cedar and cologne roused her. Still groggy, she peeled her eyes open to find Luke's coat draped over her body.

*Huh? I thought I gave it back.*

"Good morning, darlin'," he said.

She turned sharply toward his chipper voice and found him sitting so erect, bright-eyed, and bushy-tailed. *Really? How does this guy function on so little sleep?* She shook her head in disbelief. "Don't you ever sleep?"

"Sure — in my own bed," he answered.

"Jenna," Mom's voice percolated, "I swear you could fall asleep on a picket fence."

Unaware of her mother's presence, Jenna uncurled her body and sat upright. "Mom, you're here! How's Daddy?"

"In recovery. We're waiting to speak with the surgeon."

"Oh. Where's Anthony?"

"Getting coffee," Mom answered.

Luke pushed to his feet. "I think I'll get myself a cup too." He touched Jenna's wrist. "Want anything?"

Jenna yawned. "A hot chocolate?"

"Coming right up."

While Luke and Anthony were gone, the automatic doors from the cardiac unit opened with a swoosh. A surgeon in cobalt scrubs and sneakers stepped into the waiting room. He lowered his mask and greeted Jenna and her mother.

"Mrs. Rossi, the surgery went well. His left anterior descending artery was ninety-nine percent blocked. We placed a stent to keep the narrowed artery open."

Mom nodded. "Okay."

"He's incredibly lucky," the surgeon said.

"Can we see him?" she asked.

"Certainly. Once he's settled in his room, I'll send a nurse for you."

"Thank you, doctor."

The surgeon turned and exited through the double doors. Jenna leaned forward in her chair and met her mother's gaze head-on. "So, tell me, Mom. What happened yesterday?"

Mom shrugged. "He was on the job site and had sudden pain in his chest. He thought he pulled a muscle, but the pain got worse, and he began sweating. He was rushed to the E.R. by ambulance."

Jenna swallowed hard. "I had no idea Daddy was a risk."

"He's been on blood pressure medication."

"But isn't that supposed to help?"

"It's not a fix, Jenna. The E.R. doctor said his heart attack was most likely caused by stress and genetics."

Jenna dropped her head. *It was all my fault.*

Mom placed her hand on her shoulder. "It's a wake-up call — a reminder that we have to take care of our bodies and not take life for granted."

"I guess," Jenna said, standing. "I'll be right back."

She found her way to the payphone area. Her mother's words about not taking life for granted repeated in her head like a dominant chord, prompting her to clear the air with Tommy before it was too late.

She dug her calling card out of her purse and dialed Tommy. The phone rang ten times before she gave up. *Where are you, Tommy?* She glanced at her watch — only five a.m. in California. She sighed. *He probably got in late from the club.* "I get it, Tommy; I'm tired, too — tired of you not giving a damn," she mumbled.

Jenna returned to the waiting area where Luke was drinking his coffee. He handed her a hot chocolate and informed her that her mother and Anthony had gone in to see her father, but only two visitors were allowed at a time.

Jenna paced the waiting room like a caged animal.

"You're going to wear out the floor," he said.

"I can't help it."

Luke caught her arm and turned her around. "Hey," he said, gripping her shoulders. "Everything's going to be okay."

Jenna closed her eyes tight. "God, I hope so."

He ushered her to a chair and eased her into it. "It will be."

She sat there, her leg bouncing, thinking what an excellent job she had done to cause all this drama.

After ten minutes or so, Mom and Anthony returned to the waiting room. Mom smiled softly.

Jenna hesitated to stand. "How is he?"

"He's sleeping, but your presence there will do him good."

Jenna stood inside the doorway of her father's room. The beep of his heart monitor made the situation even more real. She took a tiny step forward but stopped at the closed curtain. The scent of fresh flowers made her stomach turn, taking her back to her grandfather's funeral many years ago.

*I can't do this.*

But the gentle touch of Luke's hand on the small of her back prodded her forward.

"I'm going," she whispered, then reached for the curtain and slid it along its metal rod.

With Luke's support, she cautiously approached her father's bed. She stood beside him and held his hand.

"I'm here, Daddy," she sniffled. "If you can hear me, squeeze my hand."

Nothing. His callused hand lay limp between hers. It was hard to believe someone so bold and full of life could be so weak and vulnerable. She peered up at Luke with uncertainty.

"Remember, he just got out of surgery," he said.

"I know," she said, pulling up a chair.

Luke pointed to the door. "I'll, uh, wait outside with your mother and Anthony."

Jenna nodded. "Thanks."

She turned to her father. "Please be okay, Daddy. I know we don't always get along, but I know in my heart that you want what's best for me… even though I am the one who needs to figure out what that is."

Her heart ached. She loved her father unconditionally but couldn't understand his views on life.

"Why can't we see eye-to-eye?" She shook her head. "Regardless, Daddy, I still love you." She stood and whispered, "I'll be back."

Jenna returned to the payphone area. She dialed Tommy, but the phone rang several times before Jeff answered. Loud music blared in the background.

"Hey, is Tommy there?" she asked.

"Yeah, hold on."

His muffled voice called out to Tommy. A moment later, Tommy picked up.

"Yeah," he said.

"Tommy! It's me. I, uh, just wanted to update you on my father's condition. He had surgery, and the doc said it went well."

"Oh, so he was lucky," Tommy said.

"Well, I'd like to call it blessed."

"Then I guess you left here in haste."

"I had to, Tommy! It was an emergency."

"Jenna, all I wanted to do was spend some time with you."

"Same here, but it didn't work out that way."

"Hey, you made that choice," he said.

"I had no choice. What do you want, an apology?"

Silence as thick as mud oozed between them.

"Jenna…" he hesitated, choosing his words carefully. "Let's… not argue, okay?"

"Let's not," she replied. She sucked in her bottom lip. *How do I make him understand?* "Listen, I'll call you when I get home from the hospital."

"Okay, but I'm playing tonight."

"Thanks for the heads up."

"Yeah," he said before hanging up.

Jenna blinked warily. *Who was I just talking to? Certainly not the Tommy I fell in love with.* Something about his behavior struck her as odd. She shook her head in disgust, then remembered Luke's words.

*Guard your heart,* he had told her.

*Luke… what are you implying?*

Jenna returned to the waiting room. As soon as she stepped through the doorway, Luke leaped from his chair.

"Oh, there you are," he said. "Your dad is asking for you."

"He's awake? Oh, thank God!"

"Yeah, your mom and Anthony are in with him now."

"Oh. So, I should wait here?"

"No, you can go in. They lifted the visiting restrictions."

"Cool. Are you coming?" she asked.

"I'll be along in a moment." He pointed toward the café sign. "I need a pick-me-up first."

"Wait! Luke, before you go, I just wanted to thank you again for getting me here."

He tossed his wrist. "Nah, it was no big deal."

"No, really. You went way, way out of your way for me in a blizzard to get me here safely. I can't thank you enough."

"I'd do anything for you. You're like my kid sister."

*Oh. At least I know now where this relationship is NOT going.* She smiled politely. "Thanks, Luke. You mean a lot to me, too."

Jenna arrived at her father's room but stopped at the closed curtain when she heard his fragile voice.

"You mean he drove one hundred plus miles out of his way in a snowstorm to pick her up from the airport?" he asked.

"Uh huh," Mom said.

There was a brief silence before her father reacted.

"In a blizzard?" he asked. "Now that's a good man." *Madonna mia… in una bufera? Per mia figlia?* "I don't suppose the boy came back with her?"

"Nope!" Anthony said.

"That boy's no good for my daughter," Dad grumbled. *"Amore merita di meglio."*

At her father's remark, Jenna's cheeks burned with shame.

"Shh, Nick!" Mom said. "She's going to be here any second."

Nick murmured under his breath: *"Non voglio perderla…"*

"Pfft… so what? Amore can do better."

Jenna's heart sank. She quietly stepped away from the curtain and wandered back into the hallway. She didn't need to hear any more of that conversation — nor did she want to.

She found herself at the end of the corridor near the vending machines, eyeing an almond chocolate bar. It seemed right, so she dropped a coin into the machine and made her choice. The candy bar dropped into the dispenser with a thunk, and she retrieved it.

She sat down in a chair and unwrapped the bar. As she took her first bite, she heard Luke's voice call out to her.

"Well, that's not a healthy lunch," he said.

Jenna tossed a dismissive shrug. "I'm a big girl. I think I can decide what I should or shouldn't eat."

"I didn't mean it like that." He glanced down the hallway toward the cardiac wing. "I thought you were going in to see your father?"

With a mouthful of chocolate, she answered, "I needed an energy boost first."

"You should've said something. I would've bought you lunch. I haven't eaten anything yet either."

"No. You've done too much for me already."

"So what? I told you. We're like family," Luke said.

*You keep reminding me of that.* She stood up and tossed the candy wrapper into the garbage. "C'mon, let's go."

Jenna and Luke entered her father's room. The aroma of flavorless hospital food camouflaged the fragrance of Mom's flowers. The instant she slid the curtain open, her father's attention jumped from Mom and Anthony to her. Tears welled in his eyes, and a content smile split across his face.

"There's my *Amore*," he said, holding out his hand.

"*Amore mio… sei qui.*"

Jenna's mouth trembled as she reached out to him. "I'm so glad you're okay, Daddy."

"I'm okay, but they won't let me go home," he complained.

"You will soon, Daddy."

"Not soon enough," he said, then pointed his finger at Luke. "Now there's a hero. *Un vero uomo*. First, you save my life, then you bring my daughter home."

Luke shook his head and waved his hands. "No, no! I only did what anyone else would've done, sir. *La famiglia viene prima*."

Jenna turned sharply toward him. "Wait — what?"

Dad chimed in. "He saw me collapse and called 911."

"I was at the right place at the right time," Luke said.

"Oh my gosh!" Jenna smacked Luke's shoulder. "Why didn't you tell me?"

Luke shrugged. "You didn't ask."

Jenna felt her body heat up with annoyance. Smoke must've been pouring out of her ears, because her mother intervened.

"Never mind, Jenna," Mom said. She turned her attention to her husband and placed a gentle hand on his shoulder. "Nick, you rest now. We'll be back after lunch."

## Chapter 21

After changing into her flannel pajamas, Jenna sat on the edge of her bed and listened to the frozen tree limbs outside her window creak in the howling wind. She shook her head in disgust. The winter weather in River Grove couldn't compete with the warm sunshine she had left behind in Sandy Ridge. But still, she was glad to be home; the past few days had been beyond stressful. Tonight, however, she could breathe easier. Her father had been discharged from the hospital and was recovering in the comfort of home. In fact, he was back to his grouchy old self.

Jenna glanced at her phone. No messages. No missed calls. Nothing from Tommy in two days.

*What's up with that?*

She crawled under the covers and shut off the light. Her room was still and dark except for the multi-colored Christmas lights dancing around her window. Exhausted, she drifted off to sleep.

Floating into the wisps of a dream, she heard church bells ringing. The limo door opened. Her father reached in and took her white-gloved hand. Teary-eyed, she gazed up at the cathedral. Her glorious wedding day had finally come. She lifted the hem of her satin gown and stepped forward in her two-inch heels. Excitement mounted as she climbed the soapstone steps.

Inside the dim-lit church, candles flickered, and flower bouquets adorned the altar. White satin bows hung on every pew. At the altar, her handsome groom waited in a black western tail tuxedo. The organ sounded the wedding processional, but as he turned to face her—

Her phone rang.

The dream shattered.

Jenna reached over the edge of her bed and answered. "Hello?" she mumbled.

"Hey! You asleep?" Tommy asked.

"Uh, yeah. It's like two-thirty in the morning," she said, staring bleary-eyed at the red digits on her alarm clock.

"Oh, right. I keep forgetting the time difference."

"It's okay," she yawned, secretly wanting to return to that wonderful dream. "I was dreaming we—"

"We should talk," Tommy said.

Jenna sat up and rubbed her eyes. "Sounds serious."

"It is."

"Okay. I'm listening."

"I think we're better off as friends."

Jenna blinked at the icy tone in his voice. "What? Wait — you're breaking up with me?"

"I'm sorry, Jenna."

"Why? Because I left abruptly to see my ill father?"

"No, because we're moving at different tempos."

Jenna ran an agitated hand through her disheveled hair. "Tommy, I don't get it. You sang to me on stage in front of a crowd of strangers; we walked the beach together and discussed our future. Hell, I almost gave my virginity to you."

In a wooden, distant tone, he said, "I'm not in love with you anymore."

"And you just figured this out now?" she shouted.

"Well, no. I kind of knew, but I had to see you — to know for sure."

Jenna held her heart like a knife had just stabbed it. "And you couldn't tell me this when I was there?"

"I needed some time to sort it all out."

"That's really lame, Tommy."

"Look, we can still be friends."

"Oh, no, no, no! Don't pull that card. There's somebody else, isn't there?"

"No!" Tommy shouted. "Jenna, listen to me. Our lives are going in different directions… I think we should see other people."

"Ha! So there *is* someone else — that bimbo at the bar the other night. What's her name?"

"Her name is Sheri, and no. I'm just saying that if we're meant to be together, then—"

"Then what? Do you expect me to sit and wait for you?"

"No, but we can remain friends."

"No, we can't!" she cried. "Forget it, Tommy; our song is over."

Jenna slammed the phone down without waiting for his response.

*This can't be happening.*

Her mind stirred over his destructive words. *I'm not in love with you anymore.* They were like bullets straight to the heart. At first, it didn't hurt — but then it burned.

*Why, Tommy? I was counting on forever.*

Aching with inner pain, she crossed her arms over her chest and leaned forward. "I trusted you, Tommy," she cried, "and you betrayed me."

She sat up and gathered her defenses with several deep breaths. "He's not going to break me. No, I'm not going to let him break me," she uttered.

She nodded with confidence — then huge tears rolled down her cheeks and her mouth crumpled in pain.

"Who am I kidding?"

She dropped her head on her pillow and cried herself to sleep.

Hours later, morning found her in the throes of a girl's worst nightmare. *Don't do this to me, Tommy!* She woke drenched in sweat, her bed sheets tangled in a knot.

"Oh, thank God, it was just a dream." She propped herself up with her pillows and rubbed her tired eyes. "Wait! No… it wasn't a dream. He really dumped me."

She held her aching head, trying to make it all make sense. Still foggy, she reached over the edge of the bed and picked up her phone. She dialed Kellie's number, but it rang and rang.

"C'mon, Kel, pick up."

Suddenly, there was fumbling and a delay.

Kellie grumbled, "You better have a really good reason for waking me up at the crack of dawn on a Saturday."

A lump clogged Jenna's throat. "Tom…" She drew in a quivering breath and started over. "Tommy broke up with me last night."

"What? No," Kellie said.

"Yep. He did."

"What happened?"

"I don't know." Jenna rubbed her brow to soothe her aching head. "He says he just wants to be friends. I *know* Sheri has something to do with it."

"No-o-o," Kellie said.

"I have to find out."

"Wait. Just wait," Kellie said, suddenly sounding like some kind of expert. "Let him dwell on the break-up for a while. Let him think you're over the relationship. Let him miss you."

"I can't, Kellie. I love him so much."

"I know, sweetie. I know it hurts. Stay strong, okay?"

"But I need answers." Tears of desperation flowed down her cheeks. "Kel, could you call him? Find out what really happened… for me? Please?"

Kellie let out a long sigh. "Jen-naaa."

"Plea-e-ease," she begged.

"I have work later. Gosh, I dread going in. The *Fashion Niche* is swamped with holiday returns."

"C'mon, Kel."

"Fine," Kellie sighed, "but it'll be late — and I mean late."

"Thanks," Jenna sniffled. "Love you, girlfriend."

"Yeah, yeah," Kellie said before hanging up.

Jenna paced her bedroom, thinking foolishly how she could have saved her relationship with Tommy. *If only I had lost my virginity to him in California, we'd still be together. Maybe if I call him back, we can work things out. I'd promise him a romantic evening on spring break. Besides, I owe it to him for rejecting him that afternoon in California. All he wanted was to show me how much he loved me, and I pushed him away.*

She dropped to the floor and pulled her knees to her chest. The pain of their breakup dug into her soul and tore at her dreams of forever. She cried hopeless, bitter tears.

It was late afternoon. Jenna lay in bed, no longer asleep but unmoving. The demise of her relationship with Tommy probed and poked at her, keeping sleep at arm's length.

An unexpected knock at her door startled her.

"What?" Jenna answered.

The door opened slowly, and her mother peeked in.

"You're not still sleeping, are you? Supper's waiting."

"I'm not hungry."

"Oh? Are you feeling okay?"

"I'm fine."

"Your father and I haven't seen you all day. At least join us at the table."

Jenna clicked her tongue against her teeth. "Fine. I'll be there in a little bit."

After the door closed, Jenna kicked off the covers and quickly freshened up. The aroma of dinner led her down the hall into the kitchen — grilled lamb, mixed greens, and salad. It wasn't one of her favorite dishes, but even homemade Italian meatballs couldn't comfort her broken heart.

She sat at the opposite end of the table and greeted her parents with a flat smile. Thankfully, they were too engrossed in their meals to notice her misery.

She rested her chin in her hand and watched her mother take small, careful bites, savoring each forkful. Mom was always mindful not to overeat. Dad, on the other hand, held his knife tightly in his left hand and his fork in the other, shoveling each mouthful. He loved his food — and appreciated Mom's cooking even more since his hospital stay.

Dad peered up from his plate, his eyes sharpening on her.

"Aren't you going to eat?"

"I'm not hungry."

"This is good food. Don't let it go to waste."

"More leftovers for you," she mumbled, avoiding eye contact. But she felt his gaze studying her.

"You been crying?" he asked.

"I'm fine."

"Your eyes are bloodshot. What's the matter?"

Jenna shielded her face with her hands. "Nothing."

Mom placed her fork down. "Jenna, is there something you need to tell us?"

Jenna shook her head, but her parents kept their gaze fixed on her, waiting until the silence crushed her façade.

"Fine, fine," she said, waving her hands in surrender. She tried to keep her expression neutral, but her voice gave way. "Tommy broke up with me last night."

Mom's jaw dropped.

A strange, sober expression fell over Dad's face.

"I never liked that boy," he said in a firm, honest voice.

Jenna rolled her eyes. "Please, I don't need your lecture."

"*Amore*, he wasn't right for you."

His disapproval made her feel like a little girl again.

"Daddy, if I left it up to you, no one would be right for me," she shouted.

He nodded. "You got that right."

Jenna dropped her head into her palm. "Never mind." She lifted her head and threw out her hands. "Four years… we were together for four years!"

"That was high school, *Amore*. His needs have changed."

Jenna couldn't stand to look at her father. The truth hurt too much. Frustrated, she pounded her fist on the table.

"Forget it, Daddy! You don't understand."

"Jenna," her mother said calmly, "he—"

"No, Mom!" she yelled, tossing her napkin onto the table.

Jenna stood abruptly and left before the tears flowed. She slammed her bedroom door and collapsed on her bed like a flimsy tent in a windstorm. Great sobs wrenched her body. Part of her wanted to confront Tommy, but another part wanted to shut him out for good.

At three-thirty in the morning, Jenna sat on the floor near her closet, browsing her yearbooks while love ballads from her favorite hairbands played softly in the background. She reached inside her closet and pulled out a wooden box. After unlatching the clasp, she sifted through memories of every moment she'd spent with Tommy. Concert ticket stubs, postcards, and even one of his guitar picks. It was personalized with their names and etched with the message; *I pick you.*

She held the red textured pick in her hand and smiled, thinking about how much she missed hearing him play. *I'd still pick you, Tommy.*

She reached deeper into the box and pulled out a photo from their first date. They had gone ice skating at the community rink down the road. Neither of them knew how to skate. She remembered holding his hand so tightly she nearly crushed it, and how they struggled to make it around the rink once while lone skaters raced past like it was a competition. Confident skaters made sweeping turns and twirls look effortless. And then there were the boisterous preteens who had no regard for anyone. It only took one to jostle her off balance. She remembered falling hard on the cold ice — taking Tommy down with her. After that incident, they vowed never to skate again.

Jenna studied the photo of them posing on the ice. The memory was so vivid it felt like yesterday. She shook her head. *I'd try again with you, Tommy.*

She tossed all her memorabilia back into the box and shoved it into the closet. Reminiscing only taunted her with thoughts of what might have been.

Just then, the phone rang. Quickly, she scrambled to answer before it could wake her parents.

"Hello?" she whispered.

"Hey, it's me," Kellie said.

Jenna's gut clenched with an inkling of depressing news. "So? Did you talk to him?"

"Yeah, briefly," Kellie said.

"And?"

"He needs his space."

"What? We live twenty-eight hundred miles away. How much more space does he need?"

"He says he's not ready to get married, and he needs to focus on his music right now."

"What?" Jenna's voice lifted several octaves. "But he's the one who said—"

"Let him be, Jenna."

"I can't! He doesn't make any sense."

"I know, sweetie."

"Did you ask him if there was someone else?"

"He said no, and that you were a fool to be jealous."

"Oh, puh-leeze! How could I not be jealous after seeing those girls ogling over him?" Jenna shook her finger. "I know what happened. He dumped me because I didn't sleep with him."

"What? That's ridiculous," Kellie said.

"No, he's a guy. That's what all guys want." Jenna drew in a quivering breath. "I didn't love him enough."

"Jen-naaa! That's not true."

"I have to go, Kellie," she said, hanging up.

Before turning out the light, Jenna eyed the prom picture on her nightstand. She stared at it, cherishing that beautiful evening. She remembered how Tommy embraced her so affectionately in that pose. They were so much in love, and it showed. Their friends had always said they were soulmates.

Tears came to her eyes, magnifying and distorting the photo into a hazy blur. She held the frame to her heart and wept until she fell asleep.

It was early afternoon when Jenna returned home from church, her heart enlightened and hopeful. She felt confident she could salvage her relationship with Tommy — but with caution, she promised herself she'd keep an open mind.

Missing him and needing to hear his voice, she sat on the edge of her bed and clutched the phone. *I don't care what Kellie said. I'm calling him.*

The phone rang six times before someone picked up.

"Hello?" Scott answered.

"Is Tommy there?"

There was an uncomfortable silence. "Uh, hang on," he said.

"Thanks."

Commotion sounded in the background before Tommy answered. "Hey, what's up?"

"Tommy, can we talk?"

"I only have a few minutes."

"Oh, um…" She wanted to tell him she missed him but feared his response. "Are you heading out?"

Tommy's voice brightened. "We're playing tonight. And we're doing New Year's Eve, too."

"That's awesome, Tommy!"

"Yeah. We're psyched. Oh, and I wrote a new song."

"That's cool. What's it called?"

Passion sparked Tommy's voice. "'Best Thing Ever.'"

"We were," she said. A sense of strength rose in her. "We *were* the best thing ever. Oh, Tommy, I miss you."

"Jenna, don't—" The flame in his tone smoldered.

"What, Tommy — what did I do? I love you."

"Look, I have to go," he said.

"Tommy, don't give up on us!"

"Bye, Jenna."

There was a click — then the infamous dial tone.

Jenna's body trembled, and a pit of hopelessness opened in her stomach. Hot tears pricked her eyes as reality set in.

*It's over. It's really over.*

Right away, Jenna called Kellie.

"Hello?" Kellie answered.

"I messed up."

"What'd you do?"

"I called Tommy like you said not to."

"Oh, Jenna…"

"We were talking. He said he wrote a new song, '*Best Thing Ever.*' I told him we were, and that's when everything came undone."

"You didn't," Kellie said.

"Didn't what?"

"The lyrics… it goes something like *the best thing ever was letting you go,*" Kellie said.

"What? You heard it?"

"Well, no, but I heard about it."

"How? Tommy told you?"

There was a brief silence.

"C'mon, Kellie! How do you know the song?"

"Uh," Kellie stuttered, "I, um, was getting my nails done, and Tina said—"

"Tina? How does she know?"

"Her boyfriend is friends with—"

"Oh, God!" Ignorance hit Jenna in the chest, taking her breath away. "How could I be so stupid to misinterpret that stupid song?"

"Hey, don't beat yourself up over it," Kellie said.

Jenna's vision wavered from unshed tears.

"It's really over then. My dream… gone."

"No, Jenna. Not your dream — just Tom."

Overwhelmed with sadness, Jenna wanted to slash a hole in her world and escape. "I gotta go."

"No, wait!" Kellie said. "I'm worried about you."

"I'm fine. I just need to be alone right now."

"Okay but call me if you need to talk."

"Sure," Jenna uttered and hung up.

A hot wave of shame washed over her. *Tina knew everything.* How could I be so blind?

The heartache swelling inside her was crippling, but she knew she had to move on. She stood slowly and staggered toward her closet.

She pulled open the bi-fold door and dug through the hangers until she found Tommy's black leather fringed jacket. She remembered the first time she'd ever seen him — wearing that jacket, wearing it well. His scent, his aura, his bad-boy persona had hooked her instantly.

She slipped the jacket on and stood before her full-length mirror. It hung huge on her, swallowing her frame, but it made her feel warm and safe. That was what she had loved about him, too. He made her feel secure. Confident. Wanted.

She closed her eyes. Every part of her body screamed for him — to hold her, to tell her he loved her still. But deep inside, she knew she had to let him go.

Realizing now there was no changing the inevitable, she took off his jacket. Then she removed the chain that held his class ring, along with the locket he had given her for Christmas.

Jenna drove around the block to Tommy's parents' house. She pulled into the driveway behind their hunter-green Jeep and shut off her headlights. She looked up at the gray, dormered Cape Cod with black shutters. It stood high and mighty on the hill, reminding her of Tommy's current attitude. Disgusted, she shook her head. Whatever his problem was, it didn't matter anymore.

She rang the doorbell and gave the side door a knock. Their keeshond, Mika, barked and sniffed at the door. While she waited, she recalled the last time she'd been there — the night before Tommy left for college, the night he gave her his ring and the promise of forever. She blinked back the moisture in her eyes.

*You broke our forever.*

The click of the lock and jiggle of the doorknob snapped her out of the past. The door opened, and Tommy's mother appeared wearing her teal bathrobe.

"Hi, Jenna," Mrs. Pruitt said.

Caught off guard by her loungewear, Jenna apologized. "So sorry if I woke you, Mrs. Pruitt."

"No, no, dear, I was watching a movie. Please, come in."

"Thanks, but no," Jenna said. She handed over Tommy's leather jacket and a small box holding his class ring and the locket he'd given her for Christmas. "These are Tommy's. We broke up."

A sincere frown slipped across Mrs. Pruitt's face.

"Oh, I'm so sorry, Jenna. Gee, I spoke to Tom yesterday and he never mentioned a thing." She shrugged. "Well, you know, parents are always the last to know."

Jenna steadied her composure. "I guess. Well… please let him know it's here."

"I will. Thanks for dropping it off," Mrs. Pruitt said. "And Jenna, don't be a stranger."

"I won't, Mrs. Pruitt."

## Chapter 22

It was New Year's Eve. The late afternoon sunlight streamed through a gap in the vertical blinds, warming Jenna's left side as she sat at the kitchen table stirring her bowl of oatmeal. Although her stomach rumbled, she had no appetite.

She heard the front door open and close with a thud. Immediately following came the crinkling sound of brown paper bags marching up the stairs. Mom entered the kitchen carrying an armful of groceries, setting them down on the counter. As she unpacked them, she rambled about how crowded the store was and how long the checkout lines stretched.

Jenna shot her mother a blank look as she watched her place several store-packaged platters on the counter. "What's all that?"

Mom looked at her like she'd sprouted another head. "For the party tonight..."

"What party?"

"It's New Year's Eve!" Mom said.

"So?"

"Your father, being incredibly grateful for his health, wants to celebrate."

"With whom? No one is dumb enough to stay out all night with all the drunks on the road."

"The Valentes, of course. They only live a block away."

"Are you kidding me?" Jenna ran a perturbed hand through her unkempt hair. "Well, I'm not staying up all night."

"Why not?" Mom asked. "You always do."

Jenna pushed her chair back and stood. "Because I was supposed to be in California still, that's why!" she shouted.

Jenna slammed the door to her room and blasted the stereo with sappy love songs. She sat on the edge of her bed and folded her arms across her chest. She couldn't believe it. Her whole life was unraveling around her, and her parents thought it was fitting to celebrate New Year's Eve. Unreal.

She reached for her stereo and popped in a homemade cassette tape with Tommy's song, *Holding Forever*. The memory of him singing that song to her on stage drifted through her thoughts, and an all-too-familiar tenderness swept through her body.

*What am I doing?*

She pressed the pause button. The music stopped, and the room went dead silent except for her pounding heart.

*I'm so done.*

She yanked the tape out of the player and hurled it across the room. It hit the wall with a sharp crack and fell to the floor, the plastic case splitting open like a broken promise.

As the night grew old, Jenna sheltered in her room, refusing to let the distant conversation and laughter from the living room draw her out of grieving. She was a train wreck and didn't want anyone to see her red, soaking-wet face.

Lost in sorrow, she didn't hear the subtle tap on her door.

"Are you alive in there?" Luke asked, voice soft but teasing.

"What do you want?" Jenna grumbled.

The door opened slowly. Luke poked his head inside.

"You gonna hide in here all night?"

Jenna sniffled. "Yeah, why not?"

"The ball drops in thirty minutes."

"Who cares? It's just another depressing year."

"Why is that?"

Jenna tossed him an annoyed look. "You don't know?"

"Know what?"

"My dad didn't tell you? I'm surprised he wasn't gloating."

"Tell me what?"

Her temper exploded at his ignorance.

"Do I need a billboard sign? Tommy dumped me!"

Luke dropped his gaze to the floor. "Sorry. And no, your father didn't tell me."

"Well, that's a shocker," she grumbled.

"What happened?"

"He left me dying of thirst in the middle of the ocean."

"Alrighty then." Luke pulled out the desk chair and sat down, steady as ever. "Talk to me."

"No!" she shouted.

"You know," Luke said gently, "life's experiences shape a person."

Jenna tossed her wrist. "Oh, what do you know? I'm done with you and your sermons."

Luke sighed. "Jenna, it wasn't meant to be."

She lashed out again. "You don't even know him."

"No… I don't. All's I'm saying is it makes no sense to chase after something already gone."

Jenna dropped her head into her palm. "Just go away, okay?"

"Golly, I feel as welcome as a skunk at a lawn party." He stood and walked toward the door, then paused. "You may not believe this now, but there's a big blue sky behind these dark storm clouds."

Jenna flipped her wrist. "Who cares!"

"Darlin', trust me. It's all for the good."

## Chapter 23

It was the first day back to school after winter break. Jenna's boots struck a frantic rhythm against the salty, wet asphalt, the chilling wind whipping sleet into her face as she rushed toward the humanities building. Her fingers stung from the cold, and her breath puffed out in uneven bursts. *Great start to the semester, Jenna.*

The automatic doors swooshed open, blasting her with a wave of heat from the ceiling vent—so sudden it felt like someone aimed a blow dryer at her. Feeling like a drowned rat, she scraped her damp, tangled hair into a ponytail and dug through her wet backpack for her schedule.

*Please be here…* Her fingers brushed the crumpled paper. *Yes.*

She scanned it quickly. *Art History, Lecture Hall.* She checked the signage in the lobby. *Short walk. Good.*

She hurried down Corridor A, picking up speed even though she knew it wouldn't erase the forty minutes she was already late. Her stomach tightened anyway, as if she could outrun the clock.

She slipped into the lecture hall like a thief, easing the door shut behind her. The room hummed with the professor's voice. Jenna dropped into a seat in the last row, trying to make herself invisible.

The professor stood at the lectern, pointer tapping the screen as he explained an upcoming project. Architectural concepts. Symbolism. Something she'd missed entirely. He answered a few questions, then glanced at the clock.

"I'm out of time," he said, then added, "Remember, people, punctuality is expected and needed." His gaze swept the room—and landed squarely on Jenna.

Heat crawled up her neck. *Perfect. Public humiliation before lunch.*

"Class dismissed."

Textbooks slammed shut. Backpacks zipped. Students poured out in a wave of chatter. Jenna stayed seated, hoping to catch him and apologize, but he disappeared with the crowd before she could stand.

*Great. Just great.*

She clicked her pen and squinted at the whiteboard, copying notes she didn't understand, trying to pretend she hadn't already fallen behind.

"Hey, Jenna," a voice echoed across the empty hall.

She looked up. Adam was climbing the stairs toward her, his backpack slung casually over one shoulder.

"Adam? You're taking this class?" she asked.

He nodded. "What'd you do—oversleep?"

"No. Car trouble again." Her voice came out flatter than she intended.

"Oh. That sucks." He dropped his backpack beside her row. "Say, how was Cali? How's Tom?"

Moisture pricked her eyes. She blinked hard. "We broke up."

"No-o-o! What happened?"

She shook her head. "How much time do you have?"

"I got all the time in the world for you," he said, tugging his sleeve back to check his watch. "I'm on break now."

"Me too." She packed her things quickly, wanting to escape the empty room and the sting of the professor's glare. "Let's get lunch, and you can fill me in on this class."

"I'll do better than that," he said. "We can partner for the upcoming project."

Relief loosened her shoulders. "Okay, cool."

The weeks passed, and the new semester settled into its rhythm. Jenna poured one hundred percent of herself into school—lectures, projects, late-night study sessions. Her hard work paid off. Grades climbed. Professors praised her. Even her classmates noticed her talent. Somewhere along the way, she found her niche in art design, a place where her creativity finally felt seen.

But success didn't mend everything.

She had hoped her new attitude toward school would stitch up the tear Tommy left behind, but misery kept seeping through the seams. His rejection had carved a deeper hole than she expected—one her achievements couldn't fill. Why couldn't she banish thoughts of him as easily as he had banished her?

That question lingered as she sat in her bedroom listening to the March wind howl through the frozen trees. The draft slipping through the windowpane chilled her arms and made the room feel too big, too empty. Thoughts of what could've been pressed in on her, heavy and relentless.

*Enough already.* She didn't want to face every day with pain, sadness, and self-pity. But she didn't know how to move forward either.

Her bedroom door creaked open, and her mother stepped inside holding a brown paper shopping bag by its handles.

"I hope I'm not disturbing you," she said.

Jenna closed her textbook and pushed her desk chair in. "No. I was just getting ready for bed."

"I have a sewing project for you," Mom said.

"Oh? What is it?"

"Curtains."

"For what? I just made you living room curtains."

"Yes, but Mrs. Valente fell in love with them and would like you to sew her a set—same style."

Jenna hesitated. "I don't know… I'm working on a huge school project."

"Oh, no rush. Angela said she'd pay you for your work."

"That's not necessary."

"Course it is." Mom reached into the bag and pulled out a folded sheet of paper. "These are the window dimensions. And here's the fabric—it's a rustic cabin-like pattern. Nice, isn't it?"

"Yeah, I guess," Jenna murmured, her gaze drifting toward her bridal creations still sitting untouched on the sewing table.

Mom followed her eyes. "Jenna, you okay?"

She shrugged. "What do I do with all this wedding stuff now that I'm not getting married?"

Mom shook her head gently. "Save it for when you find real true love."

Jenna scowled. "What do you mean real true love? Tommy was my true love."

"No. He was your first taste of love, but not your last."

"Why not my last? We were perfect together."

Mom shrugged. "Someday, you'll know the reason why."

"No! I'll never understand," Jenna grumbled.

Mom reached for the doorknob, pausing before she left. "Jenna, you need to let go."

"Yeah, right," Jenna muttered, turning off the light.

She climbed into bed and tucked herself under the heavy blankets, but sleep wouldn't come. Her mother's words echoed in her mind.

*Jenna, you need to let go.*

"I'm trying," she whispered into the dark. "I'm lonely without him."

She slid out from beneath the covers and padded to the window. The sky outside was clear and black, scattered with thousands of twinkling stars—quiet reminders that she wasn't as alone as she felt. A shooting star streaked across the night sky, and like a child, she made a wish.

*"Please, Lord… lead me to true love."*

The next afternoon, Jenna pulled open the glass door to the school cafeteria. The bell jingled overhead, and the greasy aroma of fries and burgers wrapped around her like a warm, guilty hug. She turned toward the serving lines and immediately cowered at the cluster of noisy students crowding the counters.

*Bad timing.* She'd never get her food before her next class.

She jumped into the shortest of the four lines and waited, shifting her weight from foot to foot. Her eyes scanned the menu for something healthy. Her bathroom scale insisted on a salad and water, but her empty stomach begged for grilled cheese and a fountain soda.

*What will it be, Jenna?*

The server at the register stared at her, waiting. The customer behind her shifted, growing quiet in that irritated way people do when they're losing patience. Jenna caved.

"Grilled cheese and a soda," she said, handing over her money. "What the hey, you only live once."

Tray in hand, she scanned the packed cafeteria for an open booth. She spotted Kellie sitting alone at a window table. Jenna waved, then weaved through the crowd, careful not to crash into anyone or spill her drink.

"Hey, bestie," Kellie said. "I saved you a seat."

"Thanks," Jenna said, brushing crumbs off the chair before sitting.

"I lucked out. English class let out early today," Kellie said.

Jenna snitched one of Kellie's fries. "Whoa, these are salty."

"I know. I've been drowning them in ketchup," Kellie said, ripping open another packet.

Between bites of her grilled cheese, Jenna rambled about her art history project with Adam.

"You should see our model. It's really cool!"

But Kellie's usual bright smile faded, replaced by a distant, unfocused stare.

"Kellie?" Jenna leaned forward. "Earth to Kellie!" She waved her hand in front of her face.

"Huh?" Kellie blinked.

"You were a million miles away. What's wrong?"

Kellie moistened her dry lips. "It's Ryan. We've been dating two months now, and…"

"And he's really into you," Jenna said.

"I know." Kellie dropped her lashes. "That's the problem. I'm not really into him."

"Maybe you need more time to get to know him?"

"I don't think so." Kellie shook her head. "I'm not feeling it. There's no spark like you and Tom had."

"Yeah, *had*." Jenna lowered her eyes, wishing the fire still burned.

"I'm sorry, Jenna. It was insensitive of me to compare."

"Forget it. It's all for the good."

Suddenly Kellie's expression brightened, as if the conversation had never happened.

"What're you smirking at?" Jenna asked.

Kellie's eyes flicked past her, motioning her to turn around. Before Jenna could, two firm hands landed on her shoulders. Goosebumps pricked her skin. She didn't need to look to know who it was.

"Gotcha!" Adam said.

A mischievous twinkle lit his hazel eyes.

"Hey, you!" Jenna said, reaching for his hand.

"I, uh…" Adam stuttered. "I just wanted to know if we're still on for tonight?"

"Yeah. Your house at six, right?"

"Yeah, great. Okay, cool!" He gave her a flirtatious wink before walking off.

Kellie gasped. "You two? On a date?"

"No-o-o! We have another project to do for Business Management," Jenna said.

Kellie stared, mouth open. "Oh, please. Did you see the way he looked at you?"

"What?" Jenna flipped her wrist dismissively. "We're just friends."

"The heck you two are. Now I know why you switched your major to art design."

"No! It's because being creative is my thing."

Kellie shook her head. "I don't buy it."

Heat crept up Jenna's cheeks. She couldn't help the tingle of excitement fluttering inside her just thinking about Adam.

Kellie pointed. "Look at you! You're beet red."

Jenna laughed. "No, I'm not!"

"C'mon, Jenna. Admit it—you like him."

"Stop! I told you before, I'm not into him."

"You obviously didn't tell him that," Kellie said, tossing her napkin onto her plate.

Jenna grabbed her tray and stood. "Adam's a nice guy with a great personality, but I'm not ready to share my heart with anyone anytime soon."

That evening, Jenna pulled into the driveway at Adam's house. The last time she'd been there, snow had blanketed the ground and the skeleton trees creaked in the blistery wind. Now spring had sprung. Trees arched their heavy green canopies over the property, and blooming flowers splashed color across the garden beds bordering his beige bungalow.

The pungent smell of freshly mowed grass itched her nose as she walked along the sidewalk toward the front door. She rang the bell, and her stomach coiled into a knot.

*Why did Kellie have to insinuate that Adam liked me more than a friend?*

The door opened, and Jenna jumped. The mere sight of Adam made her heart pound against her ribs. *Why?* He was just Adam — same jeans, same concert T-shirt, same easy smile.

He welcomed her inside with that captivating grin. As she stepped into the foyer, the clean scent of his recent shower wrapped around her, sending her pulse racing again. She followed him into the kitchen, her gaze drifting over his backside and down to his bare feet padding across the tile.

She sat in her usual seat near the slider door, but this time Adam sat beside her instead of across from her. The shift felt small, but her heartbeat didn't agree. Determined to keep things normal, Jenna dove straight into their assignment — creating a business plan.

She clapped her hands together. "So, what type of business are we going to start?"

"How 'bout an art gallery?" Adam said.

"I was thinking a catering business, but okay, we can do an art gallery," Jenna replied, keeping her tone light.

"Cool!" Adam rubbed his hands together. "It needs to be big, have lots of lighting, an area for framing art pieces, a workroom, and—"

"Whoa, dude, slow down!" Jenna picked up the syllabus. "It says we're starting off with little finances, which means small and simple."

"C'mon, Jenna. When you start a business, you have to take risks. We need huge, well-lit displays to attract elite clientele."

Jenna yawned. "Listen. If we want a good grade, we have to impress our professor with our plan. And just like genuine business partners, we have to compromise to be successful."

"Right." Adam nodded.

"Good," Jenna said, closing her notebook. "I should go."

Adam reached for her hand. "Wait! It's early yet, and it's nice outside for once. Wanna take a walk to the park?"

"Sure," Jenna agreed. "We can both use some fresh air."

Gravel crackled under their feet as they walked the trail along Timber Creek. The last splotches of sunlight flickered through the dense tangle of oak, elm, and pine trees. Fresh wildflowers scented the air. It was the kind of peaceful evening meant for a friendly stroll; a place to breathe, to talk about the day, maybe even dream a little about tomorrow.

"I'm thinking about going to an art school in New York City in the fall," Adam said.

"You are?" A déjà vu sensation washed over her. "But I thought you were going to finish two years here and then transfer?"

"Well, my dad suggested it to me last night. You see, he landed the job he was hoping for and gave me the go-ahead like we originally planned."

"Oh," Jenna said, dropping her gaze to the ground. That stranded, left-behind feeling crept back in, tightening her chest. *He'll be leaving just like Tommy did.*

"Hey," Adam said, stopping her gently. "But I don't have to."

Jenna reached out and traced the angle of his face with her fingertips. "No, no. You have to do what's right for you."

She started walking again and spotted a brood of ducklings with their momma at the entrance of a metal footbridge. "Oh, how cute! Wish I had bread to feed them."

She hurried forward, but the ducks waddled down the bank into the water before she reached them. When Adam caught up, they crossed the bridge together.

"It's beautiful here," Jenna said, watching the ducks swim away. "I used to ride my bike through here all the time."

"What happened?" Adam asked.

"I got my driver's license."

"Oh," he said with a small laugh.

On the other side of the footbridge, they followed a narrow path that cut away from the main trail. They ducked under low-hanging branches and stepped through fragrant long grass until they reached the creek bank.

Jenna sat on a rock near the water's edge, watching small fish flash beneath the surface. The rippling water whispered over reeds and twigs. Adam skipped stones along the creek, each one hopping lightly before sinking.

Jenna picked up a pebble and tossed it in, but it dropped with a dull plop. "How do you do that?"

"Watch," Adam said. He picked up another stone, stood sideways, and flicked it like a Frisbee. It skipped several times before sinking. "See? Like that."

"You make it look so easy."

"It is — but you need a flat, smooth stone."

"Okay, fine. I'll find one."

She leaped to her feet in search of the perfect stone. But as she stepped from one rock to another, her ankle boot slipped on some spongy moss.

"Oh my!" she yelped, arms flailing.

Adam grabbed her waist and locked her in a tight embrace. "I got you."

His warm touch sent her senses spinning.

"You almost went for a swim," he said, studying her closely.

"Almost," she murmured, noticing the softness in his gaze.

He leaned in, his face drifting closer. His lips brushed hers in a gentle, searching kiss — warm, hopeful, full of feeling. For a moment, her heart fluttered in response. But the ache inside her rose too quickly, too sharply.

She pulled back, breath catching. "I'm so sorry, Adam. I really like you… but I can't do this."

Adam stepped away, retreating toward the creek. "It's okay."

"I am really sorry."

"So am I." He tossed a pebble into the water. "Why'd I think I could replace Tom?"

A pang of remorse shot through her. "No, no, Adam. It's not about Tommy. I just need more time to find myself again. I hope you can understand."

"Yeah. Of course," he said quietly.

Silence settled between them, broken only by a cricket clicking its lonely song. Jenna glanced at the tiny orange sun resting on the horizon. It looked distant, indifferent, sinking lower into the western sky. As darkness crept in, the awkwardness between them softened.

Jenna rose to her feet. "C'mon. We best head back before a bear finds us on his menu."

Later at home, Jenna avoided her parents and retreated straight to her room. She shut the door harder than she meant to, tossed her keys onto the desk, and dropped her backpack to the floor. She flopped onto her bed and stared at the ceiling, disgust twisting in her stomach.

*I blew it.*

Kellie was right. Adam liked her all along, and she'd rejected him — just like Tommy had rejected her.

*Why? What's wrong with me?*

Heat flushed her cheeks as the memory replayed. Ashamed of her behavior, she let out a humorless laugh.

*No way am I telling Kellie about this... EVER.*

# Chapter 24

After two painful hours trying to balance debits and credits in accounting class, a quaking headache gnawed at Jenna's brain. She staggered her way to the library where Professor Wiley was holding Business Management class.

As she entered the room, he directed her toward her project partner. She nodded, then made eye contact with Adam. She greeted him with a smile, acting as if nothing had happened between them, but the grin twisting his lips didn't come close to the warm, easy smiles he used to give her.

*Just act natural.* She straightened her posture and hauled her aching head to his table.

"Hey," she said, sitting down across from him. She rubbed her temples. "Accounting class is making me crazy."

Adam stood and handed her a piece of paper.

"Here. This should help then. It's my half of the business plan."

"Wait—you're bailing?"

"I can't stay for class."

"Why? Is everything okay?"

"Yeah. See ya."

Jenna pivoted in her chair and watched Adam race out of the library, his bag slung over his shoulder. His abrupt departure only added to the conflicting emotions running wild through her already throbbing head.

Fortunately for Jenna, her afternoon English class was cancelled. She went home to sleep off her stress headache, but her nap ended all too quickly when the neighbor's Chihuahua yapped nonstop at the mail carrier. When he finally quieted, the Yorkie two doors down picked up the chorus.

"Ugh." Jenna sat up in bed. "I guess I can get the mail now," she muttered.

She shut her bedroom door and moseyed down the steps to the front entry. She opened the door just enough to reach into the mailbox and pull out a rubber-banded bundle of envelopes.

Step by step, she climbed the stairs again, shuffling through the stack and weeding out the junk mail. She stopped in the kitchen doorway where Mom was preparing dinner.

"Mail came," she mumbled.

"Oh? Anything good?" Mom asked.

"Nope."

Jenna was about to hand over the pile when she spotted a card addressed to her. A burst of excitement rippled through her — she rarely got anything worth opening.

"Wait," she said, tearing into the envelope.

Inside was an invitation featuring a momma bear in a rocking chair, her paws resting on her pregnant belly. A stack of alphabet blocks spelled out *we can bearly wait.*

Jenna held up the card. "Aww. It's for Holly's shower."

Mom smiled. "Anthony told me her mother mailed them. Now remember, it's a surprise."

"I know." Jenna tapped her chin. "I wonder what I should get them."

"I know money's tight for you right now, so I can add your name to the family gift. Dad and I are buying the crib."

"No. I want to pick out something special myself."

The thought of becoming an aunt filled her with a gentle warmth, a small joy she desperately needed in the middle of her heartache.

"Think I'll go to the mall after dinner and check out her gift registry," Jenna said, leaving the kitchen with the invitation still in her hand.

Later that evening at the mall, Jenna hopped onto the escalator and rode it down to the ground level toward the baby boutique outlet. As she descended, she watched a massive crowd of headbangers mingling outside the movie theater. Security arrived quickly and moved them along. She couldn't count how many times she and Tommy had been part of that same crowd.

Despite the late hour, families were still out pushing strollers, their trick for getting babies to sleep. Jenna nodded and smiled at them.

*Oh, what are Anthony and Holly getting themselves into?*

She stepped off the escalator and headed toward the baby boutique. As she passed the arcade, a familiar cackle cut through the noise. The raucous sound yanked her back to the nights she used to hang out there with Tommy — standing at his side for hours while he played the same stupid game over and over.

Despite her determination to let Tommy go, her feet turned her toward the arcade's entryway. She peered inside and recognized a few old high school friends. One of them was Brian, a lanky rocker with long, straggly hair who used to jam with Tommy in their garage band.

He made eye contact and waved her over. She shook her head, not wanting to socialize. But before she could leave, he walked toward her with his pointer finger raised, asking her to wait. She nodded, impatient and already regretting stopping.

"Hey, Jenna — haven't seen you around."

She shrugged. "Been busy with school."

"Hun, it's Friday night. Have some fun for once!"

"I'm trying."

"So, where're you headed?"

"Oh, uh…" She pointed toward the baby boutique. "I have to get a gift for my brother and his wife."

"Cool," Brian said. He scanned the mall, then looked back at her. "Where's Tom?"

The question stabbed straight through her.

"We broke up."

Brian's eyes bulged. "What? Get out!" He ran a hand through his dark, disheveled hair. "Why?"

Jenna shrugged and forced a smile. "We needed our space."

Brian looked stunned. "Wow. You two were the last couple I'd ever thought would break up."

Jenna turned sharply toward the noisy mall, fighting to keep her emotions under control. "Hey, listen. I gotta jet, but it was nice seeing you again, Brian."

"Same here," he said.

Jenna hurried off before the tears could spill. *I should've never looked back. The past is too painful.* She wiped away a tear that escaped and stepped into the baby boutique.

*It's time to look forward to what's to come.*

Later at home, Jenna tossed her keys onto her desk and noticed the red flashing light on her answering machine. She pressed the play button and listened.

"Hey girl! What's up?" Kellie chirped. "I drove past your house to see if you wanted to rent a movie or something but didn't see your car. Just making sure you're doing all right. Call me."

Jenna sucked in a shallow breath. *I was all right until I saw Brian at the mall.* She hit speed dial.

"Hey, BFF," Kellie answered. "Where've you been?"

At the sound of Kellie's cheerful voice, misery seeped into Jenna's heart. "I miss Tommy."

"Oh, Jenna…"

"I bumped into Brian at the mall, and he asked where Tommy was. He couldn't believe we broke up."

"Jen-naaa! Tom changed," Kellie reminded her.

Jenna dropped her head, letting the truth settle. She realized she couldn't be genuinely happy living Tommy's lifestyle. "I know. I have to let him go."

"You do," Kellie said gently. "Hey, it may even open the door for the kind of love you've wanted all along."

"Yeah, sure," Jenna said. *If only you knew how I screwed that one up, too.* "Listen, I've got to get some sleep."

"Okay. Later," Kellie said.

Jenna hung up and sat down at her sewing table. She picked up the plaid curtain panel she'd started a few days ago for Mrs. Valente. She ran her fingers over the neat stitches, pleased with how nicely it was coming along. A small spark of motivation flickered inside her.

She turned on her sewing machine. Keeping busy helped her mind drift away from all her boy troubles — and right now, she needed that more than anything.

The next morning, Jenna braced her hands against the shower wall and let the warm water run over her, hoping it would help her wake up. Early mornings were never her forte, especially on weekends, but her fur babies at the kennel needed her.

After she finished, she stepped out of the tub and wrapped a warm jumbo towel around herself, tucking the corner tightly. She peered into the foggy mirror and let out a long, tired breath. Dark smudges of exhaustion lay under her eyes. She really needed to stop wasting so many nights crying into her pillow over Tommy.

"Get over him," she muttered as she combed the tangles from her wet hair.

She opened the bathroom door, and a plume of steam drifted into the hallway. The aroma of freshly perked coffee greeted her. *Why is Daddy up so early on a Saturday when he's still on medical leave?* Curious, she padded down the corridor. The rustling of a newspaper grew louder as she reached the kitchen.

"Daddy, it's six—"

The newspaper dipped, revealing Luke's devilishly handsome face. A welcoming smile curved his lips. "Morning, babe."

"What? I'm not your babe! Where's my father?"

"Downstairs in his office," Luke said.

"And why are you here?"

"I'm driving him to work."

"Why? He's still on leave."

"He has to sign off on a job."

Jenna stiffened her mouth in irritation. "I've got to get to work."

Luke's bold gaze drifted from her face and roamed downward. A mischievous smile tugged at his mouth. "Don't forget to put some clothes on first."

Jenna tightened her towel. Mortified she'd walked in like that; she dropped her head. With an eye roll, she turned in a huff and stalked back toward her room.

"Whatever, Luke."

"Hey now, be nice," he called after her. "And don't let the door hit you where the good Lord split you."

Jenna slammed the front door and marched right past Luke's company truck to her car parked on the street. She got in and gripped the steering wheel.

*Ugh. That Luke.*

She started the engine and waited for the idle to drop before shifting into gear.

An old, ratty, multi-colored pickup turned the corner, crawling along at an oddly slow pace. Jenna stared at the driver, trying to place him, but she didn't recognize the man behind the wheel. The passenger, though—her breath caught. Long, feathered hair. A spitting image of Tommy. For a split second, she almost believed it *was* him.

They made eye contact.

The driver floored the truck, and it roared up the road.

*Who was that?*

She shook her head and pressed the gas lightly to kick down the idle. As she shifted into drive, the car stalled.

"Oh great! Right in front of my house." She slapped the steering wheel. "This dang car gives me more trouble than it's worth." She grumbled under her breath. "And Daddy says there's nothing wrong with it."

When Jenna arrived at the kennel, the dogs were barking more than usual, alerting her that something had changed.

Before clocking in, she stopped at each pen and greeted every pup by name. One by one, they welcomed her with wet licks through the fencing. When she reached the last pen, she found a new German shepherd pup tucked into the back corner. He couldn't have been more than four months old. Nervous. Unsure. Completely out of place.

"Hey, boy," Jenna said, crouching at the door. "What's a beautiful pup like you doing here?"

At the sound of her gentle voice, his floppy ears perked and his tail began wagging.

Jenna slowly opened the door and stepped inside. The shepherd leaped forward, greeting her with eager puppy cries and warm licks.

"Aww, you're adorable," she said, cupping his sweet face.

A door thudded shut in the distance, and approaching footsteps pulled her attention away from the pup. Out of the corner of her eye, she saw George.

"Ah, I see you met Justice," he said.

"Why is he here?"

"Owner surrender."

"But why? He's so peaceful and well-mannered."

"A bitter woman dropped him off this morning. Her ex-boyfriend was deployed to Operation Desert Storm."

Jenna's heart ached. "That's so, so sad. Didn't he have any other family who could've taken him?"

George shook his head. "No."

Jenna lowered her gaze. "That's awful." She looked at Justice. "How could she dump you here?"

Justice leaped forward again, covering her hands with wet kisses. Her heart swelled at his affection. For the first time in days, she felt needed.

She looked up at George. "Don't adopt him out yet. I want him."

"Now hold on a moment. Last I heard, you still live under your parents' roof. I need their permission first."

Jenna stood, determination straightening her spine. "You'll get it. I promise."

After work, Jenna burst through the front door like a bull in a china shop. "Mom! Mom!" she called, tripping her way up the stairs.

Mom stepped into the hallway from the living room, arms folded across her chest. "Shush, Jenna! Your father's sleeping."

"Oh—sorry." Jenna slowed her pace.

"Why all the commotion?" Mom asked.

"There's this puppy at the shelter, and—"

"There's lots of dogs at the kennel," Mom said.

"It's a German shepherd, and I want to adopt him."

Mom shook her head. "No."

"Why?"

"Jenna, we don't have time for a dog."

"But I do."

"You have school, and I'm not home enough during the day between doctor's appointments and running errands for Nonna to care for a dog."

"Mom, I can do this. Please."

"I'm sorry, Jenna, but now's not the time."

Jenna lowered her voice to a frustrated mumble. "When is it ever the right time?"

# Chapter 25

The next morning, after Sunday Mass, Jenna remained seated in her pew. Most of the congregation had already filed out, but she needed more time — time to reflect, to breathe, to figure out where her life was going.

*Nowhere. My life is going nowhere. It has no purpose. I don't know what I'm supposed to do… or who I'm supposed to do it with. I need You, God. Where are You? Please guide me.*

A golden beam of sunlight spilled through the stained-glass window. She glanced up at the risen Lord, His nail-pierced hands extended in a loving, inviting gesture.

Jenna knelt. "I am here, Lord," she whispered. She bowed her head, letting her heart speak. *My world has turned itself upside down. Tommy was my everything, but now someone else took my place. I know I need to move on, Lord… but how?*

Deep in prayer, she jumped when a gentle hand touched her shoulder. She looked up to find Father Stephen standing beside her.

"I'm sorry, Jenna," he whispered. "I didn't mean to startle you."

She nodded and slid back into the pew. "I thought everyone had left."

"Is there something you'd like to talk about?"

She lowered her gaze. "I don't think you can help me."

"Try me," Father Stephen said, sitting beside her.

Jenna stared at the floor. "My boyfriend and I were planning to get married… but instead, he broke up with me."

"I see."

"Without Tommy, I feel so lost and alone. I can't help but wonder what my life is really about."

Father Stephen opened his Bible. "Recall Romans 8:28," he said, flipping through the pages. "'*We know that all things work for good for those who love God, who are called according to His purpose.*'"

Jenna lifted her gaze. His eyes held genuine compassion.

"You see, Jenna," he continued. "God sees the big picture and has a master plan. His plan is always good.

Have confidence that He is guiding you toward your purpose."

"But I thought Tommy was part of that master plan."

Father Stephen shook his head gently. "Not necessarily. But if you're called to marriage, know that God is preparing you for someone special."

"But Tommy *is* that special someone."

Father Stephen placed a comforting hand on her shoulder. "Trust God's goodness, His power, and His will. Be patient, and He will lead you to the young man He has prepared for you."

Jenna nodded. "Thank you, Father."

Monday morning in Business Management, Jenna struggled to keep from yawning while Professor Wiley lectured about the importance of effective communication and leadership skills. She used to find the course interesting, but lately it bored her — maybe because the topic hit a little too close to home. Weaknesses in communication. Weaknesses in leadership. Weaknesses in her own life.

Fifteen minutes before class ended, Professor Wiley handed Jenna and Adam their graded business plan.

He placed a hand on Adam's shoulder. "I see you're going for the jugular."

"Sir?" Adam asked, blank expression and all.

"Remember, Adam — you're new to entrepreneurship. It's unwise to risk everything on your first venture."

Jenna fought hard not to smirk.

Professor Wiley handed her paper back and smiled. "I like that you're cautious, Jenna. Your strategy balances out Adam's aggressive behavior nicely. Fantastic job, folks."

He walked away.

Jenna grinned at Adam. "Not to be a trifle smug or anything, but I told you so."

"Yeah, yeah," he muttered, cheeks flushing. "Still got a B."

Jenna nodded. "You know, we make a talented team."

Adam didn't agree or disagree. He just gathered his books. "Later."

Jenna stood abruptly. "Wait, Adam! Before you go… do you want to hang out Friday night? Maybe watch a movie or something?"

"Sorry. I already have plans."

"Oh. Okay. Maybe another time?" she asked.

"Maybe."

Jenna chewed her lower lip. She hoped everything was okay between them.

She gathered her books and stepped into the hall, content to lose herself in the crowd of chatty students passing between classes. Thankfully, the school day was over — and it was a gorgeous afternoon to walk her fur babies at the shelter.

Sun streamed through the double glass doors, gleaming off the waxed tile floor. As she pushed the door open, she heard her name echo down the stairwell.

She turned to find Kellie barreling down the steps.

"Hey girlfriend, wait up!" Kellie said, breathless. "Wanna grab lunch in the cafeteria? I'm starved."

"Can't. I have work."

Kellie's eyelashes dropped with disappointment. "Oh, bummer. Wanted to catch up. It's been a while."

"I'm sorry," Jenna said, pushing the door open. "Maybe we can get together over spring break."

Kellie brightened. "Absolutely! And we're going out on your birthday. I'll pick you up at one o'clock, so save the date."

"Sounds good. Later, Kel."

It was a beautiful day to walk the dogs at the shelter. A soft breeze tossed strands of hair across Jenna's face and rippled the tall blades of grass along the towpath. Sunlight peeked through the canopy of trees, warming her bare arms. The air smelled of blooming wildflowers and fresh pine needles. Birds chirped, insects buzzed, and a squirrel scrambled up a nearby tree.

Instinctively, Jenna braced herself, expecting her arm to be yanked out of its socket — but Justice simply walked beside her, calm and content.

She praised him. "You're such a good boy."

They continued down the path toward the creek when an old man and a young boy carrying fishing gear approached. The boy pointed at Justice.

"Look, Pop-Pop!" he shrieked. He ran forward. "May I pet him?"

Jenna smiled and nodded. Justice sat politely and welcomed the boy's gentle pats.

"He's cute," the boy said.

The old man smiled and thanked her before they moved on.

Jenna walked on, completely perplexed by Justice's perfect obedience. *How could that woman give you up?* She scratched behind his ears. "Mom and Dad are going to love you."

Back at the kennel, George was moving in and out of the pens with a hose, filling water bowls. He glanced up at Jenna.

"Did you fill out the adoption application yet?"

"No. I haven't had a chance."

"I see," George said. "We've had lots of inquiries about him the past few days."

"Please, George! I'll get it filled out before the weekend."

George lifted an eyebrow but said nothing.

＃ Chapter 26

Spring break finally arrived. A bright shaft of morning sunlight pressed against Jenna's eyelids, pulling her into wakefulness.

*Morning already?* She was still half-anchored in dreamland — standing with Adam in front of their New York City art studio, both of them dressed in wedding attire, sharing their first kiss.

"What a weird dream," she mumbled.

She rolled to her side and squinted at her clock.

"It's nine-thirty already?" she screeched, leaping out of bed. "Why didn't my alarm go off?"

Today was her nineteenth birthday. First came an early morning jog, then dropping off Mrs. Valente's curtains. Later, she would meet Kellie—who would undoubtedly nudge her into finally hooking up with Adam.

But no. Her plans had been ruined by a stupid alarm clock.

Priority now was delivering those curtains to Mrs. Valente.

While her car idled, Jenna studied the handwritten map her father had doodled on a scrap of paper. Okay, I'm going west on County Road 914 for approximately ten miles. Melody Lake Estates will be on the left at the light. She tossed the paper onto the passenger seat. "I got this," she said, shifting into drive.

She traveled that road twenty miles daily for college. A desolate, two-lane country road — mostly straight, with a few twisty bends. The township maintained it well, especially in bad weather, but school was always closed then, so she'd never had to worry.

It was a boring drive. Nothing to see except tall evergreens lining both sides and a couple of forgotten shacks tucked in the woods, waiting for lightning to finish them off. But today was beautiful — bright sun, blue sky, a gentle breeze feathering through the wild grass.

Jenna cracked her window for fresh air and immediately caught a strong whiff of skunk. Up ahead, a vulture stood on the faded yellow line, desperate for a taste of fresh roadkill.

"Gross," she muttered, closing the window.

Finally, she reached the only traffic signal in the middle of nowhere. She stopped at the red light and startled a mother deer and her spotted fawn grazing at the roadside. The fawn scrambled and leaped back into the woods.

While she waited for the light to change, she lowered the radio volume and glanced at the scribbled directions. "Dad said to turn left here on Melody Lake Road." She looked out her driver's side window. "Duh. I'm here."

How had she never noticed the divided entrance with its island of shrubbery and the stone-carved sign reading *Melody Lake Estates*? She'd driven Route 914 hundreds of times.

She flipped on her blinker. *I suppose I never noticed it because the light was always green when I passed through.*

When the arrow turned green, she pulled into the development. A few hundred feet in, she stopped. The first right turn pointed toward the sales office — future clubhouse, pool, playground — but her father had warned her not to go there unless she wanted a pushy salesperson dragging her through model homes.

To her left were skeleton houses and active road construction. According to her father's directions, she needed to follow Melody Lake Road, then turn left onto Wolves Den. The cul-de-sac held three newly built homes: a three-story chalet, a contemporary, and a small ranch.

She checked her directions. "Okay… Daddy didn't say which house, only the number. Which one is seven?"

A number seven posted on a 911 reflector at the contemporary's driveway answered her question. A white contractor's van was parked in the driveway.

Jenna parked in the street. Before heading to the door, she stood beside her car and admired the home. The builders had put extensive detail into the exterior—earthy board-and-batten siding, and a stacked stone foundation her father had likely crafted. It was a gorgeous home, standing stout on a flat acre surrounded by towering evergreens.

She walked along the sidewalk to the front entrance, but before she could ring the bell, the door opened. Mrs. Valente stepped out and hugged her.

"Jenna, honey, so glad to see you. Happy birthday!"

"Thank you," Jenna said, stepping inside.

She bobbed her head in every direction, taking in the interior. Just as impressive as the exterior. Natural wood walls glowing with sunshine, a fieldstone fireplace chimney rising to exposed beams in the vaulted ceiling.

"Wow. This home is breathtaking."

"Yes, I must admit this model is my favorite," Mrs. Valente said. "But I no longer have a need for a home this size."

"Well, I'm sure it'll bring happiness and memories to some new family in no time."

Mrs. Valente clasped her hands and glanced toward the dining room. "Would you like a bottle of water?"

"No, thank you," Jenna said, reaching into her tote. "Here are the curtains."

"Oh yes! I almost forgot why we're here." She took the bag. "I'm so excited. These will complement the rustic vibe perfectly."

"I hope so. You'll have to show me pictures."

"Better yet, why don't you stay while I hang them up?"

"Sure. I have some time."

"Wonderful." Mrs. Valente looked up at the taller windows. "Let me find a stepstool. I know there's one around here somewhere."

"Fine," Jenna said. "I'll start with the lower windows."

While Mrs. Valente searched, Jenna hung a curtain on one of the living room windows. She stepped back, admiring her work.

Suddenly, clunky work boots pounded across the knotty pine floors. Jenna turned… and froze.

Luke stood in the doorway wearing a gray Valente Construction T-shirt, worn blue jeans, and a leather tool belt. He held a folded stepstool. His sudden presence made her heart race.

"Looking good, birthday girl!" he called in his lively southern voice.

"They do," she said. "They match the rustic décor perfectly."

A sinful grin quirked his lips. "I wasn't talking about the curtains."

"What?" Jenna asked, heat rising in her cheeks.

"You look happy. Last time I saw you, you were eating sorrow by the spoonful."

"Well, my mom always told me happiness is a choice. Find it or be the reason for it."

Luke nodded, gaze still fixed on her. "I like that."

Jenna shifted under his stare. "I should get back to hanging these curtains," she said, reaching awkwardly for the stepstool.

"I got it," he said. "Which window is next?"

"Oh. Uh…" Her composure faltered. She glanced toward the dining room, eyeing the lake view through the French doors. "How about we start in there?"

"Sure thing," he said, motioning her forward. "After you."

As she walked into the dining room, she glanced back — and caught him studying her backside. Vulnerability shot through her. She yanked her T-shirt down over her leggings, spun around, and shouted, "Would you please stop it!"

Luke halted just shy of bumping into her.

"What?"

"Stop staring at my butt!"

His face flushed like a fourteen-year-old caught red-handed.

"Sorry, but I was admiring the view."

"If you want a view, go outside," she said, opening the French doors.

"I see that view every day on the job site."

Jenna rolled her eyes and closed the door.

She wandered into the kitchen, admiring the knotty pine cabinets and butcher block countertops. "Great choice for this style home."

"You like it?"

"I do."

A proud smile tipped his mouth. "Cool. I designed it."

Jenna smoothed her hand along the blond wood, then noticed design samples on the floor. One caught her eye — pickled oak cabinets, hunter green counters, brass hardware, black-and-white checkered tile.

She shook her head. "I know green with brass is the hot trend right now, but I'm not digging it."

"You're good at this," Luke said. "We designed that kitchen in the ranch next door. Want to check it out?"

"No, I have to leave soon." She glanced around. "Where'd your mother go? She was supposed to help me."

"She got sidetracked with the painter about stenciling ivy around the doorways."

"Oh." Jenna sighed. "I need to get this done so I can get out of here."

"I'll help you," Luke said, following her back toward the French doors.

Jenna was strangely flattered — and felt a warm affection rising — but she shoved it aside. She was here for business.

She positioned the stool and stepped up. A dizzying current raced through her, fingers trembling as she unfastened the rod. *C'mon, Jenna, focus.* But Luke's nearness made her senses spin. Sweat beaded on her forehead.

*How am I ever going to finish this with him watching me?*

Her lack of confidence made her curt. "Don't you have something better to do?"

"Well, I could be hanging shelves in the garage, but this is much more exciting."

"Yeah, right," she said, glaring down at him. "You better not make me fall."

"Don't worry. I got your back."

"Yeah, I bet you do," she mumbled.

She unlatched the rod and stepped down.

"When you're ready, I'll hang it back up," he said.

"Thank you."

After hanging all the curtains, Jenna stepped back and admired the cozy, fresh look. "I love it."

"You did good, darlin'. Momma's gonna be pleased."

Jenna smiled. "Thanks. And thanks for your help."

"My pleasure," he said.

*Yeah, I'm sure.* Jenna glanced at her watch. "I should go."

"Already?" he asked. "You just got here."

"I know, but I want to get my jog in before the sun gets too strong."

"I'll join you," he said eagerly. "I got a—"

"Sorry, but I'm meeting up with a friend."

The animation drained from his face. "Oh. I was hoping afterwards I could take you to lunch for your birthday."

She heard the disappointment in his voice and bit her lip in remorse. "That's so thoughtful of you, but I can't. I'm sorry." She grabbed her car keys off the hearth. "I have to go."

"Yeah," Luke said, dimming his eyes.

Jenna arrived at the township park feeling a bit guilty for lying about meeting a friend and turning down Luke's lunch invitation, but she really did have afternoon birthday plans with Kellie and Adam.

She jogged along the tree-lined path circling the pond. Branches overhead intertwined to form a giant green umbrella, shading her from the hot noon sun. She'd left her headphones and CDs in the car, choosing instead to listen to nature. Birds sang bright little tunes, and bees buzzed lazily from flower to flower.

About three-quarters of a mile into her run, a group of kids on dirt bikes raced up behind her. She hopped off the pavement into the soft grass to avoid being run over. *Whatever happened to pedestrians having the right of way?*

After the kids passed, she heard a familiar giggle — one that sounded very much like Kellie's.

*I must be hearing things.* She shook it off and continued her run.

But as she rounded a bend, she heard the giggle again, louder this time. She stopped short. *Who is that?* It wasn't the knee-deep fishermen in the pond. It could've been the teens at the basketball court or the little kids at the playground.

Drawn to the peculiar laughter, Jenna veered off the path through the long wild grass toward the pond. When she heard it again, she tucked behind a tall maple tree for a better view.

A chummy couple sat at the pond's edge, tossing rocks into the glistening water. When the slender girl in tight jeans and a crop top stood and flipped her sandy-brown hair off her forehead, Jenna froze.

*Kellie? What's she doing here? She's not the outdoorsy type. And who's she with?*

The dark-haired guy stood and turned his head. Pointy nose. Acne complexion.

Jenna gasped.

*Adam? Huh? What happened to Ryan?*

She watched as they chatted and playfully touched each other's arms. Then Adam braced his hands on

Kellie's waist and caged her in with his stout body. They stared dreamily into each other's eyes. He leaned in — a full-contact, wet, tongued kiss — their bodies molding together like they'd done it a hundred times.

*What? No.* Jenna pressed her hand to her chest, as if that could calm her pounding heart. *When did this happen?*

It was too much, too sudden, too painful.

She hightailed it out of there.

Jenna arrived home and parked her car in the street. She stayed inside with the radio blaring, replaying what had just happened. *How could my best friend do that to me?* She dragged a troubled hand through her hair. *First I lose Tommy, and now my two best friends deceive me. Some birthday this is turning out to be.*

She turned off the ignition and opened her door just as a rumbling pickup truck lumbered around the corner. It was the same ratty truck she'd seen last week, but this time she got a clear look at both occupants.

The driver was a no-good derelict from high school.

And the passenger… was Tommy. His expression dark. Rebellious. Closed off.

*Oh, crap. What's he doing at home?*

When she made eye contact with him, the driver put on his tough-boy face and lit up the tires. The truck smoked all the way up the road, leaving long burn-out marks on the pavement.

Frustrated and annoyed, Jenna shook her fist at the taillights. "I'm done with you!" She slammed her car door. "I'm done with everyone!"

Inside the house, Jenna trudged up the stairs. Her mother poked her head out from the kitchen.

"You're home early, honey — thought you were spending the afternoon with Kellie."

"Change of plans," Jenna said, continuing down the hallway.

"Oh? In that case, do you want me to make you a special birthday dinner?"

"No thanks, Mom. I'm not hungry."

Jenna closed her bedroom door, and a cluster of mylar balloons scudded across the room. She turned toward her desk and noticed a teal envelope with her name written on it. Her eyes moistened, her sour mood softening. She opened the card, and a gift certificate slipped out. She read her parents' kind birthday wishes and later thanked them for their thoughtfulness.

That evening, Jenna lay in bed staring up at the dark ceiling. The only light in the room came from her answering machine — a red blinking dot pulsing like an accusation. New messages. Probably Kellie. She refused to play them.

*I'm through talking to you.*

She rolled to her side, closed her eyes, and listened to her alarm clock tick the seconds away. The quiet pressed in around her.

Then her phone rang, slicing through the silence.

"That's it," she snapped, snatching it up. "Hello?" No reply. "Hello?" she said again, sharper this time.

A couple seconds passed.

Then someone started breathing — slow, heavy, deliberate.

A shiver rippled up her spine.

She slammed the phone down and sat upright against her pillow, knees pulled to her chest. *What creep would do that to me?* Her heart thudded hard in her ears.

*I really need to get a caller ID service.*

# Chapter 27

It was midafternoon the next day when Jenna's shift started at the kennel. Usually, when she pulled into the gravel lot, the dogs greeted her with barking and howling, but oddly, not today. She parked near the main entrance in a spot beside George's shiny new metallic-blue truck. No other cars. No other workers.

*I better not have triple the work because everyone called out.*

Exhausted from another sleepless night, she stifled a yawn and opened her car door. The air smelled of impending rain — heavy, thick, unsettled. She glanced up. Storm clouds churned overhead, darkening the sky. A clap of thunder muttered in the distance.

Apparently, Mother Nature was just as angry as she was.

Jenna hurried inside. Only five lonely dogs greeted her with friendly, desperate cries. On a normal day, twenty-five pups waited eagerly for her. *Where had they all gone? And where was everyone?*

She walked past the empty kennels to the office to clock in. When she opened the door, George sat at his desk, buried in paperwork. He adjusted his glasses on the bridge of his nose and peered over the rim.

"Jenna, what're you doing here?"

"I'm on the schedule."

"Didn't you get my phone call?"

"What? No."

"I left you a message on your machine. You didn't need to come in today."

She stared, dumbfounded. "Oh." She pointed toward the kennels. "Where're all the dogs?"

A satisfied smile lit his face.

"The open house yesterday with the discounted adoption fees… it was a success! Now all we must do is find homes for Rosie, Lady, Daisy, Max, and Toby."

Jenna blinked, baffled.

"Wait! Where's Justice?"

George removed his glasses. His somber expression told her everything she didn't want to hear. "He was adopted two days ago."

Jenna stomped her foot. "No! How could you?"

Suddenly, rain pinged angrily on the tin roof.

"You were supposed to hold him for me!" she shouted.

"Jenna, I gave you two weeks to get the paperwork signed." He stared at the ground. "I'm sorry, but I couldn't deny him a loving home."

Jenna dropped her head. Her beloved dog was gone. Her only desire faded like yesterday's sunshine.

"Oh, and Jenna," George added, "I also mentioned on the machine that I have to temporarily cut your hours."

Jenna nodded and left. Her life was unraveling around her. Could it get any worse?

On her way home, Jenna stopped at a fast-food restaurant. The drive-thru line wrapped around the building, so she parked and dreaded the thought of eating inside alone. *I'll just get it to go.*

She stepped through the double doors. Inside wasn't any less crowded. Kids at a private birthday party squealed as they crawled through the maze of tubes in the play area. The floor shook with every pounce of their knees — and so did Jenna's throbbing head.

*Oh, why did I bother coming inside anyway?*

Her stomach growled at the aroma of sizzling burgers and fries, reminding her why she was there. *Okay, fine,* she told herself and stood in the shortest line. She scanned the menu while the customer ahead customized his order and confused the trainee cashier.

*Of course. Shortest line, slowest line.*

When the stressed cashier finally asked if she was ready, Jenna rubbed the back of her neck. "Number three with a Coke, please."

After receiving her order, she grabbed the bag and darted toward the exit. As she pushed the door open, she heard her name.

"Jenna, wait!"

*Oh no.* She turned to find Kellie, fashionably dressed in a belted mini skirt and blouse, snaking her way through the lines. Jenna dropped her gaze to her frumpy work clothes and worn-out sneakers, then ran a hand through her disheveled hair.

"Hey," she said, forcing a smile.

"OMG! It's been like forever since we talked," Kellie said in her bubbly voice. "And here it is, spring break."

Jenna shrugged carelessly.

"What's wrong?" Kellie asked.

"You blew me off yesterday. On. My. Birthday."

Kellie threw her hand to her mouth. "OMG! I'm so, so sorry, Jenna. We were supposed to go out and I forgot."

"So you forgot *me*, but not Adam... What're you doing, Kel?" Jenna asked, her voice sharpening.

"What am I doing?" Kellie pointed at herself. "Adam and I are—"

"Really? How nice. When were you going to tell me?"

"Jenna, you told Adam you only wanted to be friends, and he respected that."

"No. I told him I needed some time to find myself again before jumping into a new relationship."

"You had your chance, and now it's too late!"

Jenna gasped. "This isn't about Adam," she said, shaking her head. "I turned down a lunch date yesterday waiting around for you!"

"I said I was sorry!"

Jenna shook her head. "Whatever."

♡♡ *Chapter 28*

Jenna hurried down the hallway, her sneakers whispering against the hardwood floor. Six weeks had passed since her birthday disaster, and now finals week had arrived, bringing the college year to a stressful close. The house felt unusually still like even the walls were holding their breath. She tugged her hoodie tighter around her shoulders and stepped into the kitchen, where the faint aroma of leftover coffee lingered.

Outside, the sky had already begun to bruise. Heavy clouds rolled over the mountains, swallowing the morning light. A low rumble vibrated through the air, and Jenna paused at the back door, staring out at the shifting gray horizon.

Storm's brewing, Mom had said.

Jenna swallowed hard. *There's been a storm brewing inside me for weeks.*

The memory of Kellie's betrayal still throbbed like an unhealed wound, even after all this time. Jenna blinked, and another tear threatened, but she forced it back. She wasn't going to cry over it anymore. She wasn't going to cry over anyone.

She stepped back into her room to grab her car keys. On her desk, the red light of the answering machine blinked a steady, demanding pulse. For a moment she considered ignoring it—she didn't have the emotional bandwidth for anyone today—but habit won out. She hit the playback button.

The machine whirred, clicked, and let out a sharp beep before Kellie's voice filled the room.

"Hi Bestie, it's me. Good luck on finals tonight! You'll do great."

Jenna's chest tightened. The message was sweet. Thoughtful. Exactly the kind of thing Kellie would say. And yet it felt hollow, like a balloon with a slow leak.

Jenna's car sat at the end of the driveway, speckled with the first drops of rain. She jogged toward it, her bag thumping against her hip. As she reached for the door handle, a voice called out behind her.

"Jenna!"

She turned. Mom stood on the porch, arms folded, worry etched across her face.

"You sure you're okay?" Mom asked, raising her voice over the rising wind.

"I'm fine!" Jenna called back, though her voice cracked.

Mom didn't look convinced. "Storm's supposed to get bad tonight. Drive slow."

"I will!"

Jenna ducked into the car and shut the door. The interior felt cold, almost unfriendly. She started the engine, gripping the steering wheel as if it were the only stable thing left in her life.

*Focus on school. Focus on graduating early. Focus on anything but people who let you down.*

She backed out of the driveway, the rain beginning to fall in earnest. As she turned onto the main road, lightning split the sky in a jagged white line.

Her heart jumped.

The storm was coming fast.

Hours later, after taking exams in both philosophy and graphic design, Jenna dropped onto the vinyl couch in the vacant student lounge and heaved a huge sigh. Her finals were over. Finally. She could relax now. She was done with school — at least until the summer session began.

She sprawled out, letting her muscles melt into the stiff cushions. Her eyelids drifted shut, and she pictured herself sitting at home on the back deck in the warm sun, listening to the soft hum of cicadas and the rustle of leaves. *Just me, the quiet, and no one expecting anything from me.* It was the break she needed — a chance to rediscover who she was without constantly orbiting around other people's choices.

A sudden crack of thunder exploded overhead.

Her heart jolted violently, thudding against her ribs. She sat upright, breath catching as the wind roared outside, kicking up debris. Within seconds, heavy rain lashed the glass panes and hammered the roof like a thousand angry fists.

*Mom warned me it was going to storm tonight. Of course she was right. She's always right.*

Jenna bit down on her lower lip. Now she'd have to drive home in it. The thought made her stomach twist. *Great. Just what I need — a dangerous commute on top of an emotional meltdown.*

She stood and headed toward the lounge doorway. The lights flickered off. Darkness swallowed the room.

*Oh, perfect. Just perfect. Power outage. Because tonight wasn't stressful enough already.*

Doors slammed somewhere down the hall. Students screamed. A frantic cluster of bodies scrambled through the hallway like panicked chickens, and a few barreled into the lounge, sending Jenna stumbling backward.

"Hey! What gives?" she yelled, steadying herself.

The lights flickered on again, buzzing weakly. Jenna recognized two of the drenched students, Jasmine and Dante from accounting.

Jasmine, plump and vibrant, blurted out in her spirited voice, "It's like a monsoon out there!" She gathered up the hem of her sopping lime green dress and wrung it out onto the floor. "Girl, I am soaked!"

*No kidding.* Jenna's gaze dropped to the puddle forming beneath Jasmine's sandals. *If she's drenched, what chance do I have out there?*

Dante stood there like a drowned rat. The legs of his oversized hip-hop jeans wicked rainwater all the way up to his knees. "Dude, we ran all the way here for nuttin'. Class got cancelled."

"And I was just leaving," Jenna said, gathering up her belongings. *I should've left ten minutes earlier. Why do I always hesitate?*

"Hmm-hmm, girlfriend," Jasmine said, shaking her finger. "Don't go. That big ol' oak tree out front of the dorm fell. It's dangerous out there with all the flooding. Hmm-hmm."

Jasmine waddled across the room and flipped on the TV. A warning banner interrupted the sitcom:

Severe thunderstorm warning in effect until 11:30 p.m. Potential for 70 mph wind gusts, hail greater than two inches, and isolated tornadoes. Cloud-to-ground lightning, heavy downpours, and flash flooding possible.

Jenna's voice shook. "Oh, no, no, no. There's no way I am staying here all night."

*I can't. I won't. I refuse to sit here stewing in my thoughts until midnight.*

"Don't you live on campus?" Jasmine asked.

"No. I have a thirty-minute commute home."

Jasmine smacked her lips. "I'd wait, girl, but that's me."

Jenna stared at the window. The rain had softened to a gentle patter, almost deceptively calm. *It looks safe. Safer, anyway. And I need to get home. I need my space. My quiet. My reset.*

Jenna turned to Jasimine and Dante. "It's not raining hard now. I'm going to scope out the damage, then run with it."

Dante's face was as bleak as the storm outside. "Be safe."

"I will," Jenna said, tightening her grip on her bag.

*I hope.*

In the lobby, Jenna peered out the double glass doors and surveyed the outcome. Sure enough, Jasmine and Dante were right. The huge oak tree that once stood proudly on the front lawn of the dorm building was now uprooted, lying on its side like a fallen giant. The river below had swelled over its banks, flooding sections of the campus grounds. Siding and roofing debris from the guard shack were scattered throughout the parking lot.

A combination of yellow, red, and blue lights flickered against the black sky. Campus security, fire, and police were securing the area, their silhouettes moving briskly through the chaos. They looked tense, alert — ready for whatever came next.

*This is worse than I thought. Way worse.*

Jenna paced the floor inside the lobby, her sneakers squeaking against the tile. She kept glancing at the doors, then at the ceiling, then back at the storm. It was barely raining now, and the winds appeared to have calmed down.

*Could the storm be over? Or is this just the eye? I hate when storms pretend to be done. It feels like they're lying.*

She agonized over her decision, her stomach twisting with indecision, then finally pushed on the door.

The wind ripped it from her hand.

"Oh, crap!" she yelped, stumbling forward.

The smell of rain lingered in the air — earthy, metallic, sharp. It wouldn't be long before the sky let loose again. She could feel it, like pressure building behind her eyes.

*Just find the car. Get home. You can do this.*

As she trekked uphill toward Lot D, the wind whipped her hair across her face, stinging her cheeks and making it even harder to see. The flickering night sky charged her jittery nerves even more.

*I hate this weather. I hate storms. I hate feeling like I'm one wrong step away from disaster.*

Fortunately, Jenna's car was parked under a dimly lit lamppost, and she was able to find the keyhole to unlock the door. Her hands shook as she fumbled with the keys.

As soon as she got in, hail pounded her car — sharp, violent bursts that made her flinch with every strike.

*Seriously? Now hail? What else can this night throw at me?*

She idled in the lot until Mother Nature calmed down, gripping the steering wheel to keep her hands from shaking. When the hail finally tapered off, she backed out of her space.

*Just get home. Please, God, just let me get home.*

Jenna exited the college and was soon driving east on Route 914. There wasn't another soul out on the dark country road. The emptiness pressed against her windows like a warning. She told herself she knew the road well enough to navigate it blindfolded if she had to — *or so she thought* — before the heavy rain began to fall.

She peered miserably through the downpour. Her wipers, on full speed, slapped at the rain but barely made a dent. Water smeared across the glass like someone dragging a wet paintbrush over her vision. The smell of damp upholstery filled the car, mixing with the faint scent of her vanilla air freshener, now oddly nauseating.

With her sight reduced to nothing, she hit her brakes.

*God, I can't see. Please help me see.*

Lightning split across the black sky, and the hair on her forearms prickled. The dashboard lights flickered for half a second, just long enough to make her stomach drop, before steadying again. Seconds later, a roll of thunder shook her car, vibrating through the steering wheel and into her bones.

She cranked up the radio, hoping the music would drown out the storm — or at least distract her from the panic clawing at her chest.

*Ooh, I hate this weather. I hate everything about tonight.*

She gripped the steering wheel tighter as the merciless wind jerked her car in and out of her lane. Her tires hissed against the wet pavement. Her damp jeans clung to her legs, cold and uncomfortable.

*This is miserable, God. Please just get me home.*

Ten miles into her drive, a huge dark shadow barricaded the road ahead.

"Now what?" she grumbled, pulling into the shoulder.

She flipped on her high beams and squinted through thin wisps of fog. A tall, lean fir tree and several powerlines had fallen, blocking the entire road. There was no way around it.

*Great. Perfect. Just what I needed. And of course there's no phone booth. No flares. No cones. No warning. Because why would anything go right tonight?*

Her fingers hovered over the gear shift, trembling. She didn't want to turn around, she didn't want to stay, and she certainly didn't want to admit she was scared.

Her nerves felt as violently uprooted as the fallen tree blocking her path.

As her mind raced, she stared through the fogged-up windshield at the roadblock. What were her choices? Wait it out? Attempt a clumsy K-turn on the narrow road and head back to school? Or just sit here in the dark until the storm decided to be nice?

She threw her hands out wide. "What do I do, God?"

A fork of lightning split the sky directly in front of her, illuminating a gravel road to her right that hopped off into the woods. She had no idea where it led. She didn't even have a roadmap in her glove compartment — just her insurance card and vehicle registration.

*Would the scenic route loop me back to 914? Or dump me in the middle of nowhere? Make up your mind, Jenna.*

The rain slowed to a drizzle, almost like a sign.

*Fine. I'm turning here and hoping for the best.*

She kept her high beams on and turned right onto Turtle Creek Road. Gravel pinged against the undercarriage. Along the winding road, she passed a dilapidated shack that had finally collapsed.

*I knew one strong wind would take that thing down. Guess Mother Nature agreed.*

She continued driving along the narrow gravel road for about a mile before it changed into poorly paved asphalt. The road was an obstacle course — potholes, ruts, dips — each one threatening to yank her car into the ditch. Her shoulders tightened with every swerve.

She flipped back to her low beams. *Gosh, as if the misty fog weren't bad enough. I have no idea where I am. Please let this lead somewhere familiar.*

After another mile downhill, she came to a fork in the road. Her stomach dropped.

*Now what? Seriously?*

Turtle Creek Road continued to the right but was impassable due to serious flooding. Her only choice was to bear left onto Melody Lake Road. It was newly paved and not yet underwater.

Wait. Melody Lake Road…

*I must be at the back entrance to that housing development. So if I follow Melody Lake out, it should take me to the main entrance at the 914 light. Yes. Yes! I know where I'm at.*

Relief washed over her, until she moved her foot from the brake to the gas and her car stalled out.

"No, no, no; not now!"

She shifted into park and started it again. When she shifted into drive, it stalled a second time. The dashboard lights dimmed, then brightened.

"No! Don't do this to me!"

Her trembling fingers turned the key again. The car started. This time she put her left foot on the brake and her right on the gas, then shifted into drive. The car puttered forward.

"Oh, thank you, God!"

She followed Melody Lake Road for about a half mile when her car began stuttering. The engine coughed, sputtered, then lurched. She coasted around a corner onto a side road before it stalled again.

"I give up!" she shouted, throwing her hands in the air. "I'm never going to make it home."

Her breath fogged the windshield. The engine ticked in the silence. And for the first time all night, she felt truly alone.

The beginning of tears stung her eyes. "I don't even know where I am," she sniffled. She glared out the driver's side window into the glistening dark. The streetlight across from her shed just enough light on the reflective street sign that read Wolves Den.

*Wolves Den?* Her breath caught. She was parked at the mouth of the cul-de-sac where she had hung the curtains in the model home weeks ago. *What are the chances?* She recalled Luke telling her the ranch home's kitchen was custom designed. The owner had to have moved in by now.

She looked at the three houses up the road. None had lights on, but she wasn't about to let doubt steal her hope. *Maybe the storm knocked out the power. Maybe someone's home. Please let someone be home.*

She grabbed her purse and keys and exited the car. She slammed the door but didn't bother locking it. *Who'd want it anyway?* Using the mini flashlight attached to her keychain, she bathed the misty dark street with a narrow beam of light and began walking toward the cul-de-sac.

It was barely a quarter mile, but her imagination ran wild with every step. The shadows seemed to breathe. The wind rustled the trees, and fear crept up her spine. She froze.

*Is that a bear?*

She shined her flashlight into the evergreens and hit on two green flashes. A jolt of panic ripped through her as a couple of deer scrambled back into the woods.

Her heart hammered. She picked up the pace, her sneakers smacking the wet pavement. *Please God, let someone be home somewhere.*

As she neared the houses, the intense barking of a large dog startled her, halting her mid-step.

Someone had moved in.

A motion sensor light flicked on at the contemporary house. A four-legged shadow leaped out from behind the shrubbery. Its chain and tags jingled with each paw clicking against the blacktop as it sprinted down the driveway.

Jenna gulped a quick breath and took a nervous step backward. *Stay calm. Just stay calm.*

The dog ran full speed toward her, floppy puppy ears bouncing with each stride. His bark wasn't aggressive — more excited, eager — but her pulse still spiked.

She braced herself. "Easy boy, easy," she said, her voice soft and steady despite her racing pulse.

When the dog reached her, he halted and sat, tail sweeping the wet pavement like a broom. Jenna only knew one dog that obedient.

She crouched to his level, her breath catching as she recognized the black German shepherd.

"Justice? Is it really you?"

His ears perked at her voice. He whined softly, nudging her hand with his nose.

A memory flashed. Justice at the shelter, leaning against her leg, trusting her instantly. She could almost hear herself whispering *good boy*. The lingering grief of losing him vanished, overtaken by a wave of disbelief.

She gazed at him with hope and shock. "Oh my gosh… it is you!" Tears of joy streamed down her cheeks. "But how?" She peered into the darkness. "Where's your owner, huh?"

Someone whistled. "Dagnammit, Justice! Where are you?"

Jenna traced the voice to the contemporary house. A shirtless man wearing jeans strutted down the driveway, his bare feet slapping the wet pavement. When he spotted his dog, he shouted, "Justice, come!" Then he stepped into the street and called, "Sorry 'bout that. His butter done slipped off his biscuit. He doesn't normally run after strangers."

The southern drawl hit Jenna like a memory.

"Luke? Is that you?" she asked, shining her dim flashlight toward him.

"Jenna?" Luke asked, squinting. "What're you doing out here?"

Her tension lifted like fog burning off in sunlight. "It *is* you. Oh, thank God!"

Luke chuckled. "Golly, that's a welcome I thought I'd never hear."

She couldn't help noticing the way the rain glistened across his shoulders, the easy confidence in his stride, the warmth in his voice. Even soaked and barefoot, he looked steady, like someone who didn't scare easily.

"Wait—*you* live here?" she asked, pointing at the contemporary house. "And you adopted *my* dog?"

"Yeah, about that. I tried to tell you that day, but you—"

"Never mind!" she said, waving it off. "My car died just down the road a way."

"At this hour?" Luke asked.

"I didn't know cars only broke down during the day."

Luke sighed. "Let me get my boots and a shirt," he said, then signaled Justice to follow him back to the house.

Justice lingered at Jenna's side for a heartbeat, leaning into her leg as if reluctant to leave, then finally trotted after Luke.

Pebbles of chilly rain began to pepper Jenna's head.

"Grab an umbrella while you're at it!" she shouted.

Jenna sighed. For the first time all night, she didn't feel alone.

Of course Luke didn't bring an umbrella, and within minutes of reaching her car, heavy rain drenched them. Jenna was soaked to the skin, her hoodie clinging to her like wet paper, and her socks were sponges inside her sneakers.

"Unbelievable," she grumbled, shivering.

"Where're the keys?" Luke asked, wiping rain from his eyes.

Jenna tossed them to him. "It's unlocked. Who'd want to steal it?"

"Good point," he said, opening the driver door. "Hop in and slide over."

She scooted across the seat, the cold cloth upholstery brushing against her legs with a damp chill. Luke climbed in behind the wheel, dripping everywhere.

"This turd got gas?" he asked.

She shot him a look. "Think I'm stupid? Of course it does. It has a full tank."

Luke shrugged and turned the ignition. The engine turned over.

Jenna slapped her knee. "No way! This car makes a liar out of me every time."

Without saying a word, Luke shifted the car into drive and hit the gas. The car hesitated, coughed, then stalled.

"Ha! See? I told you," Jenna said, a little too enthusiastically.

Luke started it again and shifted into drive, but the car stalled a second time. "Third time's a charm," he said, cranking the engine once more.

This time, he used both feet like Jenna had done earlier — brake and gas working together, coaxing the car forward. It puttered, jerked, and wheezed its way the short distance to his driveway.

From the asthmatic rattle of the engine, Jenna knew her car was in serious trouble. Frustration mingled with anger, sizzling through her. *How many times had she told her father something was wrong? How many times had he brushed her off? There's nothing wrong with it, Amore.* He'd said it so many times she could hear it now, echoing in her head louder than the storm.

Luke revved the engine gently, listening. Jenna watched him — the way he leaned forward, brow furrowed, rain dripping from his hair onto his shoulders. He looked focused, capable. Like someone who actually cared enough to figure out what was wrong.

"What do you think is wrong?" she asked.

He didn't answer right away. He listened, head tilted, eyes narrowed. "She's plain tuckered out."

At that moment, the engine stalled completely.

Jenna tossed her head back against the seat with a heavy sigh. "Of course."

"I'm going to open the garage door and push this thing inside," Luke said. "I'll need you to steer, so slide over."

"Okay," Jenna said, her voice small but relieved to have help.

She watched him step out into the pouring rain , boots on, shirt clinging damply to his shoulders, then she scooted into the driver seat.

Jenna gripped the steering wheel, rain pounding the roof like a drum. *Thank you, God,* she thought. *For sending someone. For sending him.*

As Luke pushed Jenna's car into the third bay, she eyed the shiny black Trans Am tucked in next to her.

"Whoa, nice ride! When did you get this?" she asked.

Luke pulled the garage door down. "In Texas, just before we moved."

"Is it new?"

"Yep. It's a 1990. It's got a 305 engine with a five-speed manual. Fun car to drive."

Jenna poked her head inside the driver's window and inhaled that unmistakable new-car smell. Her gaze dropped to the odometer. "What?" she asked, peering up from the dashboard. "Only thirty-two hundred miles on it? I thought you said it's fun to drive."

"It is when the weather cooperates, which isn't often living here in the mountains. Most of the time it's impractical, so I drive the company truck."

"Oh," she replied, her gaze lingering on him longer than she meant it to.

Luke peeled off his rain-drenched T-shirt and winged it across the garage, belting the interior door with a wet splat. At the sight of his muscular arms and taut stomach, a warm blast of desire rippled up her spine. Losing interest in the Trans Am entirely, she backed her head out of the car—bumping it on the closed T-roof.

"Ow," she muttered, rubbing the sting.

Luke didn't seem to notice. He grabbed the button-down shirt hanging on the corner of his toolbox and pulled it on, casual and unbothered, as if standing shirtless in a storm-soaked garage was just another Tuesday.

She watched him, unable to help herself. He was the last guy she ever expected to be attracted to. She shook off her giddiness and redirected her attention to the other car cocooned in the first bay.

"What's the story with that car?" she asked.

A huge smile lit up his face. "Let me show you." He squeezed past his workbench and engine hoist and made his way into the first bay.

Luke peeled back the cover, and a gleaming white muscle car emerged from beneath it. Two blue racing stripes stretched from the hood to the trunk, sharp and vivid even in the dim garage light. The car sat low and wide, all curves and muscle, with twin hood scoops that made it look like it was breathing. Chrome trim winked at her from the fenders, and the rear spoiler gave it the stance of something built to fly. Jenna didn't know a thing about cars, but even she could tell this one was special.

"You're looking at a rare 1969 Trans Am, four speed," he said proudly.

"Sweet! What makes it rare?"

"This was the first year. It only came in white with blue accents."

Jenna nodded even though she had no clue what she was looking at. "How long have you had it?"

"Since I was sixteen. It belonged to my pawpaw."

Luke pointed to the engine stand beside him. The block gleamed a deep Pontiac blue, the enamel still giving off that sharp, chemical sweetness. Even Jenna could tell Luke had poured hours into making it perfect.

"This classic will rumble again once I get some time off."

"Cool. Can't wait to see it on the road," Jenna said.

"And in the meantime," he said, pointing at her car, "let me see what's wrong with this thing."

Jenna nodded. "Thanks."

While Luke tinkered under the hood of her clunker, she wandered around the garage. For someone who had just recently moved in, he sure had a lot of stuff—but surprisingly, everything had its place. Luke was neat, organized, and methodical. It suited him.

She meandered back to the bay where Luke was trying to restart her car. She plopped herself on a stool and watched him work. There was something about his aura—his confidence, his capability—that hooked her.

"Is there anything you can't do?" she asked.

"What?"

"I mean, how do you know all this stuff?"

Luke shrugged. "I imagine two years of tech school and two years working as a mechanic in a dealership helps."

Jenna gasped. "Then why're you building houses?"

"What's wrong with building houses?"

"Nothing," she said, shrugging. "But I can see how mechanically inclined you are."

Luke grabbed a towel and wiped his greasy hands. "Remember when I told you that we all make sacrifices at some point in our lives?"

Jenna nodded slowly. "Y-e-a-h."

"Well, after my dad had his accident, I took a leave of absence from my job at the dealership to keep the family business afloat. But eventually, I had to quit the dealership."

"Oh," she said, dropping her gaze. "I'm so sorry."

"Don't be. I'm blessed in so many ways, and I'm happy building houses—at least for now."

"Well, that's good, 'cause there's nothing more miserable than waking up day after day for a job you hate."

Luke winked at her. "You're learning."

He reached inside the car and turned the key. Suddenly a spark of life returned to her car.

Jenna hopped off the stool. "You fixed it?"

"No," Luke shouted over the noisy engine. "It's running too lean."

"What does that mean?"

"The air/fuel ratio is too low," he said, disconnecting the exhaust analyzer. "That's why it keeps stalling."

"Can you fix it?"

"Nope. The factory carburetor is junk."

"So, what do I do?"

"Replace it or learn to read the bus schedule."

"Noooo!" Jenna ran a hand through her wet, matted hair. "This can't be happening." She glanced down at her watch and frowned. "Listen, can you just give me a ride home?"

"I'm listening," he said, cupping his hand to his ear. "I'm listening to the rain plummeting the roof. So, NO. Not in this storm."

"C'mon, Luke. You drove me home in a blizzard."

"I had the truck, and it was an emergency."

"So, you have your Trans Am."

"It fishtails in the rain. Besides, then it'll get all wet."

Jenna smacked his shoulder. "Ooh, I can't stand you!"

"Speaking of wet…" he said.

His gaze dropped to the transparency of her drenched T-shirt. Jenna caught on instantly and crossed her arms over her chest.

"You're a pig," she said, slapping his shoulder.

"And you're soaking wet," he said.

"Well, I don't have any other clothes, now do I?"

"I think I can help with that," he said. "But first, call your parents so they don't worry."

Jenna shook her head violently. "No. No way!"

Luke lifted the phone from the wall cradle and handed it to her. "Your dad's fixin' tuh have a conniption fit if you don't call him."

"And if I tell him I'm staying at a guy's house, he's liable to have another heart attack."

Luke flashed his warm, country-boy grin. "It's *my* house, and I promise he'll be fine with it."

"Why? You gay?"

Luke gave a half-laugh, his face turning scarlet. "Far from it, darlin'."

Jenna huffed and took the phone. Her pointer finger trembled as she dialed. "UGH!" she yelled, slamming down the phone.

"What's the matter—forgot the number?"

"NO! I messed up. Now I gotta start all over again. Couldn't you have at least gotten a push-button phone?"

"It's my garage phone and it was free. Sheesh!"

Jenna put the phone to her ear and listened to it ring, dreading the moment someone picked up. She covered the receiver and whispered to Luke, "They're going to flip!"

He placed a consoling hand on her shoulder. "Chill, girl."

"I am—I'm freezing!" she chattered.

"Hello?" her father answered.

"Daddy," she said, swallowing the lump in her throat.

"*Amore*! Where the hell are you?"

"My car—"

"Do you know what time it is?" he shouted.

"Daddy, I know it's late, but—"

"Well, it's almost midnight!" he rumbled, launching into a lecture about needing to know her whereabouts.

Jenna frowned at his harsh tone, then drummed up the courage to speak her mind. "I know, Daddy, but—" She couldn't get a word in edgewise and was ready to pitch the phone across the room. "Daddy! If you would just listen…" Her voice trembled with anger and frustration. "My car broke down. You know, the one you said ran flawlessly?"

Dark and hot, she narrowed her eyes, locking them on Luke's face. He smiled at the temper smoldering in her eyes, then reached for the phone.

"Mr. Rossi, it's Luke," he said calmly. "Yeah, she's okay. She's here with me." He winked at her. "Yes, sir. That's correct. I hooked it up to the exhaust analyzer. The air/fuel ratio is too low."

Luke paused, listening, then sighed. "Yes, sir," he said, handing Jenna the phone.

"Daddy?" she said.

"*Amore*, you stay there for the night. You'll be safe."

"O-k-a-y," she answered, totally flabbergasted. "Good night then."

She hung up the phone, baffled by her father's response. Had she been stranded with Tommy, it would've been another long song and dance.

Luke placed his hands on her shoulders and looked at her with a know-it-all twinkle in his brown eyes. "Didn't I tell you everything was going to be okay?"

Jenna swallowed, feeling the storm inside her finally settle. God had sent help. And it had come standing barefoot in the rain.

# Chapter 29

Jenna followed Luke upstairs to the master bedroom and stood in the doorway while he rummaged through a cardboard box. As she waited, she admired his southwestern décor. He had a king-size bed made of striped pine logs that was centered in the room facing the window that overlooked the backyard and the lake below. Although it was dark and foggy outside, she imagined what it must be like waking up to a gorgeous view on a sunny day. She glanced at Luke crouching beside the closet and gave her head a quick shake. *Never mind, I don't want to know.*

Luke pulled a gray T-shirt, with *Valente Construction* logo on it, out of the box and tossed it to her. He then grabbed a white pair of crew socks out of his dresser drawer and a terry bathrobe off a hanger in the closet and handed them to her.

"They'll be big on you, but I reckon it'll do for the night."

Jenna nodded. "Thanks."

Next, Luke showed her the guest bedroom and pointed at the bathroom door. "There's towels in the linen closet if you'd like to shower."

"Yes, thanks," she said.

Luke stepped into the hallway. "You can bring your clothes down to the laundry room when you're through."

As he was about to walk away, Jenna called out, "Wait!" She reached for his hand. She gave him an appreciative smile, and said, "Thanks for everything."

A gentle finger tucked her tousled hair behind her ear. "If you need anything else, I'll be downstairs with Justice."

Warmth fluttered through her, quiet and unexpected. After the night she'd had, his gentleness felt like grace.

After a warm, soothing shower, Jenna slipped Luke's T-shirt on over her head. No doubt, the men's XL was huge on her. The sleeves fell to her elbows and the hem draped to her knees like a nightshirt.

She pulled his bathrobe over the T-shirt and tightened it. His clean manly scent enveloped her. The feel of him on her skin stirred her senses, taking her back to their first encounter.

What was it about him that attracted her? She shook her head. *I don't get it. He's not my type. Or maybe he is. I'm confused.*

Her chest tightened. Loving Tommy had carved a deep place in her heart — one she wasn't sure would ever heal enough to make room for anyone else.

Jenna stood at the top of the staircase. She took a moment to regain her flagging spirits before clutching the glossy oak banister. Thoughts of her ill-fated love weighed heavily on her as she meandered downstairs to the laundry room carrying her bundle of wet clothes.

She tossed her clothes into the washing machine. As she measured the soap powder, she sensed a presence behind her. A tap on her shoulder made her jump out of her skin. She spun around to find Luke standing there in a black B.U.M. muscle shirt and cotton pajama pants.

"Don't do that!" she shouted.

"What?" Luke asked. "I came to see if you need help."

She folded her arms across her chest. "I know how to wash clothes."

"Okay, okay," he said, surrendering his hands in the air.

His eyes gave her a once-over that made her feel exposed. Heat crept up her neck, and she fidgeted with the sash on her robe, wishing she didn't feel so vulnerable in front of him.

"Don't look at me like that," she yelled, tugging the robe tighter around herself.

"Like what?"

She sighed. "It's rather embarrassing being in a strange house with someone I HARDLY know, wearing ONLY his T-shirt and robe."

Luke pointed to her feet. "You forgot the socks."

Not in the mood for his wisecracks, she leveled him a look.

"No worries, darlin. I've seen you wearing less," he said with a spark of mischief in his brown eyes.

Jenna smacked his shoulder. "Don't remind me!"

"Hey, now. I wasn't the one running around my parents' house in only a bath towel."

Jenna clucked her tongue in irritation. "You had no business being in their kitchen at the crack of dawn."

"Whoa, there!" Luke said, raising his hand. "It WAS business with your dad."

Jenna firmly shut her mouth. It wasn't worth arguing over.

Luke curled his arm around her shoulder. "C'mon. I made you a cup of hot chocolate."

As Jenna approached the great room, a warm breath of seasoned oak drifted from the rough-stone fireplace. Justice lay curled beside the hearth, one floppy ear pitched upward like a sentry. When he noticed her, he rose and nudged her with his wedge-shaped head.

"Oh, Justice! I missed you," she said, crouching to pet him.

Luke touched her shoulder. "Make yourself at home. I'll be right back with our hot chocolate."

She nodded, though her feet stalled. The flicker of firelight danced across the walls, weaving shadows through the room. It looked nothing like it had when she'd helped him hang curtains. Now it reflected Luke himself—tan leather furnishings, southwestern pillows, a cowhide rug anchoring the space. She loved his taste. She bobbed her head in approval and wandered in, Justice padding behind her until he circled back to his warm spot and spun himself into sleep.

Jenna smiled. *You're too cute.*

She sank into the deep, cushy couch and leaned against a pillow. Closing her tired eyes, she hoped to unwind after an awful day—but instead her mind dredged up a sludge of emotions. *Oh, God…what have I done to deserve a messed-up life? Mom and Dad don't trust me. Tommy dumped me. My best friend betrayed me. Where's the love?*

The clack of ceramic mugs on the coffee table snapped her out of her spiral. She lifted her head and met Luke's tender eyes.

"You okay?" he asked, settling beside her.

She shook her head.

"What's wrong?"

A deep breath steadied her voice. "My life can't get any worse."

"Oh, c'mon," he said, patting her knee. "You just turned nineteen. How can things be that bad?"

Tears blurred her vision. "Nothing in my life ever goes right."

"What? The car? Don't fret. I'll take care of it."

"No-o-o, I'm a reject."

"Golly! Why would you say that?"

She sat in silence, fighting her tears.

"Darlin, talk to me," he pleaded.

Jenna ducked her head, refusing to let him see her cry.

"Look at me," he said gently.

She peered up—and a tear slipped down her cheek, then another. Luke leaned in and brushed them away with the work-worn pad of his thumb.

"C'mon. It can't be all that bad."

"My life's a tragedy."

He exhaled a ragged sigh. "How's that?"

"Where do I start? First, Tommy dumps me for a groupie, then my best friend steals Adam away, and you adopt my puppy."

Luke blinked, clearly caught off guard. "Hey, you can see Justice anytime. Heck, you can have visitation rights. As for your friends, I can't answer for their disloyalty."

"I can't trust anyone anymore."

"You can trust me."

"Oh, right. You're a spy for my father."

Luke took a gulp of hot chocolate and coughed. "Now why would you say that?"

"Because you're always around, like you're keeping an eye on me or something."

He laughed and shook his head. "Girl, you're about half a bubble off plumb."

She snorted despite herself.

Luke grinned. "At last, I got you laughing right back at me."

"That wasn't a laugh," she muttered, trying to keep a straight face.

"Oh, c'mon, lighten up. Sometimes life leads you down a different road."

"Yeah, tell me about it. How do you think I got here?"

"Oh, I don't know…fate. Don't cha think?"

She didn't answer, but the idea tugged at her. What were the odds that a bolt of lightning would lead her down a road she never knew existed? That an overflowing lake would force her to choose a different path? That her car would break down on the right cul-de-sac? Was it all coincidence?

A thrill of wonder fluttered through her stomach. She shook it off and reached for her mug of hot chocolate.

"You cold?" he asked.

She nodded. "A little."

Luke sprang from his seat and crouched beside the hearth to stoke the fire. Without warning, a flash of lightning lit up the room, followed by a crack of thunder that rattled the windows. Rain hammered the skylight in sheets.

"Here we go again," he said.

Jenna rubbed her stomach, trying to settle the anxiety twisting inside her. "I hate these wild storms."

"Really? Ain't you the gal who wanted me to drive you home in it?"

"Okay, okay," she sighed. "I didn't expect it to be this bad."

"You think this is bad? Don't move to Texas."

"I don't plan on it, nor do I plan on moving anywhere."

Luke wagged his pointer finger. "If I remember right, you were moving to California last Thanksgiving."

"Visiting—only visiting," Jenna corrected. "And it was only to be with Tommy."

"Uh-huh," Luke replied.

"California was his dream, not mine." She lowered her gaze. "River Grove will always be my home."

"Is that right?"

"Absolutely. I love the mountains, the seasons, the wildlife."

Luke nodded. "I smell what you're stepping in."

Jenna lifted her eyebrows. "You do?"

"Sure thing. That's why I moved back."

"Didn't you like Texas?"

Luke shrugged. "Eh. I didn't much care for watching the grass burn in one-hundred-degree temps."

Jenna nodded.

Luke tossed another log onto the fire. "There. It'll be toasty warm in here in no time."

Jenna eased herself onto the floor beside him, her back warmed by the softly burning fire.

"This is nice. Thank you," she whispered.

Luke nodded. "It's nice spending time with you."

He smiled, and his mouth curved into the most beautiful lips she'd ever seen. Longing to taste his kiss, she traced her fingers over his full lips.

Luke framed her face and leaned in. The moment his lips met hers, a cold, wet nose wedged itself between them.

"Ugh!" Jenna groaned, pulling away.

Justice pawed Luke's shoulder and whimpered.

"Great timing, boy," Luke said, glaring at his pup.

He pushed to his feet. "Sorry. It's his signal to go out."

"Oh," Jenna said, glancing up at the skylight. "Well, at least it's no longer raining."

"Yay," Luke said without enthusiasm. He pointed toward the door. "Be right back."

"Okay. I'm going to check on my laundry."

Jenna had just settled herself back down on the floor beside the fireplace when she heard the front door close and lock. Moments later, Luke stepped into the living room without Justice.

"Where's your best friend?" she asked.

"In his crate, soaking wet. He decided it would be fun to slosh through some puddles."

Jenna's mouth fell open, surprised her obedient pup had gotten himself into mischief. She shook her head. "Really?"

Luke nodded. "Yeah…so don't think he's always so well-behaved like me," he said, a playful lilt in his voice.

"Well-behaved…like you?" A burst of laughter slipped out. "You're too much."

"What?" Luke asked, dropping onto the soft rug beside her. "Look, if you were to pick up a dating résumé about me, it would read something like honest, hard-working, fun-loving gearhead, looking to build a long-term relationship with a gal who's faithful, caring, and ambitious."

"Really?" she asked, incredulous.

"Yeah, and I think I found her — if she'd give me a chance." He took her hand and placed it over his heart. "Jenna, you can trust me."

Soft wisps of his minty breath brushed her cheek before his lips touched hers. His gentle kiss filled her senses — but the phone rang, jolting her back to the memory of that awful day in the hotel room when she learned of her father's heart attack.

She winced.

"Let it go," he murmured between kisses. "The machine will get it."

Jenna breathed a soft, broken sound as he deepened the kiss, but the incoming message kept her from fully sinking into the moment.

"Hey, wonder twin," Liliana's voice chimed through the machine. "I know it's late…that is…in your time zone, but I heard you had severe weather and wanted to know you're safe. Oh, by the way, Amy Lynn stopped by the ranch asking about you. Don't be surprised if you hear from her. Anyway, call me in the a.m. Love you, bro. Bye."

When the answering machine clicked off, Jenna broke the kiss and pulled away. "You said I could trust you!"

"You can!" Luke insisted.

"Then who's Amy Lynn?"

Luke tipped his head back and closed his eyes. "My ex."

"Your ex? You never mentioned an ex."

"That's because she *is* an ex," he said, his voice honest and steady.

Hearing the sincerity in his tone, Jenna stared blankly at the crackling fire, ashamed for overreacting. She drew a deep breath, sorting through her thoughts. *Gee, everyone has a past. After all, his ex lives in Texas. I'd be stupid to let her ruin my chance at new love.*

She turned to him with softened eyes. "I'm sorry."

Luke flicked his hand dismissively. "She wasn't meant to be. Besides, then I wouldn't be here with you."

His confident response eased her insecurities but stirred her curiosity. "So, why'd you two break up?"

Luke sighed. "Let's just say my beer budget couldn't support her champagne appetite."

Jenna lifted her brows. "Oh, wow. One of those girls."

"Yeah, well, Amy Lynn had grand expectations. Her old man's an oil tycoon."

"Oh? How did you meet her?"

Luke's mouth twitched into a wry grin. "So, I'm behind the service desk at work, 'bout to go on break, when this shiny new sports car rolls in. This eager young lady in a sleek red mini dress and four-inch heels rushes inside like she's on a mission. She flashes me this 'hello there' smile, hands me her key, and says in her bubbly voice, 'I'm here for an oil change.' So I politely point out the Porsche dealership across the way."

He chuckled. "Golly, the color in her cheeks matched her dress."

Jenna smiled, not feeling threatened by his past. "So, how'd you two end up together?"

"Get this," he said. "On my way home that evening, I took the back roads through the countryside and spotted a marine-blue Porsche on the shoulder with a flat. I was like, 'Golly, it's Amy Lynn!' So I stopped. And the rest is history."

"Wait!" Jenna said, a zany thought flashing through her mind. "So this makes me your next damsel in distress." She nudged his arm. "Ha! I see how it is."

Flushing, Luke stammered, "No, no! It's not like that at all. Amy Lynn and me…we're from two vastly different worlds."

Jenna frowned. "Just like me and Tommy."

"Hey now, Jenna." Luke cupped her face and gently brushed her bottom lip with his thumb. "Give me a go, and I'll be your new knight in shining armor."

His tenderness stirred something deep inside her — a longing she'd been afraid to acknowledge. *I'm not going to mess this up like I did with Tommy.* She leaned forward in one smooth movement and kissed him, driven by fear of losing her chance at love again.

But Luke flinched, pulling back with hesitation.

"Whoa, slow down," he said gently.

"Oh…uh." Confused and embarrassed, she rolled away from him and turned her back. "I thought you wanted—"

"Stop. I'm not your ex," he said, firm but not unkind.

"I know, but all you guys—"

"No. I'm not all you guys," he said boldly. He exhaled. "Listen, if a guy doesn't know a girl's morals, then he doesn't know her well enough to date."

"What?" Jenna asked, trying to process his words. *Gee…he's not like Tommy at all.*

"I didn't think guys like you still existed," she whispered.

"This may sound odd to you," Luke said, "but some of us can be nice without hidden agendas." He paused. "Look, I see it like this: if purity destroys a relationship, then you can be sure it was never built on love in the first place."

A soft wave of relief washed over her — deeper than she expected. For the first time in a long while, she didn't feel pressured, or cornered, or afraid of disappointing someone. She felt…safe.

# Chapter 30

The next morning, Jenna rose to a sloppy wet kiss on her lips and a paw on her shoulder. She groaned and pulled the fleece blanket tighter around her. Justice whined and nudged her arm with his long nose. She groaned again. As she tried to peel her eyes open, a beam of sunlight from the skylight blinded her. When her vision adjusted, the twelve-foot ceiling framed by log timbers reminded her she wasn't home — and she was still wearing Luke's T-shirt and robe.

*So, I'm not dreaming.*

The aroma of freshly brewed coffee and sizzling bacon drifted into the great room, coaxing her upright. She rubbed the sleep from her eyes and ambled into the kitchen, where Luke stood at the stove cooking.

"Good morning, sleepyhead," he said. He pointed toward the laundry room with his spatula. "Your clothes are in the basket, and breakfast is almost ready."

"Gee, you cook too?"

"Yeah, well, my momma ain't here to do it."

Jenna nodded. "Right. I'll, uh, get dressed."

After breakfast, Jenna stepped outside to breathe in the fresh morning air. She squinted at the white, fluffy clouds sailing calm and majestic overhead. At a break in the sky, the sun peered through with its happy face. She smiled in awe. *At last, a beautiful spring day.*

The door opened, and Luke joined her on the front porch.

"Ready to assess Mother Nature's aftermath?" he asked.

She nodded and took his hand. Together, they followed Justice's lead along the concrete sidewalk past the ranch house, where a pool of water rippled across the yard. Broken tree limbs creaked in the soft breeze, and fallen leaves littered the ground. Last night's storm had left a mess.

At the end of the cul-de-sac, Justice turned left toward a break in a row of dwarf Eastern hemlock trees lining the street.

"Where's he going?"

"He knows the way," Luke said.

"But I thought we were checking out the neighborhood?"

"Nah. That would be boring."

"Don't cha think I had enough excitement last night?"

Luke slipped his arm around her shoulder. "C'mon. I want to show you something awesome."

"What?"

"It's a surprise."

"Oh, great," she muttered. *Just what I need — another adventure.*

Beyond the row of hemlocks, a woodchip path bordered by landscape timbers led them into a green arbor of freshly blooming trees stretching high against the bright blue sky. Inside the tree-arched path, evergreens dominated the scenery, but oak, maple, beech, and birch completed the splendid view. Though weakened by the thick greenery, the sunlight softened the ground beneath their feet. The air smelled of moist pine and earthy moss. Birds chirped and screeched all around.

A half mile in, the easy stone path narrowed to single file and zigzagged into the mountain. As they rounded a bend, Jenna glanced over her shoulder. The entrance had disappeared behind a rock wall covered in moss and sprouting trees. Along the rock-strewn path, she slowed her pace, ducking under low-lying branches. Raindrops dripped from leaves onto her head, and annoying gnats buzzed in her face. Swatting at them, she muttered, "Where on earth is he taking me?"

Not paying attention to the uneven terrain, she stumbled over a tree root, nearly pitching forward onto the unforgiving ground.

"Careful now," Luke said, reaching for her hand.

"You're not planning on pushing me off a cliff, are you?"

Luke let out a short laugh and shook his head. "Girl, you have a wild imagination, don't cha think?"

She shrugged.

Luke held her chin gently. "Hey, you can trust me."

Jenna saw the sincerity in his eyes and nodded.

"I want you to see this," he said, pointing with his chin.

"See what?"

"You'll see."

"Not if I trip and break my neck first."

"I promise…the trail gets easier."

Luke was right. They came to a boardwalk built to protect hikers from the fragile, treacherous terrain beneath it.

"How much further?" Jenna asked.

"Shh. Just listen."

The roar of rushing water caught her attention. Up ahead, the boardwalk led to a set of stairs. She grasped the timber railing and climbed the wet, slippery steps to an observation deck. When she reached the top, she froze in awe.

Across the gorge, a magnificent waterfall thundered down the rocky cliff. Trillions of glistening droplets tumbled seventy-five feet into the rough rapids below, sparkling like diamonds in the morning sun.

"Welcome to Symphony Falls," Luke said.

"Oh, wow. It's breathtaking. Totally worth the hike."

Luke nodded. "I've been coming here several times a week since I moved in. It's my go-to place to clear my head."

"I can certainly see why."

Luke pointed toward the swinging bridge stretching twenty-five feet across the choppy river below. "Two hoots and a holler away, there's another viewing balcony if you want a closer look."

"Sure! Let's go," she said, leaping ahead like a little kid.

The next observation deck sat only yards from the plunging falls. From Jenna's new viewpoint, sunlight glittered across the silvery water, creating a shimmering rainbow.

"Absolutely heavenly," she uttered.

She moved closer to the railing, letting the water-saturated air mist her skin. It made her think how refreshing it would feel on a sweltering summer day.

Listening to the falls crash against the rocks below, she wondered when she had last enjoyed nature in the good company of a man. Her mind drifted to the beach with Tommy — listening to waves lap the shore, talking about their futures. Looking back now, they weren't discussing a shared future at all. They were dreaming alone.

She blew out her breath. *Tommy, I wish you the best.*

She picked up a broken twig and tossed it into the water.

Another memory surfaced — Adam at the creek, trying to teach her how to skip rocks. She shook her head. *Oh, how badly I messed that up too.* But in retrospect, she understood why. He wasn't part of God's greater plan for her. Adam was meant for Kellie.

She glanced over her shoulder and watched Luke toss a stick for Justice to fetch. *What about him?* He had always been there when she needed him, especially when her father was in the hospital. *Was he part of God's plan?* She shook her head. *He can't be — he called me his kid sister.* She opened her palms. *But then why the passionate kiss last night?*

A tender hand touched the small of her back, sending shivers up her spine. She turned and met Luke's troubled gaze.

"Hey, you're quiet," he said. "You alright?"

She nodded. "Yeah, just thinking."

"About?"

She caught her bottom lip between her teeth, weighing her words. "Us."

"What about us?" he asked.

"Like…where's our friendship going? I mean, last night we kissed, but what about that kid-sister thing?"

"What?" Luke asked, rubbing the back of his neck. "Oh…that. I was just protecting myself from falling for you."

"And now?"

"Well, you're single, aren't you?" he asked.

Jenna lowered her voice to a silky softness. "I am for you."

Warmth and affection filled his gaze as he pulled her snug into his arms. At the first touch of his lips, his kiss felt like a heart-stopping plunge into the rapids below. Familiar sensations from the first moment they met resurfaced- feelings she had never had with Tommy. She realized now that Luke was the one for her.

She smiled against his mouth. "Just for the record, you stole my heart at howdy."

"Is that so?" he asked, brushing her lips with teasing kisses.

"Uh-huh," she breathed.

Abruptly, Luke broke the kiss and stumbled backward as Justice tugged the leash. The pup emitted a playful bark at a young family strolling along the bridge toward them.

Luke licked his lips. "I guess it's time to head back."

"Yeah, I guess so."

Jenna and Luke followed the community walking trail another mile through the scenic woods toward Melody Lake. Along the way, they passed several more hikers heading in. As they approached the entrance to the picnic area, sharp high-pitched squeals and shrieks from children playing tag around the pavilion pierced through the stillness of nature. Smoke from a charcoal grill drifted across the lawn, wafting the delicious aroma of barbeque ribs in their direction and taunting her growling stomach.

"What's all this?" Jenna asked.

"Families having a little fun kicking off summer."

"Oh, I forgot it was Memorial Day weekend."

As they neared the lake, Jenna shielded her eyes from the bright sun as its rays flickered across the water's surface. She watched a speedboat thump over another boat's wake, then turned at the sound of a revving engine as a second boat was launched into the water.

"How 'bout we rent a paddleboat one day?" Luke asked.

"Sure. Sounds like fun," she said with enthusiasm.

Luke's idea triggered a memory of the beach with Tommy — the day she'd asked him if he wanted to learn to surf. She recalled how disappointed she'd been when he said he wasn't interested. She shook her head. *Luke is so much more outgoing than Tommy ever was.*

Luke pointed toward the moderately filled parking lot. "The road where your car died is just over yonder beyond those trees."

"Oh," Jenna said as they headed in that direction.

She noticed a minivan pulling into a parking space. The slider doors glided open, and a bunch of youths hopped out dressed for a beach day — hats, shades, swimsuits, flip-flops. Jenna shuddered at the thought of swimming on such a chilly morning.

She lowered her gaze to the concrete sidewalk and let her mind replay last night's awful scene. It had been stormy, dark, and desolate. She remembered how scared and hopelessly stranded she'd felt. And now, twelve hours later, a mid-morning walk had brought her right back to where it all began.

A quiet inner smile creased her lips.

Luke noticed and squeezed her hand. "Hey, now that's a smile."

She shook her head. "No, it's not."

"Well, whatever you call it, you should do it more often. It looks good on you."

She smiled again, then led him off the sidewalk into the street where a swirling rainbow of fluid stained the asphalt.

"Look! This is where my car abandoned me last night." She reached up and caressed his sculpted beard. "And because it did, I discovered this charming man — making the dreadful situation all worthwhile."

Later that afternoon, Luke drove Jenna to the Deer Creek Plaza where his father's office suite was located. The parking lot was mostly empty aside from the busy pizza joint and a pharmacy. He pulled around to the back of the complex where there was no driving activity.

He shifted his car into neutral and pulled up the parking brake. "Okay, your turn," he said, hopping out.

Jenna gritted her teeth and got out. "O-k-a-y."

She dropped into the narrow, stiff driver's seat. *Whoa.* Unlike her old clunker, she felt like she was sitting on the floor with her legs straight out in front of her. She couldn't reach the pedals or see over the cowl. Her petite frame was nowhere near Luke's six-foot build, so she had to slide the seat completely forward to engage the clutch.

She familiarized herself with the dashboard, then looked at him with hesitancy. "Are you sure about this?"

He reached for her hand and placed it on the shifter.

"There's a first for everything," he said.

A hot wave of shame washed over her for thinking beyond her driving lesson — knowing how badly she wanted to shift *his* gears instead of the car's. She peered through the tinted T-roof at the muted blue sky. *Forgive me, Lord, for my sinful thoughts.*

"What's wrong?" he asked.

"I don't think I'm ready for this."

"Why? I taught my sister to drive stick."

Jenna shrugged.

"You can do it," he said with calm certainty.

She nodded. "Okay. I'll try."

She put her foot on the brake pedal, then released the emergency brake. She pushed in the clutch and shifted into first gear. "Okay," she said, looking at Luke. "Now what?"

"Now slowly release the clutch. When you feel the gear engage, give it a little gas. Nice and smooth like I showed you."

Jenna did exactly as he instructed, and the car moved forward without bucking. "I did it!" She cruised the flat parking lot, stopping and going without a single stall. "You're right. This car *is* fun to drive!"

It was nightfall when Luke drove Jenna home. He pulled into the driveway behind her mother's light blue Dodge and shut off the headlights. The house was dark except for the flickering of the TV through the partially open blinds.

Luke cupped his hand over hers. "A few more lessons and some hills, and you'll have yourself a new set of wheels."

Mystified, Jenna gazed at him. "Why are you doing this?"

"You need a car to get to school, don't cha?"

"Yeah, eventually, but this is your car. What if I wreck it?"

"Whoa now. Don't go borrowing trouble," he said.

Jenna clicked her tongue. "That's my point exactly. I don't—"

"Hey, I trust you. Besides, the car's fully insured."

She opened her mouth to protest, but before she could get a word in edgewise, he settled his mouth over hers, instantly quieting her insecurities. A pair of passing headlights strained through the tinted side glass, interrupting their kiss.

Jenna groaned and pulled away, spotting a familiar car idling in front of her house. "Oh no, it's Kellie," she said, sucking in her lower lip. "What's she doing here?"

Luke shrugged. "Go talk to her."

"But we haven't spoken in weeks."

"Well, now's your chance."

"I guess." She opened the car door, then hesitated. "I don't know what to say."

Luke winked. "The words will come."

She nodded and closed the door.

Jenna waved goodbye as he backed out of the driveway. She watched until his taillights disappeared around the bend. When she heard tires chirping between first and second gear, she shook her head and smiled. She was falling in love with a gearhead.

She traipsed across the front lawn toward Kellie's parked car. Bathed in its headlights, Kellie stood in front of it with her arms folded across her chest.

"Hey, Jenna," Kellie said. "I, um, didn't see your car, so I wasn't sure if you were home."

"It broke down."

"Oh. Sorry to hear that."

Jenna shrugged. "It was only a matter of time."

"I've left you tons of messages. Can we talk?"

"I'd like that," Jenna said, sitting down on the curb in front of Kellie's car. "I, uh, missed you."

"Me too," Kellie said, sitting beside her.

"I'm sorry for being mad at you. I was jealous and hurt…"

"Don't be, Jenna. I should've told you how I really felt about Adam from the get-go."

"Forget it."

"I can't. I was insensitive to your feelings and—"

"Kel," Jenna said with a sturdy nod. "It's all for the good."

Kellie blinked in bewilderment. "Wait!" She glanced at the vacant spot in the driveway, then back at Jenna. "Whose hot car did you just get out of?"

Jenna pressed her lips together, trying not to grin.

Kellie's brows lifted. "You met someone new."

Jenna broke into a wide smile. "Maybe…"

Kellie clapped her hands and squealed. "Yay! Tell me ALL about him."

"Well, he's not really someone new." She touched Kellie's forearm. "Remember that day in the library when you spotted that *hunk* you were drooling over?"

Kellie's eyes grew wide. "Noooo, really?"

Jenna filled her lungs with a deep, satisfying breath. "Yes! And you know that bad thunderstorm we had last night?"

"Yeah, it was freaky," Kellie said.

"So, I was leaving school and my car stalled out, and…"

# Chapter 31

It was Friday again. Oddly, the week had flown by — and why shouldn't it have? Life was exciting for Jenna. She had newfound love and a renewed friendship. Joy bubbled inside her.

Refreshed from a good night's sleep, she sat up in bed and watched the darkness fade into dawn as the rising sun peeked over the horizon. Ready to start her day with a run, she bounced to the edge of her bed and eagerly changed into her reflective athletic gear.

She opened her bedroom door, and the crispy aroma of cinnamon-raisin toast greeted her. She wondered who else was awake at five-thirty in the morning. She quietly slid down the hallway in her socks, hoping not to find Luke in the kitchen reading the newspaper again. But if she did, at least she was wearing clothes. She poked her head into the doorway and found her mother at the counter fixing herself breakfast.

"Morning, Mom. You're up early."

"I have to take Nonna and Nonno to the doctors today."

Jenna heard the exasperation in her voice. She knew her mother dreaded the long two-hour drive to Stonebridge where her grandparents lived, but she understood their desire to stay in the suburbs where healthcare was more accessible.

"Well, safe travels, Mom. And tell Nonna and Nonno hello from me," she said, grabbing her keychain and bear mace from the wooden wall rack.

"I will, thanks," Mom said, watching her bolt down the stairs. "Oh…and be careful out there!"

"Yeah, Mom," Jenna said as she sat on the bottom step to tie her laces.

Mom always worried when she took early-morning runs because the sun was barely up and there were no streetlights or sidewalks. And since most homes in their neighborhood were nestled on heavily wooded lots, Mom feared she would be a target of an attack — not so much by another human, but by a momma bear with her cubs. Although encounters with black bears were rare, Jenna always carried her mace as a precaution.

Jenna opened the front door and breathed in the crisp morning air, then set off on her run. There was nothing better than feeling the cool, tender breeze against her heated skin, the crunch of gravel under her feet, and the serenity of nature all around her.

She loved River Grove. Her neighborhood encompassed clusters of distinct-looking homes, each reflecting the homeowners' personalities. Many were well-landscaped and looked like they belonged on a magazine cover, while a select few had a long-vacant appearance with stacks of newspapers cluttering the front porch. Those homes belonged to the snowbirds who hadn't yet returned from winter.

Jenna jogged past Acorn Way where Tommy lived. According to Kellie, he was home from college — and he was the last person she wanted to have a run-in with.

Jenna turned left at the stop sign and was in the home stretch. Four houses away from hers, she noticed Mr. Valente's work van in the driveway. It wasn't unusual for him to stop by on Friday mornings to discuss business with her father.

She slowed her pace to a speed walk, panting in short, choppy breaths. She lifted her head and let the cool morning breeze wash over her face. She'd had an amazing workout.

As she approached the house, she saw her father and Mr. Valente sitting on the front porch steps with their coffee cups in hand. Bits of broken English mixed with

Italian filtered through the shrubs. The fervor and pitch of their conversation grew more intense as she got closer.

Jenna rolled her eyes. *Can Daddy ever have a discussion without conflict? I swear he'd argue with himself just for the challenge.*

Just then, Luke stepped out from behind an arborvitae bush.

*Oh, no. He's here too?* Beads of sweat dripped from her forehead. *Please don't look at me.* If she could just sneak along the row of spruce trees and slip in through the back door, she'd be in the clear. But her plan failed when he caught sight of her.

"Oh, hey, you're back," Luke said, giving her a wave.

With long strides, he walked toward her. His gaze drifted down her sweat-drenched tank top, past the smooth curves of her hips, then back up to her face.

"How was your run?" he asked.

Jenna scrunched her nose. "Don't look at me. I'm a smelly hot mess."

Luke shrugged. "So what? Do you really think I look my Sunday best after a hard day's work nailing shingles on a hot roof?"

"Probably not," she said, dropping her head.

Luke rubbed his hands together. "Got a favor to ask."

"Ask away," she said, beginning her post-run stretches.

"A buddy of mine is going to the drag strip in Belltown and invited me along. Would you be able to take care of Justice while I'm gone?"

"Sure, but when?"

Luke rubbed the back of his neck. "Charlie's picking me up at five-thirty tomorrow morning. I was hoping you could stay at my house tonight, and I'll be back by suppertime on Sunday."

"Sure," Jenna said, nodding. "My only plans are with Kellie this afternoon. We're going bowling. You're welcome to join us."

"Sorry, I work until five, but how 'bout I swing on down there, say 'round six-six thirty?"

"Perfect," she said, nodding. "See you later then."

Bowling Thunder was one of the largest in the state, sporting sixty lanes, a video arcade, and a full bar and restaurant featuring the best barbecue wings and appetizers.

Jenna hadn't been there in quite some time. She and Kellie used to bowl there nearly every day back in high school while Tommy and his buddies played in the arcade.

Using the side entrance, Jenna pulled the heavy door open and scrunched her nose against the acrid odor of stale cigarette smoke lingering in the lobby. The sound of rock music, balls dropping, and pins clattering drew her inside.

"Love this place!" Jenna said. She scanned the alley and noticed most lanes were occupied by leagues. "Gee, I hope they have room for us."

"Yeah, me too," Kellie said.

On their way to the check-in counter, they passed the arcade room where Jenna caught a glimpse of Tommy playing pool with two former high school classmates — Shane and Jake. Her skin prickled with unease. *Why's he with them?* Those two were no good. Jake had dropped out, and Shane had gotten suspended just before graduation and wasn't allowed to take part in the ceremony. Did she really want to be there if Tommy was hanging with those losers?

She picked up her pace, hoping he wouldn't see her.

Kellie nudged her. "Look who's here."

"I don't care," Jenna said, trying to act poised and relaxed. But when Kellie gawked at him like a hawk zeroing in on prey, Jenna gritted her teeth. "Don't make eye contact."

"Okay, okay," Kellie said.

At the service counter, one attendant was busy spraying shoes with disinfectant while another was clearing pins from a malfunctioning pinsetter in lane twenty-six.

"Crowded today, huh," Kellie said.

"Always on a Friday," the attendant replied, tossing a pair of shoes into the cubby. "How may I help you?"

"Any lanes available for us?" Jenna asked.

The attendant glanced at the monitor. "Lane forty-eight." He flipped a switch and asked, "Will you ladies be needing shoes?"

Kellie pointed at the shoe cubby. "Those ugly things? Heck no! We've got our own gear."

The attendant raised his eyebrows. "Can't say I blame you," he said, ringing up the register. Kellie handed him a twenty. "One hour," he said, tearing off the receipt. "Call the desk if you want to extend your time."

At their reserved lane, Jenna set her bowling bag down on the floor and kicked off her sneakers. Her mind stewed over Tommy. Of all the days she decided to go bowling, why did he have to be there? Feeling miffed, she prayed he'd stay far away from her.

Meanwhile, Kellie rummaged through her denim purse and pulled out a few crumpled-up bills. "At least the snack bar is only across the way. I'm starving. Want anything?"

"A fountain soda sounds good."

"Okay. Be right back," Kellie said.

After Jenna finished tying her laces, she sat at the game console, dumbfounded. The computer had been upgraded since she'd been there last, and she didn't take well to modern technology. She fumbled her way through the bowler setup screen, and just as she hit the enter button, an angry outburst stopped her cold.

"Hey!" Tommy roared.

Jenna's heart pounded courageously hard. She drew in a calming breath, then turned around and faced him. He glared at her like she was a fresh piece of meat.

"I saw you the other day. Who's the guy?" he asked.

Jenna crossed her arms and glowered at him suspiciously. "My friend, Luke. What's it to you?"

Tommy's eyes narrowed, burning with rabid fury. "Luke, you say?" He scrubbed a hand across his face in frustration. "You told me he was your old man's friend?"

"What does it matter? You and I are through."

"So tell me. Is he good to you?"

"Better than you were. In fact, he's *the best thing ever*."

Tommy's nostrils flared. Without another word, he turned in a huff, nearly knocking the tray of cheese nachos out of Kellie's hands.

"What the heck! Excuse me," Kellie shouted, pivoting to keep her snack from going airborne. She looked at Jenna. "What'd I miss?"

"Nothing!" Jenna grumbled.

Kellie set her tray down carefully. "Okay. Well, if you don't want to talk about it, then let's try to have some fun."

"Oh, I will," Jenna sneered. "That is, after I blow off some steam first."

Kellie shot her a look. "I know where this is going."

Jenna picked up her bowling ball. She was furious now, her temples pounding thickly, her throat tight. She stepped up to the approach and aligned herself with the pins. She tuned out the metal music blaring overhead and the screeching preteens to her left. With her ball heavy in her grip, she pictured Tommy's face and delivered it down the freshly oiled lane.

A perfect hook.

"Yes! A ten in the pit!" she shouted. "This is going to be a good game!"

An hour passed, and all lanes were occupied. It was a rocking evening. People were laughing and spewing trash talk in friendly competition. Kids ran everywhere, tugging on their parents' sleeves asking when it was their turn. Then suddenly, the lights dimmed and were replaced by neon strobes for glow-in-the-dark bowling.

"Cool!" Kellie said, gripping her ball.

She walked up to the foul line, ready to start their fourth game. She released her ball with a thunk and watched it rumble down the lane, making a last-minute swerve into the gutter. The bar came down and the lane went dark. Their hour rental was over.

Kellie slapped her hands to her sides. "Darn!"

"Want me to call the front desk and extend our rental?"

Kellie tossed her hand. "Nah. Wasn't a good start to a new game anyway. Besides, Adam's expecting me. We're going to see that new battleship movie tonight."

"Okay," Jenna said.

Kellie flung her bowling shoes off and packed them into her bag. "Are you sure you don't want a ride home?"

"I'm sure. Luke will be here around six."

"Ooh, la-la!" Kellie said, putting her hand to her chest. "And I'm going to miss meeting him."

Jenna felt her face heat up. "Oh, stop! You have Adam."

"And I'm very happy," Kellie said, stepping into her flats. She grabbed her bowling bag. "Gotta jet. Enjoy your sleepover."

Jenna scrunched her nose. "It's just a pet-sitting job!"

She reached for the phone to call the front desk to request more time on the lane but was denied due to the huge line of bowlers waiting. She hung up and shook her head. *What's the point of Luke coming here if he can't bowl?* She glanced at the clock and realized it was quarter after six already. *He should've been here by now. I hope he didn't blow me off.*

She gathered her belongings and wandered the long alley toward the center hub where the front desk, pro shop, and restrooms were located. *This is crazy!* Wannabe bowlers occupied every lane. She stalked through the crowd, hoping to find Luke amid the bustle and chaos.

She made her way to a phone booth near the front entrance and slid the bifold door open. About to drop a quarter into the slot, she heard a familiar male voice with a little southern twang shout her name.

"Jenna!"

She turned to find Luke waving her down. When their eyes met, a sudden gleaming smile lit his face, putting her at ease. She stepped out of the booth and greeted him. He hugged her close, a quick grasp before letting go.

"It's busier than a hound in flea season. I thought I'd never find you," he said.

"I know, and they wouldn't let me keep the lane because of it," Jenna said.

"That's okay," Luke said, reaching for her bowling bag. "You hungry? Wanna grab a bite to eat while we're here?"

Jenna shrugged. "Can we stop for take-out instead?"

Luke dug into his jean pocket, pulled out his car keys, and handed them to her. "Whatever you want. You're driving."

She quirked her eyebrows. "Me?"

"Sure. Practice makes perfect, right? You know…in case you need the car over the weekend."

She sighed nervously. "Okay."

Luke pointed to the main entrance door. Jenna nodded, relieved she wouldn't have to traipse back through the bowling alley past the arcade again. The last thing she wanted was another encounter with Mr. Personality.

Luke held the door, and Jenna stepped outside. The evening air was thick and moist, yet easier to breathe than the smoky, stuffy bowling alley. Across the rural county road, the mountains stood in their spring glory, decorated with yellow-green budding trees. Through the gaps, a pale crescent moon slipped in and out of view. It was a pretty night, but she sensed the smell of approaching rain.

Since the main entrance was only a drop-off/pick-up U-shaped driveway, Jenna and Luke followed the sidewalk along the brick building toward the side parking lot where she had entered earlier. A gentle breeze drifted past, carrying the stench of cigarette smoke and the sound of cuss words their way. A loud cackle erupted, and one guy stepped backward into view. She recognized the auburn curls.

Shane.

Jenna's heart leaped into her throat. "Great," she muttered.

"What's wrong?" Luke asked.

"I know that guy. He's trouble."

"How so?" Luke asked, calm and collected.

"He's friends with Tommy, so please...don't say anything, okay?"

"What's there to say? He ain't no corn-fed country boy."

Jenna shook her head. Luke was right — and there was nothing to fret about. She slid her hand silently into his and continued walking.

"I'm parked over there," Luke said, pointing with his chin.

"Okay."

As they reached the side entrance, Tommy leaned against the brick building, smoking and talking nonsense with Shane and Jake. Their conversation stopped instantly, and all three pairs of eyes jumped to Jenna. She dropped her gaze, but when she stepped off the curb, Tommy's hostile voice bellowed.

"Hey, cowboy!"

Jenna squeezed Luke's hand. "Just keep walking," she whispered.

But Luke stopped abruptly and spun around. "What do you boys want?"

Tommy hitched the collar of his denim jacket and stepped forward. Though he smiled, trouble simmered in his eyes.

"A word — with you," Tommy said.

"I'm listening," Luke replied, setting the bowling bag down.

Tommy took a drag on his cigarette, then crushed the butt beneath his heel. "What's with you and her?"

Luke gave him a once-over. "What's it to you, poser?"

Tommy jabbed a finger into Luke's chest. "She used to be mine. That's what."

"With a Texas-sized chip on his shoulder, Luke replied, "That's right…USED to be."

A chilling smile surfaced on Tommy's face. He laughed bitterly. "Don't expect much. She doesn't put out."

Jenna's breath caught. Luke's eyes narrowed.

"You son of a gun." He grabbed Tommy by the collar and shoved him against the building. "Boy, you watch who you're playing with. This ain't my first rodeo."

Tommy threw his hands up. "Alright! Alright!"

Luke dropped him. "Dangit, now you got me all worked up for nothin'." He pointed at Shane and Jake. "All y'all try anything silly, and I'll be fixin' to knock you losers into next week."

He turned to Jenna. "Let's go."

"But what if they—"

"Don't worry. They're big hat, no cattle."

Luke crouched to pick up the bowling bag — and Shane lunged. He grabbed Luke's shoulder and swung a punch, but Luke dodged it. Jake attacked next, clumsy but powerful, sucker-punching Luke in the gut. Luke gasped for air.

"Luke!" Jenna screamed.

Fear coiled in her stomach. She screamed again, hoping someone — anyone — would help, but no one was out there — just rows of parked cars and the echo of her own voice.

She pressed a hand to her mouth as Luke stumbled forward. He swung blindly and missed. He dodged another fist but caught a boot to the side of his head. The sound alone made her flinch.

"Get up, get up," she cried.

Resilient, Luke bounced back, angrier now. He delivered a punch that knocked Jake to the ground, leaving him moaning.

Then Shane stormed toward him, arms outstretched — a switchblade glinting in his right hand. Luke spun and delivered a well-placed kick, dropping him instantly.

Just when Jenna thought it was over, Tommy lowered his shoulder and charged. She couldn't bear it.

Adrenaline surged, and she jumped on Tommy's back, beating him with all her strength.

He grabbed a handful of her hair and flung her onto her backside. "Stay down, bitch," he demanded.

Shaken, Jenna huddled on the ground, knees to her chest, crying as Luke took over.

"I didn't start this fight," Luke said, grabbing Tommy and lifting him off his feet, "but I'm damned well gonna finish it."

Tommy shook his head violently, gasping.

Luke dropped him. "You dang fool. I told you this wasn't my first rodeo."

Jake glowered from the sidewalk. "Next time, I'm gonna jack you up."

"Looking forward to it," Luke said.

Shane spat blood. "You'll be leaving in a body bag."

Luke reached for Jenna's hand. "Let's go, sweetheart, before I change my mind."

At Luke's home in the Melody Lakes community, Justice announced the pizza delivery man's arrival before the doorbell even rang. Jenna handed the kid a ten, then carried the pizza box to the coffee table where Luke sprawled in his recliner with an ice pack pressed to his head, resting, half swooning.

She sat beside him and rubbed his forearm. "You okay?"

He blinked his eyes open. "I feel like I got hit by a dump truck. Golly, that one punk is bigger than Dallas."

Jenna let out a short laugh. "Yeah, in high school, Jake sold the most chocolate for the PTA fundraiser. Class joke—he bought it all for himself."

Luke burst into laughter, then grabbed his head with a groan.

"I'm so sorry," Jenna whispered, raking her hand through his matted hair. "Maybe I should take you to the E.R."

"No."

"But you might have a concussion."

"I'll be fine."

Jenna frowned. "This wouldn't have happened if I didn't ask you to meet me there."

"Stop. It could've been worse if I wasn't there."

Jenna tossed her wrist. "Tommy's not like that."

Luke's mouth dipped into a troubled frown. "Trust me. After what I saw tonight, your no-account sorry excuse for an ex-boyfriend *is* like that now."

Jenna dropped her head. Although she was totally over Tommy, a twinge of disillusionment pricked her heart. *He's still a good guy.*

"Hey," Luke said gently, stroking her cheek. "How 'bout a slice of pizza before Justice learns how to open the box."

She laughed. "Sure. Coming right up."

♡ *Chapter 32*

Jenna tossed and turned, trapped in the grip of a terrible nightmare. *No, no!* Her own voice echoed through the darkness as she begged for mercy. But Shane's switchblade flashed, finding its mark. Luke staggered—one step, then another—before collapsing in a lifeless heap.

She jolted awake, drenched in a cold, clammy sweat. Her breath came in short, shallow gasps as she hovered on the edge of consciousness, unsure for a moment what was real. She pressed a trembling hand to her forehead.

"It was just a bad dream," she whispered, though the words felt fragile.

She rolled onto her side and glanced at the alarm clock. 2:30 a.m. The red digits glowed accusingly in the darkness. She closed her eyes, desperate for even a few more hours of sleep, but last evening's showdown with Tommy and his thugs replayed in relentless loops.

Every sneer. Every threat. Every moment she feared Luke might not walk away.

Sleep refused to come.

Minutes crawled into hours as she watched the clock tick the night away. Frustration surged. She kicked off the sheets and sat up, rubbing her arms to chase away the lingering chill of fear.

She slipped her bathrobe over her summer pajamas and padded downstairs, hoping a glass of milk might settle her nerves. The kitchen was dim and quiet, the hum of the refrigerator the only sound. She opened the door, letting the cool air wash over her.

Just then, the back door opened. Luke stepped inside with Justice trotting at his heels, both of them carrying the scent of early morning dew.

"What're you doing up so early?" he asked, brow creasing with concern.

"I couldn't sleep."

"I'm sorry. Is the bed uncomfortable?"

"No, no," she said, pouring milk into a glass. "I, uh…had a bad dream."

"What about?"

She looked away, voice small. "Tommy and his thugs."

"Why? It's over." Luke leaned against the counter, calm and steady. "I told you—they're all hat, no cattle."

"But Shane threatened you."

"So what?" Luke stepped closer and placed a consoling hand on her shoulder. His touch was warm, grounding. "Look, if it bothers you, we can file a report with the police."

She shrugged. "I guess."

"You need to relax, darlin."

She sighed. "I know."

Luke pointed toward the French doors. Through the paned glass, the pool shimmered under the patio lights, a quiet oasis in the predawn stillness.

"It's gonna be hot and humid today," he said. "Go swimming later. Enjoy the peace."

Jenna shook her head. "But I didn't bring my swimsuit."

"So? Skinny dip."

She half laughed, startled by his innocence.

"What?" he asked. "It's private."

"I don't think so."

"Look," he said, nodding toward the wall hook where his car keys dangled. "Take my car and get what you need."

"Fine," she sighed, though her nerves fluttered at the thought.

A dark pickup truck with a classic Camaro on a trailer rumbled to a stop in front of the house and honked twice.

"Charlie's here," Luke said, grabbing his cooler. "Have fun but remember—no parties."

Jenna planted her hands on her hips. "C'mon, you know me better than that."

Luke grinned. "Yeah, I do. And I know your father, too!"

Mid-morning, Jenna walked Justice along the trails toward Symphony Falls, but the sweltering heat wrapped around her like a suffocating blanket. Sweat trickled down her temples, and every breath felt thick and heavy.

*I need gills to breathe in this humidity.*

Justice slowed, panting hard. Jenna turned back before they reached the overlook, grateful for the thought of air-conditioning and cold water.

When she returned to Luke's house, she ushered Justice inside where the cool air revived them both. He hurried to his bowl, waiting eagerly while she refilled it with fresh water and dropped in a handful of ice cubes. As he drank, she drifted toward the French doors.

The pool shimmered beneath the sunlight, a sparkling oasis that looked more inviting by the second. *Luke's right. It's a perfect day to go swimming.* Maybe a little rest and relaxation was exactly what she needed.

But skinny dipping? Absolutely not.

She opened the door to the garage and paused. Her old four-door clunker sat in the first bay, hood propped open like a defeated soldier. She shook her head. Luke had enough on his plate—his own projects, his own responsibilities. Fixing her junker wasn't exactly top priority.

Her gaze shifted to the second bay.

Luke's black Trans Am gleamed like a polished onyx stone. She smiled. His car was so much more fun to drive. But then reality hit. She'd be driving it alone.

What if she stalled out? Rolled back on a hill? Hit someone?

Luke said he wouldn't be angry, but she knew herself—she'd never forgive the damage.

She reached for the garage phone and dialed her mother, hoping she could bring the swimsuit to her instead. The phone rang and rang with no answer.

*Guess I need to get it myself if I want to go swimming.*

Jenna stepped off the front porch just as her father made his first sweep across the front yard on his lawn tractor. When he looped back around, he stopped, cut the motor, and wiped his brow.

"*Amore*, I thought you were dog-sitting?"

"I am. Just came home to get something." She glanced around. "Where's Mom?"

"She went shopping. Didn't she call you?"

Jenna twisted her mouth. "Daddy, I haven't been home, remember?"

"She was supposed to call you at Luke's house." His face brightened. "Holly had her baby. It's a boy—Anthony James!"

Jenna spun around, unable to contain her excitement. "Oh, my goodness! When? How much does he weigh? What did—"

"Slow down, *Amore*!" Dad chuckled. "Mom has all that."

"Aww, okay." Tears welled in her eyes. "I can't wait to meet my new little nephew!"

Before she could say more, that loud, obnoxious multi-colored truck rumbled around the corner—stereo blaring, tires squealing. Shane was behind the wheel, Jake riding shotgun.

"Those punks again," Dad muttered, jaw tightening.

"What do you mean, again?"

"It's the third time today they drove by."

The truck slowed to a crawl. Jake stuck his head out the window, shouting trash talk and making obscene gestures toward Jenna.

Her father turned crimson. She thought he might blow a gasket. He shook his fist and hollered, "Come back again and I'm calling the cops!"

Shane flipped him the bird, cackled, and sped off.

Mortified, Jenna could hardly bring herself to meet her father's gaze.

"How do you know those punks?"

She swallowed hard. "High school," she mumbled.

"They're trouble. You stay away from them. Got it?"

"Yes, sir." She pointed toward Luke's car. "I, uh…got to go now, Daddy."

He stared at her for a long moment, then nodded. "Okay, but be careful."

"I will."

"Oh—and *Amore*," he added, "when your mother gets back, we'll be leaving for Stonebridge to meet the baby."

She nodded. "Okay, Daddy."

Jenna unlocked Luke's car and tossed her tote bag onto the passenger floor. Just as she was about to slide into the driver's seat, a horn honked. She turned to see Kellie pulling up in her mother's maroon car.

Kellie rolled down the passenger window, lowered her sunglasses, and flashed her *tell-me-everything* smile. "How'd last night go?"

Jenna shook her head and walked toward the car. "Oh, you have no idea."

Kellie grinned mischievously. "Ooh, must've been good."

"No, seriously, Kel. Tommy and his thugs started a fight with Luke."

Kellie's eyes nearly popped out of her head. "OMG! What happened?"

"Luke kicked their butts! That's what happened."

As Jenna spoke, a flashy red Mustang with dark limo tint cruised by. Not far behind, Shane's ratty multi-colored truck sputtered around the corner again.

"Really, jerks?" Jenna muttered. "This is the fourth time!"

Kellie flipped her wrist dismissively. "Who cares? They're sore losers."

"I care." Jenna pointed to her chest. "I'm telling you, the weirdo is watching me."

"Oh, you're just paranoid."

Jenna looked away sharply. "You would be too if someone was leaving you creepy phone messages."

"You're crazy," Kellie said, rolling her eyes. "I got to get to work. Call me later."

Jenna nodded and waved as Kellie pulled away. She watched her car disappear around the corner, then trudged back up the driveway to Luke's car.

She dropped into the driver's seat and mumbled, "Nobody takes me seriously."

She backed out carefully and headed down the street toward the stop sign. Instead of turning left onto Pinecone Road, she turned right. Another right onto Acorn Way brought her past Tommy's house. She drove at a snail's pace, peering at the closed blinds and empty driveway.

The car bucked. She quickly pushed in the clutch to keep it from stalling.

*What am I doing? I better go before trouble finds me.*

She downshifted and sped off.

On her way back to Luke's house, thoughts of Tommy raced through her mind in a relentless loop. *How could someone I loved so much turn into such a jerk?* Unable to answer, she popped Luke's hillbilly cassette into the player, hoping to redirect her thoughts toward her newfound love. But anger and frustration toward Tommy stole her focus and robbed her of contentment.

When she arrived at Luke's house, she parked the Trans Am in the garage and secured the door. Still stewing over last night's scuffle, she reached for the garage phone and dialed Tommy's number, ready to give him a piece of her mind.

The answering machine picked up.

"Hey, it's Tommy. You know the drill."

His friendly voice recording sent her spiraling back to happier times—when he was gentle, kind, attentive. *Where'd that guy go?* The machine beeped, snapping her back to reality.

*What am I doing?*

She slammed the phone into its cradle. *Have I lost my mind?* She shook her head hard, trying to free herself from him.

Inside, she greeted Justice with her high-pitched hello and a few pats. "Ooh, I just love you so much, boy."

The phone rang. Justice barked. Jenna blinked at him. "Gee, am I supposed to answer it?"

She reached for the phone just as the answering machine clicked on. A few seconds later, she heard raucous race cars revving in the background—and Luke's voice.

"Hey, darlin…you there? Pick up the phone."

Jenna answered. "Hey, you. How's it going?"

"Awesome! But it's hot as Hades here."

"I'm sure. I just got back. I stopped home to get my suit."

"Oh." Disappointment colored his tone. "So, no skinny dipping then?"

"No, I told you!" she laughed.

"Darn. And here I thought I'd come home to exciting footage on my security cameras."

Jenna's jaw dropped. "You pig!"

"I'm kidding!" Luke laughed. "Justice is my only home surveillance—"

"That's not funny, Luke," she scolded. "Some weirdo has been leaving me disturbing messages on my private line."

"Who?"

"I don't know! But it's creeping me out."

"Maybe I should come home early."

"Why? Think I should be worried?"

"No…" He hesitated. "I…miss you…I love you."

The words stunned her.

"Ditto," she blurted, unsure how to respond. "I, uh…" She glanced at Justice sprawled over the A/C vent. "I need to take Justice out. Talk to you tomorrow."

She hung up quickly and pressed her hand over her pounding heart.

*He loves me? Really?*

She slapped her hands down at her sides in frustration.

*And all I can say is ditto? I blew it. I really blew it this time.*

Jenna floated on a double inflatable lounger in the deep end of the pool, letting the cool water cradle her as the heat of the afternoon pressed down. She closed her eyes and imagined Luke stretched out beside her, his steady presence warming the space between them. No matter how hard she tried, she couldn't turn her mind off—not after their phone conversation.

She gazed up at the drifting clouds, soft and white against the endless blue, and let her heart speak.

*So, God… Luke says he loves me. Does he really? Isn't that ridiculous considering we've only been seeing each other for a couple months? I mean… everything feels right, and I've never felt so peaceful in a relationship before. I don't know, God. I think I love him, too, but I once loved Tommy, and look how that turned out. I'm scared to love again... scared of getting hurt. Please help me learn to trust again.*

The clouds shifted, parting just enough for a warm beam of sunlight to break through. It kissed her cheeks with a gentle heat—soft, comforting, almost like a father's consoling touch. A tender breeze swept across the water, brushing her skin with cool relief.

Jenna smiled, her heart loosening just a little.

"Amen."

Gray clouds smothered the afternoon sun, and the air carried the heavy scent of impending rain. Jenna swam to the shallow end and climbed the steps, shivering as her dripping body met the cool breeze. She crossed the pavers toward a lounge chair where her warm, soft towel waited.

Bundled in the chair, she let the towel absorb the water from her skin. Justice trotted over with a tennis ball clenched in his mouth, tail wagging in eager arcs. He dropped the slimy ball in her lap and stared up at her, ready for a game of fetch.

Jenna scanned the backyard for the best spot to throw it. Straight ahead was the pool—Justice had already had his fill of swimming. To her left stretched the only patch of green where he could run. She grasped the ball and flung it across the yard, landing just before the wrought-iron fence. Justice spun and bolted after it, returning proudly with the ball in his mouth.

She threw it again. And again. Half a dozen more times until a low rumble of thunder rolled across the sky. Justice barked in alarm.

"Yep," Jenna said, "it's time to go inside."

She pushed open the patio door, and the ringing phone immediately grabbed her attention.

"Ooh, that's probably Mom calling me."

Holding the door for Justice, she hurried toward the phone—only for it to stop ringing.

"Darn it! Hopefully she leaves a message."

Later, after a refreshing shower, Jenna returned to the kitchen to feed Justice and fix herself dinner. She opened the pantry and smiled at Luke's organizational skills. Each shelf was perfectly categorized—canned goods, baking ingredients, boxed cereals, pastas, snacks. Every label faced outward in neat alphabetical order.

She spotted the jar of peanut butter and shook her head. *This guy has some serious OCD problems.*

A short while later, Jenna settled into Luke's recliner with her PB&J sandwich. She glanced at the wall clock. *I should call Kellie.* She reached for the phone on the end table and dialed her number. After three rings, the answering machine picked up.

At the tone, Jenna left a message. "Hey, Kel. It's me. When you get this, call me back at Luke's…555-7268."

She hung up and took a bite of her sandwich. Naturally—Murphy's Law—the phone rang. With a mouthful, she answered, "Hey, Kel."

Silence.

"Kel…is that you?"

The eerie sound of heavy breathing filled her ear. Heart-wrenching fear consumed her. She slammed the phone into its cradle and stared at it, unseeing.

Immediately, the phone rang again, but Jenna was too shaken to answer. Moments later, the machine clicked on, and Kellie's voice filled the room.

"Hey Jenna, it's me."

Jenna snatched up the phone. "So, it's YOU cranking me!" she shouted.

"What? No!" Kellie said. "I'm calling you back."

"That creep just called me! How'd he get this number?"

"Maybe…the phone book. How should I know?"

Jenna threw her hand out, palm up. "But he wouldn't know Luke's last name to find it."

"Maybe from his company truck parked in your driveway," Kellie suggested.

Jenna shook her head. "No way. Seems too far-fetched. Besides, his work truck is labeled with the business number, not his house line."

Suddenly, a loud crash sounded in the backyard. *What the—?* Jenna twisted in the recliner and glanced out the French doors. A random jerk of wind had flipped a patio chair onto its backside.

"Oh crap!" Jenna said, rising to her feet. "I left the patio umbrella open and another storm's coming."

"And I forgot to close my car windows," Kellie chimed in. "I'll call you right back." She hung up.

Jenna called out, "C'mon, boy!" then opened the patio door. "Last chance to do your business before it rains."

Justice leaped to attention and followed her outside.

The thick, moist air carried an eerie stillness that scraped across Jenna's taut nerves. "Okay, so where's this horrific storm that disrupted my phone call?"

She tilted her head toward the sky. Ugly dark clouds had swallowed the beautiful sun she'd enjoyed earlier. Lightning lashed the sky in jagged streaks of gold, raising goosebumps on her arms.

"Okay, God. Sorry I asked."

She hurried to close the umbrella and secure the chairs, then chased after a beach ball that had skimmed across the water into the grassy area where Justice stood like a guard dog.

"What do you see, boy?" she asked.

He stood at the gate, tail stiff, staring through the thick evergreens that separated the side yard from the road.

"What's out there?" she asked, approaching the fence.

Justice emitted a low, threatening growl.

Jenna froze; afraid a bear might be lurking in the woods. Just then, the throaty roar of a vehicle vibrated through her nerves. "Oh crap!" She clutched her chest.

But when the red glow of brake lights illuminated the darkness, she realized it was just a car idling in the road.

"It's okay, Justice," she said, patting his head. "It's only the neighbor."

She watched the taillights gleam through the trees as the car circled the cul-de-sac and sped off.

"C'mon, boy."

But Justice remained at the gate, still on high alert.

A stunning roll of thunder boomed overhead, and fat raindrops began to fall.

"Hurry up!" she called.

Justice finally obeyed and followed her to the patio door.

Inside, while Jenna was locking the French door, the phone rang again. She rushed into the kitchen and answered on the third ring.

"Perfect timing, Kel," she said.

"You can't hide from me," the familiar creepy voice replied.

Jenna sucked in a breath, fighting the panic clawing up her throat. "Who is this?" she asked, her voice trembling.

The line went dead.

She dropped the receiver, letting it dangle against the kitchen wall. Heart pounding, she scurried through the dining room into the living room, flipping on lights, closing blinds, double-checking locks—anything to make the house feel less vulnerable.

She leaned against the front door, stricken. *How did he find me here?* A cold chill settled over her as a troubling thought crept in. *It's got to be Tommy. I called him from Luke's garage phone. I know he's got caller ID.* She shook her head hard. *No. He wouldn't do that to me.*

She returned to the living room. Justice lay curled in his bed, sleeping without a care in the world. *If he's calm, why shouldn't I be?* She tried to convince herself, but her nerves refused to settle.

She grabbed the red-and-black checkered throw blanket from the couch, plopped onto the cushion, and tucked herself in. Outside, raging winds and heavy rain slapped against the windows, adding to the unease twisting inside her.

*As if the creeper's phone calls weren't enough… now I have to deal with this wacky weather.*

She tried to calm her anxiety by reflecting on her tranquil afternoon, but exhaustion finally overtook her. Her eyes drifted shut.

Thunder—loud as cannon fire—rumbled the entire house, jerking Jenna out of a deep sleep. At once, the lights flicked off and the house went dark, sending her into a blind, whirling panic.

"Oh, no!" she gasped, her heart pounding painfully hard.

Justice barked.

"It's okay, boy," she called, forcing courage into her voice. "It's just a quick passing storm."

But minutes passed, and the power stayed off.

"Oh, great!" she grumbled, bouncing to her feet. "Now where does he keep the flashlight?"

Justice barked again.

"Do you know, boy?"

She stumbled through the darkness, flinching each time lightning flickered its eerie glow and thunder rattled the walls. In the kitchen, she rummaged through the junk drawer until her fingers closed around a working flashlight.

*Amazing how this guy really has his crap together.*

She shined the beam on the battery-powered wall clock in the dining room. Midnight.

*Boy, I must've been really zonked before this storm woke me up.* She covered a wide yawn with her palm. *With no power, I'm going to bed.*

She pointed the flashlight toward the foyer and followed its beam upstairs to the guest room.

Tucked under the covers, she listened to the soft patter of rain tapping the windowpane and the low rumble of distant thunder. Relief washed over her — the worst of the storm was passing.

She closed her eyes, trying not to dwell on negative thoughts. Weariness pulled her under.

But as she slid into sleep, Justice's frantic barking jerked her awake.

She shot upright, mouth wide open, ready to scream. "Now what?"

Justice's barking grew more urgent. Something was wrong.

She grabbed the flashlight from the nightstand. One flip of the switch sent a beam slicing through the shadowed corners of the room. Nothing was out of place.

Justice bared his teeth and growled.

"Shh, boy," she whispered, setting the flashlight down. She padded across the cool wood floor to the front window. She parted the mini-blinds for a full view of the cul-de-sac—but without porch lights, everything was pitch black.

"Justice, there's nothing out there," she muttered.

She looked again—and froze.

A red glow from a cigarette pulsed in the shrubs.

She pressed her hand to her mouth. "Oh—my—gosh! There is someone out there!" She stepped back from the window.

"I'm calling the cops."

She opened the bedroom door. Justice sprinted down the stairs ahead of her. By the time she reached the bottom step, he sat vigilant at the front door.

"Good boy. You guard the house while I call 911."

As she stepped into the foyer, bright headlights streamed through the front window, followed by a powerful thud and muffled voices.

*Who's out there?*

She turned toward the sidelight glass to sneak a peek. The illuminated mist revealed a shadowy figure strutting up the driveway.

Panic knotted inside her. "Oh, dear Lord! He found me!"

She stumbled through the darkness, stubbing her little toe on a chair leg. "Dang, that hurts," she cried, limping to the kitchen counter. She yanked open a drawer and grabbed the first object she touched—her makeshift weapon—then ducked into a corner and waited.

Justice's silhouette sat attentive at the door. But instead of growling, his friendly tail swept the tile floor.

*What is WRONG with you? Why're you giving me mixed signals?*

Suddenly, the lock clicked twice. The doorknob turned. The door slid open in deafening silence.

"Justice, attack!" she whispered, warning spasms erupting inside her.

But instead, Justice let out enthusiastic cries as the intruder stepped inside.

"Easy, buddy," Luke whispered as Justice jumped like a pogo stick. "Shh! You're going to wake up Jenna."

Jenna recognized Luke's soothing voice and sagged with relief. *Oh, thank God.* She scrambled from her hiding spot and fumbled her way into his protective arms.

"Oh, Luke! It's you. Thank God it's you!"

"What's going on?" he asked.

"Didn't you see him?"

"See who?"

"That creep!"

"No, I didn't see anyone."

"You had to have. He's out there! I just saw him from my bedroom window."

"Shh," he murmured, clasping her tightly.

She buried her face in his chest. "I'm telling you, he was here," she sniffled. "Justice heard him. I saw the light from his cigarette."

"Okay," he whispered.

"You think I'm crazy, don't cha?"

"I didn't say that."

"No, you didn't—but Kellie did."

"Sweetheart, just because I didn't see anyone doesn't mean you didn't."

"Amen," she mumbled.

"What was your guy driving?" he asked.

"Wait!" She pulled back. "First, he's NOT my guy. MY guy drives a Trans Am. I have no idea what this creep was driving."

"I didn't mean it like that," Luke said. "But I just remembered… when Charlie turned into the cul-de-sac, a Mustang blew past us like a bat out of hell."

"That's him!"

"It could've been the neighbor."

"No," she said firmly. "You have two neighbors — one owns a minivan, and the other has a sedan."

Luke didn't respond.

Jenna placed her hands on her hips. "Ha! I rest my case!"

Suddenly, a clicking sound echoed through the house. The lights flickered — then came back on.

"Finally!" she said.

Luke narrowed his eyes. "What's that in your hand?"

"Oh, this?" Jenna asked casually. "My weapon."

"You were gonna beat me with a meat mallet?"

"It was a last-minute decision!"

Luke rolled his eyes.

"Never mind," she said, walking into the kitchen. She set the meat mallet on the counter and turned around.

"So tell me—what're you doing home in the middle of the night?"

"Y-e-a-h… about that," Luke said, stepping into the kitchen. "I tried calling you, but all I got was a busy signal. I even tried making an emergency breakthrough, but the operator said the line was disconnected."

He spotted the receiver dangling off the hook. "Well, that explains that."

"Sorry," Jenna said, lowering her eyes. "That creep kept calling me, and I freaked. I'm so sorry I wrecked your plans."

"Oh, heck!" he said, pulling her into his arms. "This was a drop-everything kind of thing."

"So you *do* believe me."

Luke nodded. "I do. And to make you feel better, we're filing a report after sunup."

Jenna shook her head. "No, I don't want any more trouble." She breathed in his soothing cologne and sighed. "Besides… I'm okay now that you're home."

♡ *Chapter 33*

Hours later, instead of going to the police department, Jenna convinced Luke to take her to Sunday Mass—to reclaim her dignity from the clutches of Tommy and his thugs.

On the drive back to Luke's house, she sat in peaceful silence, gazing out the passenger window. Father Stephen's homily—*Love Thy Neighbor*—echoed through her thoughts. His words gave her the strength to release the anger, fear, and resentment she'd been carrying toward Tommy.

Luke pulled into the driveway and shut off the engine. He shifted in his seat and took her hands in his.

"Feel better now that you went to church?"

Jenna nodded. "I always feel better after seeking God's forgiveness. Thank you for taking me."

"Yeah, no problem... So, what do you want to do today?"

She shrugged.

Luke leaned back against the headrest, tilting his face toward the tinted T-top glass. "It's a gorgeous day. What do you say we drive to Stonebridge? We can meet up with your folks, see your brother and Holly, and meet your new little nephew."

Jenna broke into an easy smile as tears filled her eyes. Heaven help her—Luke was the most thoughtful man she had ever met. His presence brought her more joy and contentment than Tommy ever had in all their years together.

"Yes, I'd love to!"

"Alrighty then," Luke said, opening the car door. "But first, I'm taking off the T-tops."

Jenna handed him an ice-cold bottle of water, then sat on the shaded porch step with Justice and watched him unlatch the glass panels. His powerful, muscled body moved with easy grace as he slid each fragile piece into its storage bag. She tried not to stare, but she couldn't help it—his passion for cars, his care for his possessions, his quiet strength… it captivated her.

Normally, he wasn't the type of guy who drew her interest. Yet something about him made her feel complete.

*Could it be I've found true love in only a couple months?* She bit her bottom lip, pondering. *Maybe I have.*

She looked up at him securing the T-tops in the trunk and remembered Father Stephen's words: Love is patient; love is kind… Jenna nodded. Luke was all of the above. He was the most considerate man she had ever met. He drove her through a snowstorm to see her father; sheltered her during a thunderstorm; stood up for her in a fight… and never asked for anything in return. With Luke, she didn't have to pretend to be someone she wasn't.

He met her gaze and smiled before wiping the beads of sweat from his forehead. "Dang sun is hot!" he said.

"It sure is."

He unbuttoned his shirt and tossed it over the car door. *Whoa.* His tanned, corded muscles made her pulse skip. Even with a split lip and a shiner, he was undeniably handsome.

Luke closed the trunk, guzzled some water, then poured the rest over his head. "Ah, that feels good," he said, shaking his hair dry.

Jenna laughed. "You're crazy; you know that?"

His carefree expression softened into something more serious. "I'm, uh… gonna go in and wash up so we can go."

Jenna nodded. "Okay."

But before Luke stepped into the garage, the familiar sound of a throaty engine caught their attention. A flashy red Mustang with tinted windows pulled into the court.

Jenna's stomach dropped. She was certain it was the same one she'd seen yesterday cruising past her parents' house.

Justice let out a warning growl.

"Looks like we have company," Luke said, tightening his grip on Justice's leash.

Uncertainty made Jenna's voice shake. "Is that the same car you saw last night?"

Luke shrugged. "It was too dark and foggy to tell."

The Mustang parked inside the court, about two hundred feet from their driveway. The engine shut off. The driver's door opened.

Tommy stepped out—black jeans, white shirt rolled at the sleeves, hair rumpled like he'd slept in his thoughts all night.

"Good heavens! What's he doing here?" Jenna whispered.

Luke shook his head. "I wouldn't trust him any farther than I can throw him."

As Tommy approached, Jenna studied him. He looked tired, edgy, beaten down. When he reached them, she caught a whiff of his aftershave—and a flood of unwanted memories.

"How'd you find me here?" she asked.

Tommy dropped his head. "I, uh… followed you yesterday."

"So that was you," she snapped. "Whose Mustang did you steal?"

"Mine—I earned it." He lit a cigarette. "Case you haven't heard—got my song on the radio."

Jenna blinked. "Well… I guess congratulations is in order." She planted her hands on her hips. "So, let's cut the bull—what do you want?"

"Can we talk?" he asked.

Jenna glanced at Luke, then back at Tommy. "There's nothing left to say."

Luke brushed her cheek with his thumb. "It's okay. I'll walk Justice around the cul-de-sac while y'all talk."

Jenna nodded and gave him a kiss-me look.

Luke lowered his head and captured her mouth with his, pouring everything he was into the kiss. The wonder of him swirled through her. Reluctant to break away, she whispered, "I'll be along in a moment."

Luke nodded and walked off with Justice.

Jenna turned to Tommy. His eyes held dismay.

She folded her arms. "So… what'd you want to talk about?"

Tommy's mouth turned down, sour. His voice cracked. "Gimme another chance."

Jenna shook her head. "Don't do this."

"C'mon, babe, I miss you. Backstage, I'm surrounded by people—women mostly—but I feel all alone. I need you."

Jenna sighed. "Tommy… you did me so wrong."

"I know." He stared at the ground. "I messed up… big time. I thought you were holding me back—"

"No, Tommy," she said, steadying her voice. "I always believed in you. I would've left River Grove to be with you."

"I wouldn't have let you. This was my dream, not yours."

"And it still is your dream," she said.

Troubled lines gathered at the corners of his mouth. He reached for another cigarette.

"Well," she said, "isn't it? After all, your song made the radio."

"The band… we're having some problems."

"That's too bad. What're you going to do?"

"Ask you to forgive me."

Jenna blinked. "Tommy, you know me. I'm not one to hold a grudge, but—"

"I appreciate that," he said quickly.

"We can't go back. Like you said, we're moving at different tempos."

Tommy shifted, awkward and uneasy. "I know… but together, we can move forward."

"Tommy—"

"I'm sorry, Jenna. Letting you go was the *worst thing ever.*"

"I thought so too, at first. But now I realize you letting me go was the *best thing ever*. I just didn't know it at the time."

"What?" Tommy asked.

"Just like seasons change, we've changed. You're where you are now… and I'm where I'm meant to be."

"And where's that?" he asked.

Jenna pointed toward the front lawn where Luke was playing fetch with Justice. "With them."

"So he's the lucky guy taking my place?"

"Yep," she said softly. "And he's waiting for me." She squeezed her eyes shut, fighting the urge to cry. "But it's okay, Tommy. It's all for the good."

Tommy's shoulders sagged, the fight draining out of him. For the first time, she saw not arrogance or anger—

but acceptance. He flicked his cigarette into a puddle, nodded once, and turned back toward his Mustang. Without another word, he climbed in and drove away, the engine's rumble fading into the summer air.

Jenna let out a long, trembling breath.

As she walked toward Luke, her heart settled into a quiet certainty she hadn't known in years. He stood there in the sunlight, Justice at his side, his smile soft and steady—like a promise she could finally trust. When he reached for her hand, warmth spread through her chest, gentle and sure, as if God Himself were guiding her steps.

Luke didn't say a word. He didn't have to. The tenderness in his eyes told her everything—how deeply he cared, how fiercely he would protect her, how patiently he would love her. And in that moment, Jenna felt God whisper to her heart that every storm, every heartbreak, every sleepless night had led her right here. To this man. To this peace. To this love.

She squeezed Luke's hand, her voice barely a breath. "I'm exactly where I'm meant to be."

Luke brushed his thumb across her knuckles, and the simple gesture sent a flutter through her soul. As they walked toward the Trans Am, sunlight broke through the clouds, bathing the road ahead in gold. Jenna lifted her face to the warmth, grateful tears gathering in her eyes.

Whatever tomorrow held, she knew God had woven every step of her journey into something beautiful. Something healing. Something meant. And as Luke opened the passenger door for her, she whispered a quiet, joyful truth to herself— *All for the Good.*

## Epilogue

The roar of Symphony Falls rose in a steady, soothing rhythm as Jenna and Luke walked along the familiar trail, Justice trotting happily ahead of them. Sunlight filtered through the trees in soft gold ribbons, warming Jenna's shoulders and stirring memories of the first time she and Luke had walked this very path. Back then, she'd been fragile, uncertain, trying to outrun the ache of her past.

Now she felt whole.

They reached the overlook where the water crashed into the pool below, sending shimmering droplets into the air like tiny diamonds. Jenna paused, leaning on the railing, letting the mist kiss her cheeks. Luke stepped beside her, close enough that she felt the quiet strength of him.

For a moment, neither spoke. The falls didn't need words.

Luke brushed his thumb across her knuckles. "You ever think about the future?"

The question drifted through her like a soft echo — a memory of another place, another man, another life. She had once asked Tommy the same thing on a California beach, her heart full of naïve hope. She'd imagined a future that never came to be.

But this time… her heart didn't tremble. It settled.

She smiled up at Luke. "More than I used to."

They stood together, watching the water rush forward, always moving, always renewing. Jenna felt Luke's presence beside her — steady, faithful, safe. The kind of presence she had once longed for but never truly had.

"I don't know what tomorrow holds," she said softly, "but I know who I want in it."

Luke's eyes warmed, deep and sure. He reached up and tucked a loose strand of hair behind her ear, his touch tender. "I'm right here, Jenna. And I'm not going anywhere."

Her heart swelled. God had led her through heartbreak, confusion, and fear — but He had also led her here. To this man. To this peace. To this love.

A breeze lifted across the falls, carrying the faint sound of distant music from somewhere down the mountain — a familiar melody she hadn't heard in months. Jenna paused, listening. It tugged at an old memory, but it no longer held her.

Luke noticed. "You okay?"

She nodded slowly. "Yeah… just a memory."

The music faded. Peace returned.

Jenna leaned into Luke, resting her head against his shoulder as the falls roared below them. She felt God's presence in every breath, every heartbeat, every step that had led her from the past into this new beginning.

And with a quiet, joyful certainty, she whispered the truth she now lived by. *All for the Good.*

Thank you for spending time with Jenna's story. As I wrote *All for the Good*, I often found myself reflecting on seasons in my own life— times when God's plan felt unclear, yet His faithfulness remained steady. Many pieces of Jenna's journey were drawn from my own experiences: her unreliable clunker car, her longing to be understood, and the complicated relationships that shaped her heart.

I set this story in 1990 because that era still lives vividly in my memory. Life moved slower then—no smartphones, no constant connection, no instant answers. Jenna's world reflects the one I grew up in: handwritten notes, pay phones, cassette tapes, CD's and cars that stalled at the worst possible moments. Writing in that setting allowed me to revisit pieces of my past and the lessons God wove through them.

Jenna's father was inspired by my own Italian dad— old-school, tough-love, and often quick to criticize or control, not out of indifference, but out of fear and the only way he knew to protect. And just like Luke's steady, level-headed presence in Jenna's life, my fiancé once showed me that same quiet strength. When my own clunker kept breaking down, he didn't dismiss my concerns. He listened, trusted my instincts, and handed me the keys to his brand-new car so I could feel safe. Luke carries pieces of him: calm, dependable, and eager to provide stability when it's needed most.

As I wrote, I felt Jenna's emotions echoing places in my own heart where God had gently restored what I once thought was broken beyond repair. If you've ever walked through a season that felt heavy or uncertain, I pray her story whispered hope to you. God never wastes our tears or our waiting. He is always working behind the scenes, even when we can't see it yet.

Thank you for joining me on this journey. Your encouragement and support mean more than you know. May God continue to work all things for good in your life.

Janet

1. How does the title *All for the Good* reflect the story's themes and Jenna's journey?

2. Which character did you connect with most, and why?

3. Was there a character you especially liked or disliked? What shaped your reaction?

4. Jenna faces a moral decision that affects her relationship with Tommy. What choice does she make, and why?

5. Choose one character who faced a moral dilemma. Would you have made the same decision?

6. Both Jenna and Luke experience heartache yet hold onto their faith. How might their healing have looked without it?

7. How does Jenna mature throughout the novel? Which events or relationships spark her growth?

8. What do you consider the story's peak event? What conflicts lead to it, and how is it resolved?

9. Which scene or passage felt most profound or meaningful to you?

10. If you had to describe the book in one word, what would it be? Would you recommend it?

Janet DiFabio writes Christian romance with a heart for showing how God gently weaves hope, healing, and purpose into everyday lives. A wife, mother, and learning coach, she draws inspiration from the joys and challenges of family life in northeastern Pennsylvania, where faith is the foundation of her home.

She is the author of *Always Faithful and True*, its sequel *In Good Times and Bad*, and *All for the Good*, and she is excited to soon share her first Christmas romance, *Finding Hope at Kringle's Crossing*. When she isn't writing, Janet enjoys time with her family, quiet moments with the Lord, and the simple blessings that spark her stories.

**Abiding Spirit Press** was founded on a sacred promise to honor the enduring power of faith, loyalty, and eternal love. It was born from a deep personal vow: to walk beside a beloved friend to the very end of his earthly journey, and through that friendship, to share with him the gift and fullness of the Catholic faith.

Our mission is to publish Christian romance that gently guides hearts toward faith, hope, and everlasting love. Our novels reflect the beauty of God's timing, the gift of companionship, and the peace of the Holy Spirit, standing as testaments to His mercy and grace.

Through the stories we publish, we strive to create a haven of hope for readers traversing life's most difficult journeys. Our characters face good times and bad, grow in grace, and discover that no matter how uncertain the path may seem, they are never alone. In every season—both joyful and wearisome—we affirm that God is always faithful and true, continually working all things for the good.

At Abiding Spirit Press, every story is an invitation to encounter love that endures, faith that strengthens, and hope that never fades.

*Where the Spirit leads and grace redeems.*